A SLEIGHT OF HAND

A Novel

RAYMOND S FLEX

CHAPTER ONE

I DREW THE PEAK of my cap down to disguise my face and pounded the pavement, doing my best to hold my own against the crowds. Women clutched bonnets to their heads, the ribbons fluttering in the warm early-evening breeze, while men walked with a firm gait, their jackets unbuttoned, dabbing their perspiring foreheads with crisp, white handkerchiefs.

Dante Gobornik's likeness appeared on a billboard above the crowd. He stood with his hands clutched together, head bowed, eyes closed and top hat almost keeping the whole of his face in shadow. Still, his steepled cheekbones projected out through the dark rendering—those cheekbones which told stories of his apparent Eastern European origins, as one story had it, before he had come here, to England, and made his fortune as a magician.

I eyed the venue up ahead: *Smartsbridge Theatre*, and then examined the pair of ushers, dressed in ties and tails, but nonetheless looking threatening—their large muscles and thick faces betraying the veneer of elegance they hoped to project.

I reached into my pocket and withdrew the folded up flyer. I glanced around me, still not quite trusting that someone might snatch it from me at the last moment. I dodged out of a large lady's path. Her scarf tailed down over her shoulder and I felt the brush of fox fur against my cheek.

I waited until I'd got to the entrance of the theatre, when I was almost standing in front the ushers, before I felt safe enough to unfold the flyer completely. The air here was a mixture of motorcar fumes, cigarette smoke and ladies' perfume. I've always been highly attuned to smells—been able to keep a good record of them. For example, back home, those smells of Mum's washing powder and the coal-burning stove. Sometimes it was damp, when Mum had been boiling hot water for a bath or for dinner. Not that that happened much those days. Times were tight. Everyone needed to stand up and be counted right then. I was sick and tired of feeling like I was weighing my parents down—just another mouth to feed.

The usher who saw to me had a bushy moustache which he would twitch just before he'd speak. His waistcoat was tight against his chest and I could make out his lumpy pectoral muscles down below. When he spoke he had an accent just like where I'm from—Grunly Borough. "What we got here, then?"

I thrust the flyer into his hands, taking care not to meet his eye, and to keep my hands hidden within the sleeves of my shirt, and then sat back on my heels, glancing around me, worried that something might happen—that I might be prevented from going inside.

The usher read the flyer. "Mister Dante Gobornik: Great Purveyor of Mind Tricks and Conjurings of Nationwide Renown

Searches for a Young Boy to Take on the Mantle of his Assistant. Please Present this Flyer at Any of the Matinee Performances Whereupon the Holder Shall be Granted Entrance to the Spectacle and Later Meet with Mister Gobornik to Determine the Suitability of Said Boy to the Post. Full Compensation Shall be Granted to the Family of the Chosen Candidate." The usher glanced over the flyer at me once again, and I made the mistake of meeting his gaze. "And you think he'd be interested in, what, you, a coloured?"

I felt my cheeks burning, but stood my ground. I knew I was different, but I didn't care. My mum, she always told me to be proud, and so that was how I was. I just needed to act it and I would get respect.

The usher sighed as if this was a great inconvenience. "Where'd you find this, then?"

"It was pasted up on a pub wall."

The usher nodded to himself, appeared to scan the flyer once again. He brought his fingers up to the side of his head and rubbed away a strand of sweat leaking out. "Thing is, Mister Gobornik, he ain't said nothing about no post to us. How's we supposed to know if this is genuine or what?"

The breath squeezed from my lungs. "Please, it's the truth. I found it there."

"Yeah, but thing is anyone might've put this thing together. How'd we know whether or not it's the real thing?"

The prospect of returning home, empty-handed, just wasn't a possibility. Things were tight—too tight—and I was our family's last chance. The night before I had overheard Mum and Dad talking, the last coals crackling away, a light so dim as I could only make out their basic forms from where I lay shucked up in my sleeping bag against the wall. They said we'd need to move out of the house, maybe stay in the street a while, till we could find something cheaper—we couldn't afford the rent anymore, even with Mum working repairing clothes. Not now with the new babbie.

Still gripping the flyer in his fist, the usher turned to a couple who held out tickets for him to inspect. The man wore a top hat and a monocle. I watched the silver chain snaking out of the man's pocket to where it harnessed itself to a button on the breast pocket of his waistcoat. In that chain, I saw weeks, months, of rent. Enough to keep us all going for a long time. But, before I made my move, the man, and his lady wife— garishly dressed in a lemon and lime dress—disappeared inside the theatre. And not before the usher had clocked me staring a long while at that silver chain, dreaming of the pocket watch at the other end.

He scrunched the flyer into a ball and tossed it into the street where it landed in the sewage-ridden gutter, floating along the filthy water, sinking and growing grubbier all the time, to where it finally dipped into a drain and out of sight forever. He turned his ire on me, forehead knitted into wrinkles. "Hop it you, now, before I call a copper over!"

I stood my ground, feeling the heat rush to my cheeks, the tears well in the corners of my eyes. But the usher had no time for my sentimental outpouring and seized hold of my forearm, twisting it behind my back before tossing me out into the same gutter I'd watched the flyer sail down.

The stench of piss and shit singed my nostrils. I felt my coat damp with the sewage, the warmed sludge ooze against my skin. I helped myself up to my feet, stumbling several times, splashing sewage all around me.

A woman shrieked as a spot landed on her pristine cream

dress. Over all the commotion I heard a gentleman call out for a policeman. I observed the usher standing at the door to the theatre looking like he might tear me limb from limb if it hadn't been for the possibility of me getting his nice clothes sullied—and if he really was from Grunly then I knew he wouldn't easily be able to afford for them to be cleaned, let alone buy a new set.

A policeman's whistle screeched through the air.

I stood there, stunned for several seconds, unsure quite what to do. Unlike other kids from Grunly I never made much of a habit of running from the police—in fact they used to scare me quite a bit.

The policeman bundled through the crowd of theatregoers. He wore his navy blue cape which came down just below his knees, his helmet was neatly perched right on the tip of his forehead, the smooth leather helmet strap tucked beneath his chin. A whistle dangled from his lips as he set about getting information from the frantic ladies in dresses and their smirking male companions, standing a few feet back from them and nudging one another in the ribs.

It felt like my heart was swelling up. In that same second I caught the policeman's glare, I turned on my heel and beat a hasty retreat, almost hurling myself into a passing taxicab, and only narrowly avoiding being crushed by a passing horse and cart. I made it to the other side of the street where I paused, catching my breath, already feeling knackered—I hadn't had any meat for weeks, we'd made do with gruel and water, and small quantities at that.

The policeman, however, looked to be made of sterner stuff. He blazed his way across the street, already making up the distance between me and him.

I took off running again, already tasting blood in my mouth, feeling like my heart might pop out from between my ribs.

As I ran onward, I was afraid to look back, convinced that it would only be to see the policeman standing right over me, ready to swoop down, knock me off my feet and then drag me, kicking and screaming, to the workhouse. So, instead, I concentrated on the road opening up before me, concentrating on avoiding the vendors pitching their tents, laying out their goods on rickety wooden tables and, when they couldn't get hold of wood, overturned cardboard boxes. Inevitably, I tipped a couple of them over, sending trinkets flying. The worst collision saw me rip through a table of kitchenware. Pots and pans clattered over into the gutter and the vendor swore himself blind. But I had no time to pay attention to the curses, as I saw my opportunity to get away—a narrow alley beside a pub called *The Tom Cat*. I slipped inside, instantly finding myself with piled rubbish: fish bones, empty beer barrels, squidgy guts of indiscernible origin. I closed my eyes as I trod over all the foul crap, losing the light from the street as I went. And then, all at once, it all seemed in vain, as I came up against a ten-foot-high brick wall, with broken glass set into the top.

My heart bobbed in my throat and I knew it was all over. I stared back along the darkened alley, into that faint ray of light from the main street. I held my breath waiting for the inevitable, the policeman to find me there. I forced the extraneous sounds out of my hearing, the horse and carriages, the taxis from the street—the babble of conversation and tinkling of beer glasses coming from *The Tom Cat*. The steady policeman's bootfall filled my hearing. I watched him prowl up to the entrance of the alleyway and stare down it, right at me.

Every nerve in my body seemed to catch fire. I thought I

might burst from apprehension. In my mind's eye I saw my mother, my father, each of them sitting at home around the coal fire, wondering where I was—why I hadn't come home for dinner after school. Did they feel some guilty wish that I would be gone? That their shared mistake would slip from the face of the Earth? That the babbie would be their only child? They would no longer have to carry my financial burden.

I noticed the nightstick the policeman held down by his side, the way he had it tied about his wrist. He stared deeper into the gloom—I was sure—making eye contact with me. He took a step forward. I heard a *squelch*. He retreated, drawing his foot back. He resettled himself at the entrance to the alleyway, obviously not wanting to come any closer. "You there," he said. "I can see you, don't think you're hidden away. Maybe you're all night-coloured, but you sure as hell ain't invisible." He scaled his tone back a touch. "Why don't you be a good lad, now, and come out here. I'll just take you home, to your ma and pa, how's that sound?"

I drew breath into my lungs and held it there, wishing myself invisible. If only I could make myself disappear now I could simply wander out past the policeman. In my panic I watched the fantasy unfold in my mind's eye: the slightly comic sight of the policeman looking all around him, mouth latched open, arms flung up in disbelief. But this wasn't a fantasy. This was real.

The policeman addressed me again. This time his tone was a touch sharper. He was growing impatient. "Look here, you, come on out here now or I'll see to it personally that you're locked up tonight and taken to the workhouse first thing tomorrow morning." Then he seemed to realise that he might be losing the diplomatic battle and said, "Let's not make this any more difficult than it needs to be, eh, child? Come along now."

7

Still, I stayed my ground. If he did wish to come fetch me then he would need to steal his way across that same filth I had crossed. I valued the price of my freedom at least on par with the inconvenience of dirty boots. This was one arrest he would have to earn.

The policeman rested his hands on his hips. "Well?"

Over his shoulder someone shouted something—moments later I realised it was another policeman. The policeman chasing after me appeared conflicted, unsure whether to go after his companion or to stick with me, to make the arrest. He looked down into the alleyway with a new intensity. "Get a move on."

Not a chance.

The other policeman—the one out of sight—called out again, and the policeman took one last look along the alleyway and then turned around to shout something back. He lingered for another couple of seconds in the opening to the alley before, reluctantly, with a final glance back at me, he sprinted off in the direction of his companion's voice.

I held my position, still unsure whether or not this might be a tactic. Perhaps, somehow, he had communicated his situation to his companion and both of them, right then, waited for me at the entrance, backs flat against the wall, ready to nab me the second I busted out of the alley.

I considered my options. Of course I could stay just where I was, wait things out until they died down, but what if the policeman came back later to check? I decided that my only chance at evading the policeman was to shift from my hiding place at that moment, to risk that he was attempting to trick me.

And so, taking a gulp of air, I trod back along the rubbish, wincing at the sound of the cracking bones and the suck of waste liquids. I thought of myself as being somewhere else—crossing a lightly burbling stream in the countryside. It worked for a few steps until I heard a *"Psst!"* coming from the entrance to the alley.

My whole body froze where I stood. I set my left foot down and it got stuck in a half empty barrel of beer. I felt the hops swishing about through the holes in my battered old shoes, but I had no urge to squirm as all my attention was drawn by the figure darkening the alleyway.

"There's not much time," the figure said.

I gulped back a lump in my throat and thought over my next move—if there was one lesson that had sunk into me over years of Mum's scolding it was that I was never to trust a stranger, especially at night. Nonetheless, what could I do? I could retreat, squidge my way back to the end of the alleyway. And then there was the question of my stuck foot. I didn't have an option. For better or worse I would have to trust this stranger. "Can you help me?" I said, sounding even more exasperated than I felt.

Now that I'd made up my mind, I found that my panic subsided to a degree, I could take in the stranger's appearance more easily. They wore a ragged brown cloak with the hood drawn down over their face, leaving it in shadow. A beggar? Despite their humble appearance, the fact that this might be a person of the street, I doubted that they would be willing to wade through this rubbish even to help out a stranded child. And yet, they did just that.

I listened once more to those gut-wrenching *squidges* and sucking sounds as the stranger made his way toward me. I was so dumbstruck by this feat that I instantly accepted their outstretched hand as they helped me back along the strewn rubbish and to the entrance of the alleyway. As I stood back on the cusp of the main street, my nerves got the better of me and I looked about for the policeman who had pursued me. I soon picked him out, with the companion who had called out after him, not more than twenty paces away, remonstrating with the owner of a nearby stall selling woven goods: mittens, hats, stockings.

The stranger laid his arm around my shoulder.

I flinched.

"Come," they said, in a low drawl. "There's not much time."

But, before we could steal away lightly, I overheard the vendor pipe up. "That's him! Over there, with that child!"

My knees buckled beneath me and I would have collapsed if it hadn't been for the stranger's steady hold, *his*—as I'd established from the vendor—muscular arm sweeping my up into his arms. No longer did he resemble the doubled-over beggar. Now he was a much younger man—much younger than I'd first anticipated in any case.

He carried me across the street, easing his way between the traffic, the flaring nostrils of horses, the outraged faces of cab drivers, the caterwauling of onlookers, and over to the other side before the policeman had even set off at a trot.

He weaved his way along a series of alleyways, sure-footed and swift. It was like being carried along by a stallion. As I felt the stranger's fingers dig into my wiry frame I tried to get a glimpse of his face but it remained obscured by the hood, somehow unmoved by all the frantic motion. We carried on our way until I was sure that we'd left our pursuers behind. Indeed, the stranger seemed contented too, as he plonked me back on my feet. I had a moment to look around.

This was one of the better-lit alleys of the city. The flickering orange light chased the shadows into the corners. I thought I could hear the hum of voices coming from the street beyond. I looked back up at the stranger. "What . . . How did," and then, the gushing emotion, the exhilaration at having escaped the police—and the workhouse—rushed out of me and I lurched forward and grabbed the stranger in a hug, pressing my face up against the ragged robe. "Thank you for saving me!"

The stranger lingered a moment before prising my fingers off him. He looked up and down the alley, a gesture which brought my nerves back, made me think that, perhaps, we weren't quite as safe as I'd believed. He addressed me again. Even though I couldn't see his face I imagined that he wore a sly smile. "It was nothing," he said. "It's remarkable what an effect a common thief can have. Very useful at creating a diversion."

"But what if they find you?"

"Find me? No, that will never happen."

"How can you be so sure?"

He steadied himself before me and, very slowly, brought his hood down to reveal his face. I had no need for questions now, because I had seen that face spread out on billboards since forever, those same well-set cheekbones, those oily pupils. I was staring into the features of none other than Dante Gobornik.

He shrugged off his cloak and then, somehow, made it disappear—maybe he had shoved it into a trouser pocket without me having noticed, but I would've sworn it simply disintegrated into thin air. He straightened up his waistcoat and then shot me a grin. "I'm running a little late for the show, I'm afraid, but I simply must ask what you were doing lurking at the entrance to the theatre this evening."

I recalled the flyer, that flyer that had slipped away from me forever, and I felt my spirits dip once again—I had let it get away. But I still had to try. "The assistant," I said, "I've come about the assistant's job."

He pouted then tilted his head to one side. All of a sudden, in a single fluid motion, he knocked the cap from my head and looked me square in the eye. "I'm sorry to be impertinent, but I must declare that the advertisement stated, quite unambiguously, I thought, that I was looking for a *boy*."

And there, right then, I felt my dreams slipping away. Dante Gobornik had seen straight through my disguise, the disguise I'd thought would hide my twin shame, and so smashed all my dreams to smithereens.

CHAPTER TWO

I STOOD THERE before him, stunned. My body was still recovering from the escape from the police. I turned my attention to my flat cap, lying facedown on the ground and I stooped to swipe it up. I set it back on my head, took one last look at Dante Gobornik, and set off along the alleyway, tears already building inside me—ready to burst from my eyes. Just as I got close to emerging onto the main street—the street just outside the entrance to the theatre—Gobornik called out to me. "I *am* sorry, my dear, I never thought to ask you your name." He took a step toward me then halted. He put on a look of confusion, scrunching up his forehead, taking all the intensity out of those cheekbones.

"Sara," I said, automatically, not even thinking before speaking.

"Sara what?"

"Blind. Sara Blind."

He bowed his head, put his hand on his chin, as if considering the implications of this. I thought I could hear him muttering, "Sara. Sara Blind," over and over to himself, and then he said, with that sly smile of his, "So, Sara, you wouldn't be at all interested in partaking of my show?"

My breath hung in the air before me. Everything told me to keep going, to run all the way home, back to my family. Who had I been kidding coming here? But, instead, I continued to look back over my shoulder to where Gobornik stood.

He straightened up and jabbed his thumbs into the pockets of his waistcoat. His grin widened. "Yes," he said. "I thought so." And then, without waiting for my response, he jerked his head toward the stage door before disappearing inside.

I waited there, unsure what I should do now. My brain had just about caught up with things. Dante Gobornik had invited me in to see his show. I could hardly believe that little more than half an hour ago I had been stressing about whether or not I'd be able to get into the theatre—and here was Dante Gobornik *himself* simply asking me in.

Behind me there were several loud *clangs* of a bell. I heard the familiar, upper class voices on the street—that polite sound of hustle and bustle that only rich people can make: the smart *clack* of heels accompanied by delicate apologies, and the even more withering acceptances of those apologies. In a matter of minutes the front of the theatre would be cleared and I could easily slip back along the main street, head my way back home—perhaps snatch a ride on the back of a horse-drawn carriage some of the way. And yet that open door—a world of possibilities—played on my mind, sucked me inward, and before I knew it my feet were carrying me toward it and, a second later, I was crossing the threshold, inside the theatre, immediately into the backstage area.

A single candle flame illuminated the place I found myself in. A dishevelled, sun-faded violet curtain draped down before me, covering, I presumed, the way to the stage area. The air smelled of furniture polish and cigarette smoke. My breath came quick and fast as I saw no sign of Dante Gobornik. My mind began to play tricks on me, I thought the hurried *scuttle* of footsteps all around would be a precursor to some stagehand or other ducking their way behind the curtain and catching me there, whereupon they would snatch hold of me and deliver me to the same policeman as before, who, in turn, would escort me to the workhouse. But, much to my relief, no one came. As I took a tentative step forward, the door through which I had entered swung shut with a smart *slam*, apparently of its own volition. The flickering candle flame extinguished and I was left—all alone—in the all-consuming darkness.

Not for the first time that day, my heart rapped faster, my spine tingled with anticipation. I half-expected Dante Gobornik to appear in the gloom, with that reassuring smile of his, and lead me to somewhere safe. But no one came.

Strangely, as I proceeded through the backstage area, shoving curtains and trailing ropes out of my face, while treading lightly around indiscernible boxes on the floor, I imagined myself in a kind of human-created, mechanical jungle—one complete with savage and silent beasts. A thousand pairs of beady eyes watched me from the shadows.

In the middle distance I sensed light. A steadier glow. Not candlelight. Indeed, as I got closer I realised that it must be a gas lantern. I approached with great care, not wanting to bring anyone's attention to my presence. In my mind I began to wonder whether this might be some sort of spiteful game, if Gobornik had welcomed me into the theatre only to have me frightened before having me snatched by the police and carried away for trespassing. But, thinking over how he had saved me from that alley, I doubted that interpretation. Still, I continued onward with great care.

I reached the gas lantern and paused, still standing in the shadows, afraid to move from where I was. There was no one about from what I could see, and yet there was a gentle *burble* of conversation drifting through everything. When I dared take a couple of steps toward the source of the noise I was rewarded with a brief peak onto the stage, the expectant audience, chattering away to one another, leaning into their companions. That's another thing about rich people, I've always wondered why they do that, compete to be heard, one over the other, shouting each other down. In our house, whenever there's a discussion, there's a clearly defined hierarchy, first Dad, then Mum, last me, Sara. The babbie doesn't count, yet. But I suppose as he gets older, being a boy, he'll have me relegated to the last heard.

I retreated from where I stood, afraid that one of the members of the audience might see me—might recognise me from outside—and I returned to the obscured objects at the side of the stage. Over my shoulder I could hear the steady *thud* of approaching footsteps. I hid myself behind a cloth-covered piano, peeking out around the sides.

Dante Gobornik, now wearing a sable jacket and a towering top hat, buttoned his cuffs as he trod toward the stage—sending the aged wooden planks squeaking beneath his feet. He waited, out of sight of the audience, in the wings.

I watched on as the stage slipped into darkness, as someone cut the houselights and the frantic murmuring of the audience ceased and the excited whispers broke out. Soon enough, though, even the whispers were curtailed. A dark, booming and otherworldly voice addressed the audience from a location unseen—by myself anyway.

"Ladies and gentlemen, good evening to you all. Please permit me the pleasure of welcoming you to *Smartsbridge Theatre* this glorious summer night."

Only then did I realise that, Gobornik, with his back turned to me, was addressing the audience himself. But, the voice. It was completely different from the one in the alley. There was no sign of the slightly inflected accent, the reedy quality it had had to it, the voice which had reminded me of my own neighbourhood. Now it was sure and proud. A little disappointedly, I admitted to myself that he sounded just like them—those noble members of the audience. And I wondered who he really was.

Gobornik continued, "Now, please put your hands together and give a warm welcome to this evening's entertainment, Great Purveyor of Mind Tricks and Conjurings of Nationwide Renown, Dante Gobornik."

The audience broke out in a frenzy of applause.

And then it all happened so fast. As I leant around the piano, watching this all take place, Gobornik glanced back at me then gave me a wink. I was a little embarrassed to find myself shrinking back, into my hiding place out of sight, blushing all over. When I summoned up the courage to look out again he had, of course, set out onto the stage.

I tried to slow my breathing, to get my heart rate under control. I remembered at school how once a doctor told me I have asthma, that I have to keep myself calm under pressure or I might just stop breathing. I closed my eyes and thought of my warm blankets down by the coal fire and Dad's steady snoring, Mum's almost imperceptible breathing, the sounds of the mice scuttling about the kitchen, picking off the scraps that we hadn't consumed ourselves. But then there was the voice again, and I felt myself growing increasingly uneasy, I felt so out of place, so uncomfortable. I wondered whether I might still be able to simply cut and run, or if that time had long passed.

Silence lingered about the theatre. It was so complete that it sent a shiver up my spine. I looked about me, sure that someone was watching me, a stagehand, just waiting to toss me out into the street. I fixed my gaze on Gobornik, who trod over the stage.

The stage was empty except for a single wooden stool, which came up to about Gobornik's waist. He approached the stool and shrugged off his jacket, which he then draped over it. Next, he removed his top hat and set it on top. Looking more or less as I'd encountered him in the back alley, he twisted up his shirt sleeves and rolled them to just below the elbow. Then he held his hands up to the crowd.

I wished I could see their faces—to see how they reacted—but I was sure that their expressions were ones of wonder, spellbound: open mouths, gaping eyes, nails digging into armrests. At least that was how I imagined myself. I had to wake myself from my daze and detach my fingers from the material covering the piano—once more I told myself to calm down.

Still facing the crowd, Gobornik took several steps backwards, and then brought his hands down by his sides. He rested his chin upon his chest so that his face lingered in shadow—just like in all the posters. When he spoke he maintained that same upper class drawl he'd addressed the audience with at the start, only he dropped his volume so that it was only just above a whisper. "I will need a volunteer. A lady."

The houselights turned up to about half power, I judged

from the gleam on the stage, and there were sounds of stirring within the audience: mumbled remarks, the shuffling of feet and dresses. Finally, there was the sure, yet light, footing of a 'lady.' Slowly, she entered my line of sight, climbing to the top of the steps to stand, with her back to me, at the side of the stage. She wore a light pink dress and a frilly, netted hat. Even from behind I had a stirring inside me that she wasn't—she just *wasn't*—one of them, one of the audience. Not really.

As she stepped toward Gobornik, she raised her high-heeled feet and set them down with a slight curvature of motion. She reminded me of how the whores strut out on Basket Street, the times I'd seen once when coming home after dark with a loaf of bread clutched to my chest—one of those times when I'd had to steal.

The lady turned to face the audience in half-profile, a nervous smile on her lips, her shoulders arched and her sleek neck slick with sweat. Perhaps she hadn't fooled me, but she was —by all accounts—an accomplished actress.

Gobornik reached toward her and took her hand in his. With a lightness of touch, he led her further toward the centre of the stage, reached out and took hold of her shoulders and bent her to his whim, like a shop mannequin, so that she faced the audience. Only I could see his fingers linger in the small of her back —just for a second—but just long enough for me to confirm my earlier suspicions. This was all part of the act.

Done with her presentation to the audience, Gobornik drew her back so that she faced up to him and, again in that voice just above a whisper, said, "Keep your eyes on mine. That's it. Pretend that a pair of strings tie mine and your pupils together. An unbreakable, iron string. Yes, good, do just that."

As I stared at Gobornik's face, that intense expression, I felt my stomach churn and squeeze. His eyes were solid as marble and yet as wild as flame. My heart fluttered and I felt my throat contracting. I took a couple of deep breaths and felt a little better, but still weak—like a passing draught might be enough to topple me.

"Now," Gobornik said, a little louder, "I wish you to think of three numbers from one to a hundred—three numbers, just keep them to yourself for now." He waited a beat. "Have you thought of them?"

The lady nodded vigorously and then uttered, "Yes."

Gobornik maintained the intense eye contact several seconds longer before closing his eyes and pressing his fingers to his eyelids. His face contorted into a series of wrinkles and then he seemed to awaken, to blink sleep from his eyes, before saying, "Seventeen. Fifty-four. Seventy-six."

The lady's shoulders stiffened once more and her gloved hands went straight to her lavender lips. I watched on as her breast heaved, first inflating then deflating. She shuddered a touch and then nodded to herself. "That . . . that's right!"

A few claps broke out in the audience and then there was a faint applause. This was something these people had seen before, and probably done better. Already there were mutterings among them, I picked out a few: "Hackery, nothing more," "If I'd wanted to watch a cold-reading I'd have sent for a medium—and I know one who would charge a fraction of this ticket," and then, another, "That's enough for me. Might make a steal on an early supper. Restaurants should be pretty reasonable at this hour—what with all the shows still going off."

I clenched my teeth and dug my fingernails into the palm of my hand. I wanted to shout at those people, to ask them how they could possibly run out on this show after all that money they had paid—money enough to buy my family time. Pigs, that's what they were. Nothing more than a bunch of pigs all shoehorned into those rows of velvety seating.

But Gobornik didn't look phased in the slightest. He just kept up his stare with the lady—a stare which was making me feel increasingly uncomfortable. I wished he would stop, that he would choose another volunteer from the audience, that he had some other stooge.

And then something remarkable happened. All the lights went down.

It was so sudden, the flapping of the flames were lost in a single swift drawing of a sheet—it seemed as though dozens of ghosts, all replete with a snuffer, had extinguished every last one on a cue from Gobornik. I knew then that it was no accident, although I have no real way of explaining how. If only to confirm this, Gobornik raised his voice so that he spoke over the worried tones of shock spreading through the theatre. "Stay where you are. Keep quiet, do not move—I cannot stress that enough. Please do not move whatever may happen. If you can help it keep your lips sealed. I beg this of you."

Now, for the first time in the show, I found myself growing a little agitated. There was an edge to Gobornik's tone now, one which suggested that he was on the brink of losing control— really losing control. I wondered whether it was just my perception, my growing uneasiness, the tightness in my chest. And then, just about that time, the lady—the volunteer, the stooge he had brought on stage—let loose a blood-curdling scream, I knew that this was no act. At least, Gobornik's nervousness didn't seem to be.

More screams followed, all ladies at first, until the gentlemen joined in with their manly groans of fright. It appeared that Gobornik's advice—his suggestion to stay quiet—had been quite suddenly forgotten.

I remember quite clearly gripping hold of the piano, feeling its reassuring, sturdy wooden frame akin to the safety of a ship's mast in a storm, which was to say that I still felt in danger of being swept overboard at any moment of the storm's choosing. Still, I stared out into that darkness, trying to make sense of something. And, in the end, I did.

Well, I summoned up my guts and snuck out from my hiding place, crawling on all fours to the wing of the stage so that I could look out into the theatre, where I assumed the reason for the scream to have emanated. And as I crouched there I felt like screaming myself.

The only way I can come up with describing them was as shadows. And I know how little sense it makes to say that of forms in the darkness. There was no light—none at all. So they couldn't have been. It was an impossibility.

The shadows took the form of dough-like men, walking their way along the aisles of the theatre. There were dozens of them. My eyes soon grew accustomed to the gloom and I made out the audience, just as transfixed on these beings walking among them —occasionally pausing to stare into one of the members of the audience, inciting a scream, and then moving on. They all approached the stage in a calm and efficient manner, apparently unmoved by the reactions occurring about them.

Then I moved my focus onto Gobornik, who crouched on the stage, one hand to his brain while the other supported himself on the boards. He bore all his teeth, as if he were suffering a grave migraine. I could almost taste his pain, the blood in his mouth from his gritted teeth.

One of the shadows trod onto the first of the steps leading up to the stage and I hurriedly retreated, back into the wings, not wanting to get in the way of whatever was happening there. The shadow slunk by me, and then, all of a sudden, stopped dead and stared me right down. A winter's chill rattled my bones and I cuddled myself with my own arms, trying to warm my chest. I would never have suspected such a sensation, not here, in the theatre, on a pleasant summer's night such as this. The shadow lingered another second, two, and then lost interest, proceeding on his way. I had more to worry about than my own comfort now because those beings—those shadows—were slowly but surely stealing their way closer and closer to Gobornik.

Gobornik remained in the same position, unaware of these shadows bearing down on him. Soon they formed a circle right around his prostrate stature and I had the most horrible feeling that they were about to . . . about to feed.

It was strange. I think that I was so traumatised at watching the whole scene play out that I'd gone beyond belief, beyond fear —much like the rest of the audience—and now I was simply engrossed in the drama.

Maybe twenty minutes passed, perhaps an hour or more, but those shadows circled Gobornik—around and around they went, like a demented second hand on a clock. Then, all of a sudden, they ceased their motion and, all at once, dived into him.

Gobornik shrieked, tipping his head back as they appeared to fly into his chest, to soar right into his very being. He clutched his skull in both hands, unable to cope with whatever it was that these shadows were doing.

Out in the audience, I heard once gentleman remark, "A doctor! Someone call a doctor!"

I watched another lady, a few rows back from the gentleman, faint from the extremity of the display, only prevented from falling by the sure catch between a pair of her chaperones.

Gobornik stayed where he was, still screaming, no sign of letting up the intensity. I wondered at his lungs, how they must've stung with such an effort.

"The lights, the lights!" said another gentleman in the audience.

There was much stumbling about in the darkness, ladies fleeing for the exits, gentlemen lingering before, a little reluctantly, following. And then, without any announcement, Gobornik ceased his screaming and slowly, ever so gradually, the gas flames sparked up and then burst back into full light— bringing up the houselights.

While the exodus from the hall didn't cease completely, it certainly slowed somewhat. The gentlemen first, some of them succeeding in retrieving their wives, or mistresses, gingerly leading them back to their seats. Others, I noted, remained out in the lobby, too terrified to return. Gobornik slowly rose to his feet, his whole face soaked in sweat, his waistcoat seeming to hang limply off his frame and, amid the terror, a few buttons had burst right off his shirt. His dark chest hair billowed from the rip, not a little romantically. I suppressed a deep and sudden yearning within me and retook my position behind the piano— hidden once more.

This time the clapping started almost all at once. The semi-emptied theatre added a thick resonance to the sound of flesh beating flesh. The audience had no need to rise to their feet because they already stood on their feet.

Gobornik, his eyes wandering the crowd, dark blotches marking his face, making him seem decades older, raised his hand in a wave and then bowed to them all. He waited out the long five minutes or riotous applause before calling back his lady volunteer. As she crept onto the stage I noticed her exchange a wink with him before turning to face the crowd, her face illustrated with widened eyes and slightly parted lips—to the best of their knowledge just as taken aback by what had happened as the audience.

All at the same time realisation sunk into me, like an ointment, through my flesh, into my bones, and I knew—whatever this was, witchcraft, whatever it be—I needed to get myself as far away from it as I could. And yet, at the same time, I couldn't leave behind those mesmerising eyes of Gobornik's, those sharp cheekbones. Then I felt a hand on my shoulder.

CHAPTER THREE

M Y HEART LAPPED at my tonsils. I would've spun around, but the steady grasp the stranger held me with was sufficient for them to perform that task themselves. I found myself eyeball to eyeball with a portly man, wearing a tuxedo. He had a bushy, grey beard—a few flecks of ginger in it—and he had azure eyes that suggested he'd been good-looking, even handsome, as a youth.

My whole body shook with terror. This man. In his grasp, I managed to jerk my head around to get a glimpse of the stage—a look at Gobornik—but he was still addressing the crowd, leading them through, what I supposed to be, his final trick of the night, another tired mentalist act involving that stooge.

As I met the man's eye again, I found weak words in my throat. "Please," I said. "Don't take me to the police. Just throw me out into the alley. I promise I'll go away and never come back. I . . . I could never see that again."

The man increased his grip and then released me completely.

He continued to stare at me and then, with a quick look at the stage, said, "Come on, let's get you away from here. He'll be finished soon enough."

I managed a final glance at Gobornik on the stage, infuriatingly running his hand against that lady's cheek, reading her mind in some other way, before the man seized hold of my elbow and whisked me off, back through the darkened backstage area toward the door leading out into the alleyway.

As we passed the doorway, I bent my head up to him. "Please, please!" I said. "I'm begging you. My family needs me," I said, feeling the words burn in my brain as I said them, because I knew that getting shot of me would only be a case of lifting off a welcome burden—although I knew my parents would never so much as breath a thought like that. "Let me go, please."

The man grunted and dragged me on. For his age he was strong, although I suppose—being a fourteen-year-old girl—I had limited strength to exert on him myself, and as such was as poor judge. The man tugged me into a thin corridor, past a few doors with labels I had no time to read, until he brought me before the final door in the corridor and stopped. This time I did have time to read the label: Dante Gobornik, written out in a florid hand.

I searched the man for what to do next.

He sighed then rolled his eyes. "In!" he said, giving me a little shove.

And, suddenly, I was standing in Dante Gobornik's dressing room.

The door whispered shut behind me, a precaution that seemed

beyond the man's normal capacity but necessary given the circumstances—the almost silent stage and its enraptured audience. I listened to him snort and then spit, and then his footsteps plod up corridor and out of earshot. For the first time in what seemed like an age, I allowed myself to breathe freely and fully, and took in the room.

I sniffed the air, it was a sweet odour that I'd later find out was cinnamon, as I walked the floor of the dressing room I found the soles of my shoes sticking to it—where someone had dropped some liquid or other, who knew when. There was a mirror, a gas lamp burning away above it, and then a series of powders and other makeup items that I wouldn't discover the use for until later on. But it was the trunk in the corner of the room that caught my attention.

It was a big old trunk, the colour of spinach with hefty leather straps binding it closed. Looking around the room, I decided that this must be where Gobornik kept all his belongings, everything he owned in the world—from what I'd read about him in the newspaper I'd found in a gutter once, he toured the entire country, sometimes even crossing the Channel to Europe, never keeping a fixed address. The romance of that travelling lifestyle wound me up in knots. I thought of all the things that trunk had seen, the different landscapes: snow-capped mountains I'd only seen in paintings or heard about in stories at school, crowded towns where it's impossible to make head or tail of what people are saying because they speak a different language, but, more than anything, it was the concept of constant motion. I just couldn't comprehend moving on all the time. Never stopping except to visit the theatre, entertain the residents there. It sparked something in me—a sense of childlike wonder that I'd believed long dead, eroded away following my hard upbringing, when I'd seen my future stretched out before me—a life like my mother: kitchen, children, cleaning up. In that moment I dared to dream again.

In the distance I heard muffled applause, and then loud cheers, whistles. The cacophony startled me. I shifted away from the trunk and stood, feeling deeply awkward, in the centre off the room, hands clasped at my waist like I'd seen the posh, young girls do on occasion. Those steady footfalls trailed all the way through backstage. I trailed their locations with my mind, creating a map inside my mind. And then the door creaked open.

I guess I must've closed my eyes at some point because the first thing Gobornik said to me was, "You can look now."

He stood in the doorway, one hand lingering on the door-knob and the other hanging down by his side. His shirt was still unbuttoned, that black hair sprouting from the pearl-white material. He waited another second or so and then brought the door closed behind him. He stepped into the dressing room, toward me.

I felt every breath jerk through me. I was afraid that I would just faint away, fall to the ground and never even hear the *thump*.

He shot me a winning smile, which was still winning despite his gaunt complexion, the fatigue he showed in his eyes. "You're looking a little pale," he said. "Which is quite some achievement for someone of your colour."

I stayed quiet, knowing that I was treading on thin ice. If I said the wrong thing I might break my welcome, be turfed out into the street again. Although I knew that logically Gobornik had invited me in, saved me from that policeman, I couldn't help being suspicious of his behaviour, that at any moment he might snap around and bite.

Gobornik slumped into the chair and stared into the mirror. He snatched up a rag soaking in a dish of water and dabbed at his face. As he washed himself, he glanced at me in the mirror. "So, what did you think of the spectacle?"

Only then I noticed that his accent had returned. It was the same voice he had used with me in the street—the one that felt like home, at least it betrayed the same uneasiness, the same disjointedness that united our community.

"I thought you did pretty well. All the others I've brought here, the others I've considered, have fainted right out of hand."

Questions stirred within me like glowing coals, but I hadn't yet allowed Gobornik right into my confidence. First I needed to feel comfortable with him—my situation here—and then I could probe deeper.

Gobornik replaced the rag in the dish of water and rolled his shoulders. He puffed out his cheeks and then said, "So, do you want the job?"

All the breath leaked from my lungs. "What?"

"The job," he said. "If you want to be my assistant, the job's yours."

"Just like that?"

"Just like that."

I turned the offer over in my mind. What should I do? I had come here with such low expectations, glad to take whatever bone I might get thrown, that I might meet with Gobornik, let alone have him offer me the post, was so far off the mark that I hadn't even indulged the fantasy. And now I had a decision to make.

"Well?" he said, his tone a little sharp this time.

My throat felt inflamed, but I still got the word out. "Yes," I said, hissing the 's.'

Gobornik gave me the briefest of smiles and then returned to inspecting himself in the mirror. He moved to stretching his skin with his fingers, as if trying to work out one or two of the few wrinkles he had there.

I stood there in the uncomfortable silence, those same questions burning away, but unable to go answered. And so my mind moved onto practicalities. "Mister Gobornik—"

"Please, Dante."

"Dante, I . . . you see, I read in the advertisement that my family . . . well, that they would be . . ."

"Compensated?" he finished.

I nodded, giving him a glum smile, showing too many teeth—too many teeth for a *lady* in any case.

He squinted at himself in the mirror, as if perplexed by the notion, and then he eased back into a slight smile. He turned in his chair and eyed me, one of his arms dangling down over the back. His twinkling gold rings caught the light and dazzled me. "Yes, that's right," he said. "I think I remember now. That was the wording I had the newspaper man take down." He thrust a finger in the air. "Yes, your family shall *certainly* be compensated."

A weight lifted from my chest, but my logical mind stepped in. I had heard promises my entire life so what reason did I have to think that this one was sincere. I suppose the answer was that, right down in my deepest of deep guts, it sounded right. And yet, and yet, I wanted that confirmation. I wanted to hear him speak the words. I summoned the courage and said, "When?"

"Pardon me?" Dante said, busying himself untying his shoelaces.

"The . . ."—the word stuck in my throat—". . . *compensation*."

Dante hauled off his shoes and then shifted onto the edge of the chair, rested his elbows on the arms. "I don't see any reason why we shouldn't go there now."

"Now?" I said, almost unbelieving.

He nodded and then bounced onto his feet. He crossed the room, breezed past me and set about unlatching the trunk, undoing the leather straps. He flipped open the lid and reached inside, frown lines sketched across his face. Finally, after a good minute's rummaging, he came back up, face declaring victory, clasping a bunch of notes. More money than I'd ever seen at one time in my life. He shuffled back toward me and paused, still holding the money. "All right then," he said. "Are you going to tell me where your parents live, or what?"

Dante finished undressing, now putting on a simple, loose tunic and draping a greatcoat around his shoulders. He plunged his feet into a pair of rugged-looking brown, ankle-high boots, then clasped hold of my hand and led me through the darkened backstage area. As we proceeded on our way, I heard a familiar voice drift along the corridor—the man who had intercepted me behind the piano and escorted me to Dante's dressing room. He shifted from the shadows, a glow from the oil lamp he held before him accompanying him. His quick azure eyes found mine and then slipped, just as quickly, to Dante's. "Master, the coach is ready to go, if you'll permit me to take your trunk out?"

"Yes, yes," Dante said, with the flourish of his hand, still lugging me forward, carrying me away from the warming light as if he were allergic. "We've got a little errand to run first, that's all."

The man grunted and then I supposed he slipped into Dante's dressing room—to fetch the trunk—since the glow from his oil lamp disappeared. But I found, whereas alone in the darkness I had felt vulnerable, now in Dante's company I felt all-powerful, like nothing in the world could frighten me, which I realised—even then—was mad considering what I'd just witnessed, those shadows in the theatre. But that was the truth.

Dante leant into me conspiratorially. "Don't you worry about Farol, he's been with me since I started out. He's reliable, much quicker, stronger than he looks, but he doesn't like strangers. But he'll warm to you, I can promise you that."

I listened out to the earthy *thuds* and coughs emanating behind us, back in Dante's dressing room, and I allowed Dante to steer me further with, I thought, a more-determined step.

We walked through the now-silent theatre, along the aisles, half-lit by the houselights, and then out into the lobby. I absorbed the careful wooden curves of the bar, the plush crimson carpet beneath our feet. As I walked I felt myself bounce a little—I wondered whether that little leap in my step was because of my circumstances or because of the carpet. Perhaps it was a bit of both.

The air was a little sour, a stench that I'd learn was the smell of gin, whisky, a long way from the beer that my father would earlier—when our financial situation had been better—come home smelling of.

The air outside was thick, humid, I eyed the bulging storm clouds above us, fit to burst. I felt the sweat seep out from my pores, run in rivulets down my neck and dampen my shirt. Seemingly from nowhere, a darkened carriage popped out of the night and Dante waved his hand. He helped me up the step and inside. I got a last glance of the theatre, the words *Smartsbridge Theatre* set in a kind of twilight glow now. Beneath my bottom I savoured the springy cushions. This would be my first trip in a carriage, but by no means the last.

A feeling akin to shame shredded my nerves as we spiralled downhill, deeper into the underbelly of the city. The money, the *compensation,* rested between the two of us: a vulgar pile of notes, lightly rustling together with each movement of the carriage, each foray over lumpy ground. Every so often a beggar would jog alongside the carriage, shout obscenities at us—the occupants—and then have the cheek to demand we throw them something. Each time this happened, without fail, Dante would reach inside his tunic and withdraw a little purse he kept on a string about his neck. He would fish inside and then toss a few of the coins through the tiny gap in the carriage window. I would listen to the *tinkle* of coin against cobbles and think about how, only hours ago, that sound would've driven me insane in a crowd, that I would've dropped to my hands and knees and scoured the floors for those sacred few chunks of metal.

Soon enough the carriage drove between the leaning slate roofs, the jutting fronts of Grunly Borough. The road narrowed and, pressing myself back in my seat, for the first time concerned about moving through my home at night—because I was marked now, riding in a carriage, to them I was just another upper class *twassock*, ripe for bleeding all that he carried. Dante, on the other hand, seemed completely unmoved by the situation, he made no motion to demand that the driver speed up, neither did he riddle me with questions as to where my home was located—whether we were growing close or not, so that we might flee in the quickest manner possible. No, if I had to comment on some aspect of Dante's demeanour, it would be to say that he looked quite *at home*, as if this was really where he belonged. And that sent a warmth through me.

As we trundled through a particularly narrow alley I noticed a dark figure leaning up against a wall, quite clearly looking out toward me. But, before I could get a look at their face, see any detail, the carriage had rolled onward.

The carriage bucked its way up my street and then came to a sudden halt outside the front door of my home. I had never had much of an opportunity to scrutinise the façade of my house before, always being in a rush to either get inside or get away, but now, in the uneven light from the carriage's oil lamps, I had a chance to observe it, for the final time, to meld that image to my mind as a kind of pre-emptive nostalgia.

The door hardly fit its wooden frame and I could make out the profound darkness inside the house—I guessed that my parents hadn't thought to wait up for me to return home, having already given me up for lost. Although it sounds somewhat cruel, it was no more than the truth that children went missing every day without explanation—only to crop up in the workhouse, in prison or, if they were luckier, dead in the roadside, relieved from a life of pure misery.

And I impressed that final image of the house on my mind. Its steady loping bulkiness, the window that seemed to open out toward its edges, narrowing towards its middle. The front that had once been whitewashed but was now more of a battle-hardened, dirty grey. And this house had fought battles, of that I had no doubt. My family, we fought a fresh battle every day.

"This the place?" Dante said, with the sliver of a smile, apparently failing to grasp the gravity of my emotions connected with this place.

"Yes," I replied.

Dante reached forward and tapped the front of the carriage twice with his knuckles. I watched, through the window, as the coach driver allowed his reins to fall down by his side. Next Dante hopped up onto his feet, grabbed the pile of cash in one clenched fist and seized hold of my hand with the other. He escorted me out of the carriage. We stood together, alone in the street, outside my front door and, without hesitation, Dante knocked a pair of heavy and distinct knocks.

I waited with my breath ragged in my mouth and I closed my eyes, focussing on the sounds coming from inside the house— trying to pick out any sound of stirring from within. There was no sound. Dante knocked again, his grin widening, obviously anticipating this occasion with great relish—and why wouldn't he have? It wasn't every day that a knight rode in on a gleaming stead and emancipated a poor girl's family from that heaviest of burdens: its unwanted daughter.

But there was still no sound.

He looked to me, his smile faltering a touch. "Don't you have a key?"

In all the pent-up tension, the life-changing direction this evening had taken, I had completely forgotten about practicalities. As I reached into my pocket and withdrew my key, I noticed my hands shaking. I wondered whether my parents slept soundly or if I had misjudged them, that they had gone out to the public houses in search of their daughter. Maybe I had misinterpreted the situation completely—perhaps their love for me was unconditional, beyond reproach of practicalities.

I stuck my key in the door and listened to the ancient mechanism *click* and *creak*. I gave it a couple of wiggles and then the door burst open, trembling on its hinges as it rocked into the darkened room. Not even the coal fire burnt away. It was then that I knew my parents were not in the house.

I held back at the threshold, too afraid to take the first step, to be the one to solve all of my parents problems in one fell sweep, and now, of course, that I had plunged my understanding —my interpretation—into deep doubt, I was having second thoughts about the whole thing, having sold myself out to a magician.

"Don't you have a gas lamp?" Dante asked.

I shook my head.

"An oil lamp?"

Again, I shook my head.

"Right," Dante said, shading his way back out of the house before returning moments later carrying an oil lamp he had pilfered from the coach driver. He shone it on the interior of the house.

It was funny. At first I picked out my own place, the bundled rags, the wall marked with my hands prints—the wall which I had used uncountable mornings to help myself up to my feet. It was empty, of course, but who else would be occupying my place? It was only when I followed Dante's gaze, to those lumped-up forms on the floor, occupying the places where my mother and father, and the babbie between them, would sleep. And I knew, instantly, without having to step any closer, that they were dead. All three of them.

CHAPTER FOUR

I THINK I SCREAMED, although I cannot be sure. I recall quite clearly the sensation in my throat—the vibrating vocal chords, the exasperation that followed. I ended up on the floor, knees hunched up to my chest, letting loose wave upon wave of sobs. And then I felt his reassuring hands on me, that touch of warmth through that blisteringly cold room—impossibly cold given the muggy evening. It was the same feeling I had had with those shadows, back in the theatre, but I thought I had escaped. It was so out of place there. It took me several moments to work out the words that Dante was muttering in my ear. "Come," he said. "Come."

I allowed him to help me to my feet, to tug me close to his body so that once more I could bask in his warmth. I cradled my head upward at him then said, "Help them, please, help them."

Dante stared at the dead bodies, at the people who had once been my parents—at the babbie that had once been my brother. In the glint from the oil lamp I made out their faces, the colour of charcoal, their lips, the cracked pink of human warmth shortly extinguished. Again, I implored Dante. "Help them."

I'm not sure whether or not he shook his head, if he responded at all to my wishes, but the sum of it all was that there was nothing—simply nothing—that he could do about my family. They were gone, slipped into an abyss. No longer of this earth. And, in that moment, I felt that I wanted to slip down into a crevice, to go to the same place they had gone. Because, now, I was utterly alone in the world. Or was I?

This time Dante took hold of me with a greater strength—that strength that he kept so well-hidden most of the time, but which could startle whenever he brought it out on the occasions he deemed it necessary. On that occasion it was necessary.

I beat my fists against his chest, screamed in his face, I felt my mouth froth with saliva—that self-made cushion which eventually reduced my words to mere babbling idiocies. And, not for the last time, his strength simply overwhelmed me. He led me away from the house, placed me back in that carriage, and gave the order for us to ride away, into the night, out into the capital, away from the scene.

It was strange, but arriving back at the theatre, it felt like I was returning home for the first time. Dante hurried me from the carriage, paying the driver with one of the notes, before slapping one of the horses—sending the man, clawing for the reins, bucking and rushing into the night. Once more, he placed his arm around my shoulders, steering me into the back alley of the theatre where the carriage awaited, a pair of horses stomping their hooves impatiently, Farol at the reins, pulling on them to keep them in place. Dante barely grunted a greeting to Farol as he led me around the carriage, to the door, where he bundled me inside.

I found myself sitting beside the lady, the stooge from the stage, who now wore a satin dressing gown and a hairnet. She greeted me with a thin smile then hoiked up a cushion and rested her head against it. Her eyes fluttered closed.

Dante brought the carriage door closed with a *slam*, straightened up in the seat and faced forward. None of his light jubilance remained, indeed his whole complexion had paled and, if I'd guessed as to his mental state, I'd have said he looked anxious. What had he seen back at my house? Did it have something to do with those shadows I had seen earlier? Or was it mere coincidence, the trauma of coincidence plaguing his mind?

Outside Farol brought the reins down hard on the backs of the horses and I listened, for a long time, to the rhythmic fall of their hooves, the *clop-clop*, *clop-clop*, as they drew us out of the city. A little while later, Dante swished the curtains shut, grabbed a cushion for himself and set himself to sleep against the opposite window to the lady. Sitting there, in the middle, I simply allowed my head to fall back against the cushion and felt sleep overwhelming me.

I guessed it was early in the morning when I awoke, judging by the clean light dripping in around the edges of the curtains. The lady was staring at me through half-opened eyes. My heart jittered as I recalled what had taken place the previous night—and where I was now. We just looked at each other to begin with, before the lady's voice came out as a dusky whisper, no louder than a feather brushing a tablecloth. "Who are you?"

I listened to the tick of my pulse, and then tuned into the rhythmic breathing of Dante beside me. He slept just as I suspected, mouth closed, eyes shut tight, nostrils barely opening as he respired gently. Everything about him had the appearance of control.

I turned my attention back to the lady. "Sara," I said, the word already feeling dead in my throat.

"And where'd he rescue *you* from."

I pondered the question, not quite sure what she was getting at—and then thought of my family. I held back another moment before saying, "He rescued me from death."

The lady blew a little air from her nostrils, just the approximation of a laugh, nothing more. Then she jerked her head back onto her cushion and closed her eyes again.

I guessed that I wasn't going to get anything by the way of a formal introduction from her. When I turned my head to look at Dante sleeping away, I was surprised to find him, apparently fully-awake, bright eyes searching out mine. "Don't you worry about, Jessica," he said. "She's just jealous, that's all."

Jealous, that was one way of putting it. Another was that that look she had gave me communicated one thing, and one thing only, that she wouldn't be satisfied until she had ripped me from limb to limb.

Around midmorning, the carriage stopped and I listened to the gravelly *crunch* as Farol chucked himself out of the driver's seat and down onto the road. He picked his way around the carriage and threw open the door beside Dante. He gave me a drawn-out, searing look, then said, "Anyone for breakfast?"

As we sat about of a few logs, rubbing our hands together in the morning chill, I had a chance to take in our surroundings.

Trees, hedges, rolling hills, for as far as the eye could see. I traced the dirt road we had come along with my eyes, followed it right back to the point where it could no longer be made out— where it slipped around a bend. The capital was beyond there, a long way behind us now.

This was the first time I'd ever left the city, the first time I'd really ever seen this much space, this much *green*, all about me. The air was so fresh and tasted of nothing—no smoke or shit stenches. And, as I surveyed the landscape, my new hard-to-believe life, the sun broke through the mounted cloud above and the whole day just opened up before me.

For breakfast we had bacon and eggs, cooked by Farol on a gas stove. When I accepted my portion from him, on a chipped porcelain plate, I gave him a hearty thank you, and all I got for my trouble was a brief shrug, before he moved onto serving Jessica. I supposed I would be an outsider for a while.

Jessica scrabbled through her snap-shut purse—featuring an interwoven green and gold pattern—and fished out a cigarette case. She opened it up and then slipped a cigarette between her lips.

I was shocked. Sure, I'd seen a few women down the pub smoke once or twice, but Jessica, a lady, I had expected different from her. But, then again, I reminded myself that she was merely acting as a lady, and now the curtain had come down she could do as she wished.

Jessica sucked long and hard on the cigarette, blowing out a seemingly never-ending stream of bluish smoke as she exhaled. Then her quick eyes found mine and she arched her eyebrows. "You want some of this?"

I looked to Farol, then Dante—the closest thing I had to a father figure now, I guessed—and not getting any sort of guidance from either of them I stretched over and accepted the lit cigarette. I inhaled, feeling the smoke instantly tickling my tonsils. I wanted to sneeze but, looking into Jessica's face, I knew that would be just what she wanted. So I held the smoke in for a few seconds before spluttering it out and passing the cigarette back to her.

A slight smile tweaked her lips as she accepted the cigarette and I was glad that our relationship was thawing somewhat—just a little, but it was a start.

Farol wandered down the hillside with an empty bucket and returned with the same bucket, but this time with water slopping over the sides. He laid it between the two horses, who fought briefly before one of them gave way. As he straightened up from leaving the water there, he looked to me and said, slapping the neck of the horse who'd lost out having a drink of water first, "This here's Old Billy, a softy if ever you saw one. He'll do anything to avoid a fight. Sure and steady, though, a good worker. Oh, he'll trot all day long without a word of complaint."

I guessed by 'word of complaint' Farol meant a *whiny*, a *snort* or a *whine*. Despite everything I'd seen the night before I'm not sure I was completely willing to be taken in with talking horses. Not just yet, anyway.

Farol continued, ruffling his hand through the other horse's mane, the one drinking away, "This fella, though, he's a different story. He's a mean old brute at the best of times, but he's got us out of some sticky patches in the past, got the wheels spinning, if you see what I mean." Just as Farol's hand wandered further down his head, toward the horse's nose, the horse snapped its head back and tried to get a chomp of Farol. He missed. Though, only just it seemed. Farol managed to lunge out of the way just in time. He chuckled to himself as he regained his footing. "Silver, this boy is, and goodness, doesn't he know it."

I watched on as Silver drank the bucket dry, and as Old Billy, looking slightly wronged, did nothing to stop him. Once the bucket was empty, Silver knocked it over with a *clang* and Farol stooped to collect it. He was still smiling—I guess he got most of his joy out of those horses—and then he slouched back off to refill the bucket. As he went, he addressed Dante, saying, "I'm not feeding them till the evening. They'll work all the harder on an empty stomach. What'd you think boss?"

"Fine," Dante said, using an almost stiff rasher of bacon to mop up the remainder of his fried egg yolk.

Farol inclined his head, touched his cap and then proceeded down the hill.

There was so much burning inside me, so many questions—not least what had become of my parents, I guess that was top of the pile then. I wondered whether I should be sad, be in some kind of mourning, but I just couldn't summon anything for them. It wasn't that I didn't love them, that I didn't already miss them, but being here, out in the countryside, I felt so far removed from who I had been yesterday, that whole setting of my home. And then there was all that I had witnessed in the theatre, what I had seen last night. I guess it was a little overwhelming, hard to believe that I was really here—that this wasn't just some brilliant dream. I did opt for one question, though, and I directed it at Dante. "How come you move on so quickly after shows?"

Dante deposited his now empty plate on top of the rest of the dirty dishes then eyed me over the pile. His eyes were like a pair of twin jet-black flames. "It's all about leaving the people wanting more. We have to go elsewhere, if we stuck around, did two, three, four days, a week of shows, then the mystery would get lost, people would get bored. No, what's kept this unique for the handful of years we've been going's the *mystery*, that's the one concept I would focus on. As a magician, mystery is everything."

I wasn't quite sure that I believed all that, there had to be something else there. The 'magic' I had seen the night before I knew hadn't been a show, or at least I could see no way at all that he might've done it. And, if it were all just an elaborate act, I just couldn't believe that the audience would manage to unravel it so quickly—even going to multiple performances.

Dante broke out into a grin, as if to curtail any further questions, and he snatched hold of the plates and, the crockery toppling as he walked, he said, over his shoulder, heading in the same direction as Farol—down to the same stream, I supposed, "We share the chores around, washing the dishes, cooking, all of that. Only thing we don't share is that Farol's the driver, Jessica's the stooge and I'm the main act. I guess you're going to work out where exactly you fit in." He paused as I watched one of the plates on top wobbling precariously, apparently moments away from toppling right over. "Today I'll do the dishes since you're just starting out. But you're going to have to start pulling your weight soon."

As I watched him go, I thought on my situation, how I had lost my parents. I suppose, looking back, there's a way of seeing him as being insensitive, unfeeling to what must've been going through my mind at that point, but, in a way, I was kind of glad that he made no fuss, just got on with life—didn't see it as his business to go raking up emotions.

"I'd take care around Dante," Jessica said, lighting up a new cigarette and inspecting her nails.

The statement caught me off guard and then, a second or so

later, I prompted myself to ask, "Why?"

She smiled lightly and parted her lips. Just as I thought she was about to speak, she puffed out a cloud of smoke. It hung there, in the air, right before us. As it tumbled about, writhing within itself, we watched it tear itself apart. Finally, she held her cigarette down by her thigh and looked out over the stunning scenery, deciding to focus on a bird twittering away on a nearby branch. "He's different from us, that's all."

"In what way?"

Again, she paused, and I made out Farol making his way back up the slope, carrying the replenished bucket of water for Old Billy. She spoke quickly and under her breath. "There's a darkness which lurks around him, follows him wherever he goes."

"What does that mean?" I said, my heart juddering in my throat, already having a pretty good idea of what she was suggesting—about how it might relate to the constant moving.

Before she formulated a reply, Farol was upon us, still grinning away, and he set the bucket of water down before Old Billy, who ducked his head and drank long and hard. He approached us wiping his hands on his trousers and said, "Well, that's enough sitting about in a field for one day. Are you two just going to laze about or help me get all this kit back into the carriage?"

I climbed up into the carriage, beside Jessica, and watched on as Dante climbed the hill, lips pursed, whistling as he went, carrying those cleaned plates before him.

The evening was drawing in as we cranked our way down a precariously narrow path—two great drops to either side of the carriage—toward a town nestled in the valley below. Gas lamps blinkered on as we went on our way, lighting up as we rocked through the streets. I pressed my face up against the cold window and stared out.

The houses to either side of us were in the old style: wooden beams, chalky plaster, like a series of forgotten things, many centuries old. But it seemed cosy, homey, so different from where I'd grown up—where everything had seemed temporary, functional, never binding. And I started to wondering whether, somewhere in my past, I had a connection to this place. But I knew that couldn't be: Mum had often told us about our relatives, from long away, in much warmer places than here. Still, I had my fantasies.

Farol steered the carriage through the bending streets, beneath the lopsided houses, which seemed to lean in on us, threatening to topple over and crush us at any second. I looked to Dante, who seemed to read my mind—a phenomenon which I would begin to notice more and more as time went on.

"We're on our way to the theatre," he said. "We'll be there soon. I came here, a few months earlier. I decided that I've left things long enough, that the people will be crying out for more by now."

Still, he was choosing to continue with that pretence—to string me along. Now I had that bit of information brewing in my mind, that 'darkness' which Jessica had suggested to me, I found it impossible to listen to anything at all he said without a relentless voice nudging me, telling me that it was all a lie. All the same, I just smiled lightly at him and continued to watch the town scenery passing by.

It was completely different from the capital's streets—oh sure, there were the people selling, the market stalls, a few beggars sprinkled about here and there, rattling their tin cups at passing strangers for coins, but the underlying harshness—that sense that told you someone or something might slip from the shadows at any given moment and slit your throat—was missing. In short, there was simply no edge to the place. If this town had been an animal, it would've been a docile housecat—to the capital's prone tiger.

The carriage banked to a halt and we got out. Again, as was becoming his habit, Dante helped me out, down onto the cobbled street.

I observed the theatre front stretched before us and read off the name, all illuminated: *Ditchfurth County Theatre*. It was all made out in dark marble, its steps well-polished. I realised that this must be the shiny jewel in this town's crown—for on my journey through the town in the carriage I hadn't seen any other building so proudly maintained. With the grace that can only be brought on through deep familiarity of place, Dante swooped through the front door of the theatre with the rest of us in tow. I noticed that Jessica had plonked a wide-brimmed bonnet on her head—so as to keep her association with Dante something of a secret, I supposed, although I knew that her being a stooge had nothing at all to do with the marvels of his act—that whole introductory part was merely a misdirection and even then I wondered how necessary it really was.

Dante led us through the doors and into the gallery, where the velvet-upholstered seats sat, bowed at an angle, propped toward the stage. As we passed them, at quite dizzying speed, I found myself a little hypnotised by the rows zipping by. I heard the steady footfall of Jessica behind me, driving me on, and the marching heels of Dante before me, leading us further into the depths of the theatre.

We leapt up the stairs and onto the stage, where Dante took

a moment, stopped and pivoted around, taking in, breathing in the air of the place. Then, apparently satisfied, he'd led us into one of the wings.

Immediately I felt a great difference standing in the back-stage area. It was totally different compared to *Smartsbridge Theatre* from the night before. That's to say that the entire area was ablaze with light, people—stagehands—scurrying to and fro. I compared it with the near-emptiness of the previous night and couldn't help feeling a little warmer, a little more relaxed in this atmosphere. Dante, on the other hand, was simply livid.

It's funny, back then I could never really imagine what Dante might look cross, but I got a severe lesson. The moment that that bright light touched his face he squinted—no, utterly screwed up his eyes in disgust. He snatched hold of the nearest stagehand's collar—a blond boy with delicate features, thin pink lips—and demanded that he bring someone called Knightly, straight away. Upon being told that Knightly had, most unfortu-nately, left the theatre, Dante demanded that the boy bring whoever it was that was in charge.

I found myself standing a little unsteadily, beside Jessica, wondering what was going to happen next. I snuck her a glance and got a knowing wink in reply. Was this the darkness she'd been talking about? This thinly concealed anger?

I felt dumbstruck as Dante paced back and forth, writhing his hands, his easy composure that I'd thought was simply an effortless extension of himself, smashed to smithereens. Was this the real Dante I was seeing on show?

Finally, the blond boy returned skittering before a severe-looking woman who wore her hair in shaggy curls, had deep, dark makeup about her eyes. She had broad shoulders and wide hips, and when she spoke she held her arms down at her sides, smoothing her thighs. She had a thick—what I'd describe as—country accent. I got one of those out-of-place stares I was so used to, before she looked Dante up and down and said, "What seems to be the problem, Mr Gobornik?"

Dante reeled himself in slightly, though I could still make out his deep breathing, the way that his shirt rose and fell with the rapid motion of his chest. He gesticulated all around him, throwing up his hands. "*This*," he said. "This is just totally unacceptable."

The woman puffed out her cheeks in a manner which suggested she had quite long and tiring experience of dealing with performers, and that Dante was just another one in a long line to be dealt with. "I'm sorry, Mr Gobornik. You're going to have to be a bit more specific than that, I'm afraid."

Dante flinched, his eyelids doing a double blink. "Look," he said, taking deeper and deeper breaths. "I can't have all these lights up back here. All this . . . *brightness*. It needs to be dark, it needs to be lonely, I simply cannot go on with things as they are."

The woman frowned. "Mr Gobornik, I must ask how you'd expect all these people to do their jobs under such circumstances. Are you seriously suggesting that these people snoop about with an oil lamp before them, tripping over whatever gets in their way—tripping over themselves. I mean, blimey, we might well have a *fire* under such conditions."

Dante shook his head vigorously. "That's another thing, I cannot have these people here. Too many of them. Buzzing about." He let loose a long-held, heavy sigh. "If Knightly were here he would understand. There wouldn't be any misunderstandings."

"Knightly passed away a few months ago, so you're going to

have to make do with me. I'm sorry about that, but that's just the way things are."

All of a sudden, Dante's nervous tension retreated. He clutched his hands at his navel, as if someone had run a sword through him, and turned even paler. "Knightly's . . . dead?"

"Yes, I'm afraid so."

I remained fixed on Dante, trying to read into his expression what was going on. That look of shock, that utter disbelief. I had seen that last night when we had visited my parents house, found them all dead.

The woman was glancing about now, obviously growing impatient with the conversation. "Look here, we've got a full house tonight, I've had messengers from all the surrounding counties rocking up here asking whether there might be tickets for whichever noblemen they represent, and I've turned them away. It's in both of our interests that this performance go ahead. I'm willing to arrive at an agreement with you on some matters." She paused. "But there shall be compromise, Mr Gobornik. My employees must work safely and you must realise that *Ditchfurth County Theatre* is not a place that merely exists for Dante Gobornik. We have protocol, processes which ensure the smooth-running of all performances—the safety of its guests and staff. Do I make myself clear?"

"An agreement?"

"Yes," she said.

"Minimum staff. No lights."

She sucked in her cheeks, eyed me and Jessica then said, "Fine. But you'd better put on a damn brilliant show."

As Dante led us through the still-bright backstage area, he broke into an uneasy smile, then turned to me and Jessica, saying, "I guess she hasn't seen me perform before."

CHAPTER FIVE

I SET MYSELF to working out what my role would be within Dante's setup. I slunk back and observed both Dante and Jessica getting ready—Jessica slipped out of the dressing room, pausing to give Dante a peck on the lips, about two hours before the curtain raised, I guessed she went off to mingle with the rest of the crowd gathering in the bar, to at least put up some semblance of a façade that she was a genuine member of the audience. I watched Dante sponging on some powder—I saw that he was making his features less gaunt, the shadows etched on his face less pronounced. In the corner of the dressing room, propped up on a battered old leather armchair, stuffing poking out all over, Farol slept with his head propped up on his elbow. I guessed that the way this team worked, what with Farol driving through the day, was that he got a chance to catch up on sleep during the performance. How anyone could sleep knowing of the things that Dante was performing on stage defeated me.

Then again, I guess, somehow he had grown accustomed to the spectacle.

In my quest for some meaning as Dante's assistant, I strode out through the backstage area, into the night-time alleyway where the horse and carriage—fully prepared and ready to leave at moment's notice—waited. Both horses looked content enough. Having eaten they now slept on their feet, all bridled up, blinders fitted to their eyes. I thought how their tender, Farol, was in a similar stupor at that very moment and the idea tickled me enough to elicit a smile. With nothing to offer in terms of the horses—the carriage looked pristine too—I returned inside, to the dressing room where, with Farol in a deep sleep, I found myself alone with Dante.

He remained fixed on his image in the mirror, still holding that sponge, taking care of little spots. He replaced the sponge into the smooth shell of powder and turned in his chair to face me. There was no sign of that nervous tension which had previously had him so wound up about the lights backstage. He had his easy aspect, his stage face on—everything about him spoke confidence. "I suppose you think me a little odd, what with all that having the backstage area darkened, not letting people around back there."

Although I wouldn't have dared say as much, he had locked me down well—read my mind in that way of his. It took me a little off guard that he had so readily assumed that posh accent too: it felt as if I might be speaking to a different person entirely.

"The thing is," he said, "being a magician—a *conjurer*, that's how we sell it to the upper class folks—the most important aspect to keep in check is the secrecy surrounding your tricks.

And, with people watching, one can never tell who's standing by, ready to look for all the secrets which hold up the trick. The darkness, why, that's just a precautionary measure. If I'm truly honest about then I have to say that it puts me at ease as much as keeps things hidden from the audience. The secret is the key, though. Because without secrets, why, a magician is nothing but a fool."

I decided that now was my time to speak up. If I couldn't, as Dante's official assistant, then no one could. "Even if the secret to the trick is that there's no secret at all?"

His smile faltered a moment, then he seemed to shake that moment's hesitation and he gave me his full, all-out grin. He inspected the cuffs of his dress shirt and then, in that way of his when an idea had struck him—in a comic way that made me think more of a clown than a magician—he stuck his finger in the air. "I know just the job for you," he said. "Tell me truthfully, how did you find watching the stage the evening before?"

My stomach squeezed at the thought, but I knew I had to put on a brave face. "Oh, I quite liked it."

"Good, good," he said, rising from his chair, only half-listening now as he draped his jacket around his shoulders. "Then that'll be your job—you'll be on the look out for anyone troublesome, anyone lurking backstage who's not supposed to be there." He nodded to the sleeping Farol. "That used to be up to him, but, to be honest, I can see that it scares the bejesus out of him—and what with all the driving during the day I think he deserves a good block of sleep, last night wasn't the first time he's been caught sleeping on the job, only just caught you in the end, didn't he?" He eyed me then, his razor-sharp gaze that sent bubbles frothing through me. "What do you say?"

"Yes," I said.

And so, that was how I found myself—much as the previous night—crouching in the wings, watching the stage. The *Ditch-furth* had a more open design than *Smartsbridge* so from where I stooped, behind a large wooden crate, I could make out the audience too. Although I felt a little silly, knowing that Dante had surely invented this role for me, and also the sensation that I was stepping on Farol's toes so early on—having only just joined Dante's troupe. But Dante was my boss, so it was his rule I had to follow, and I didn't need to worry myself with any melodrama surrounding the others. At least that was the theory.

The audience filed in slowly, some of them with glasses of whisky in their hands, others with programmes dangling from their fingertips. I thought I could sort the gentlemen who had visited previously. While the ones I pinned as not having been to one of Dante's shows before laughed themselves silly with their companions, the ladies on their arms chortling along with whatever the joke was, the ones I was sure had been to see Dante before quietly took up their places, clenched their knees together—their female companions mimicking them. I traced the dark circles around their eyes, the pasty skin about their jowls, and I imagined them not having slept the night before, having woken every fifteen minutes in clammy sweats, dreading the show and at the same time driven by some deep compulsion to attend—that they were attending something truly *spectacular*. That was the power of Dante and what he did. For whatever other pretensions he put on, what with the tired, old mindreading tricks, the main act that he offered could not be beaten anywhere else—at least that's the assumption I live with, even to this day. And so, feeling more apprehensive than ever, I settled down, behind that wooden crate, ready for the night's performance: like those who had witnessed the show before, with a mixture of dread and excitement.

The bell rung—more like a chime than the *thronging* echo of the *Smartsbridge*. It reminded me of Christmas time, in fact, such was its lightness of touch, and I found myself spiralling about in a little storm of nostalgia—because that was what it felt like, as if there was already a great distance, that the butter of time had long spread itself between me and the past—for my parents and my past life. It twinged inside me, turning my guts cold, making me shiver. The houselights turned down and the audience slipped into uneasy silence.

Without warning, Dante appeared behind me.

My heart did a flip.

He laid a gentle hand on my shoulder, smiled and then ventured out onto the stage to raucous applause. Already I found myself revising my previous interpretation. Could it be that more of these people than I had imagined had come to the show before, and that they really did believe it was a mere 'illusion?' Or was it that they were merely riding the wave of hype and publicity, that they had great expectations for Dante Gobornik: Great Purveyor of Mind Tricks and Conjurings of Nationwide Renown?

Just as he had the previous night, he trod lightly over to a stool already standing on the stage. He removed his coat and his top hat—it seemed strange to me that he seemed only to wear them from the dressing room until the moment he stepped onstage. I guess, as with everything involving the upper classes, it was all about appearance.

A polite round of applause rippled around the audience. Dante took a few bows before rolling up his shirt sleeves and peering out into the audience. He called Jessica back up onto the stage, and even this time I had to admit that he did it in such a way—that looked of blank ignorance sketched over his face—that if I hadn't known of their relationship I never would've guessed. And, looking over the audience, I guessed they'd been taken in just as equally.

Dante went through another of his mind trick routines, calling on Jessica to think of several names. In the end he identified them—correctly according to Jessica—as various members of her family. Again, as had happened the previous night in the *Smartsbridge*, the audience clapped and there were a few muttered words, remarks along the lines that this wasn't anything as remarkable as the posters had made out. I searched for those anxious faces and picked them out of the crowd. They, like me, said not a word to those sitting beside them, just as aware that this was all a ruse to throw the audience off the scent of the true illusions—conjurings—to come.

After another short trick of the mind, Dante thanked Jessica and had her take up a position toward the back of the stage, in the shadows. I noted that, surely under Dante's orders, the only light which shone on the stage was a single monochrome beam, directed right at him—the protagonist. I watched as cigarette and cigar smoke twirled up into the ray of light, like this was some night in a parlour, and not the stirring of some unsettling force.

My spine tingled and I crushed my fingers into fists.

Dante swiped his top hat off the stool, carried it to the front of the stage then set it down, top first, on top of the boards. I wondered whether he was going to pull a rabbit out of it—do something else rote and mundane from the magician's locker. But, of course, this being Dante Gobornik, he had no such idea in mind.

He sat on the stage, crossing his legs before the overturned top hat. Some members of the audience murmured and I had the urge to reach out and shake them, to tell them that now—for once in their lives—they had to be silent and watch the spectacular scene that was about to unfold. Soon enough, Dante did silence them.

He leant back, eyes clasped shut, mouthing some indiscernible words. And I watched on as a thin coil of black smoke rose in the spotlight. Unlike the cigar and cigarette smoke, it rose in a single line, undisturbed by any breaths or draughts. It rose right to the roof. When it reached the ceiling it stuck there for a few moments, reminding me of a rope held taut. As I inhaled, I felt a chill enter my lungs, like a winter's morning. So I decided to hold my breath. Looking out across the audience, I saw that others did the same.

The black rope hung there before the murmuring Dante, who remained otherwise unmoved by this conjuring. And then, all of a sudden, he wrenched open his eyes and glared out at the audience.

His eyes were like pickled eggs, no pupils, a slight green tinge to them as if . . . as if he had recently passed away. The dark circles beneath his eyes seemed to become more pronounced— they reminded me of the sockets of a skull I once dug up in a heap of rubbish. He reached out his hands, toward the black rope and seemed to shape it, like a baker forms dough. The black rope responded to his gestures, manipulating itself, thickening itself, slowly taking on form.

First it changed near the very top. It fattened into what I suppose I'd describe as a head, next its shoulders, and then its chest took form. And, finally, the stomach, rather wide and stodgy, then the legs. Before us stood a sable, phantasmal giant: the size of the theatre, which was at least three storeys tall. It appeared to glare out upon the audience.

As with the previous night, several members of the audience reacted to this with muffled *shrieks*, *groans* of terror. No one made for the exits, though. It seemed that this being, whatever it was, pinned people to their seats—suggested that if they were to so much as stand it would strike them down.

Having got over the sight of this static phantom, I turned my attention back to Dante, who sat in the same position, apparently awake, what with those wide open eyes. I felt my whole body tremble as I took in his appearance, and I wondered whether this conjuring was hurting him, if it was affecting him in any way. What would happen if this being, somehow, managed to take control of him? Those were the irrational fears spreading through my mind like a cancer.

Dante slowly found his feet so that he stood between the legs of the conjuring. He stepped right up to the edge of the stage so that, from my perspective, he appeared as only a silhouette against the spotlight. He raised his arms into the air and, to my abject horror, I observed the *being* doing just the same. The thing was mimicking him.

Dante brought his arms down, his phantasmal puppet doing the same of course, and he took off walking down the steps, into the aisle, between the people with their faces opened wide like shredded tin cans. I watched as a couple of ladies fainted as he passed by them. Although the gentlemen among the audience remained conscious, their composition faded and their lips trembled. This wasn't the night of frivolity they'd bargained for. And some part of me took a sick sense of pleasure that this conjuring had set all these people straight.

Dante trudged his way between them all, the phantom appearing to be a great burden. The spotlight followed him the whole way around the theatre, discounting any chance that this being might be a combination of showmanship and some trick of smoke and mirrors.

As I forced myself to breathe in that freezing air, I heard a *scuffle* over my shoulder. At first I paid no attention to it—there were bound to be hundreds, if not thousands, of rats and mice back here, and they didn't scare me, not when I'd been used to hearing them at home going through the kitchen all night. In any case, I think that the conjuring which Dante was bringing through the hall absorbed the majority of my attention at that moment in time. But I heard it again and again. I kept on hearing it. In the end, I had to tear myself away from the spectacle unfolding before my eyes to look back over my shoulder. What I saw there was a shape, a form—a person—skulking about in the darkness. Whoever it was they obviously hadn't noticed I was there, trusting that they wouldn't be overheard backstage by the commotion, the absolute attention concentrated on the theatre.

I recalled that I was supposed to be doing a job back here, to be keeping an eye on people doing the very thing that this person was doing. I held back a few seconds, suddenly frightened that I might get myself into trouble. I played out little fantasies in my mind, that this might be a policeman, that he might've tracked me down, that he might have come all this way to haul me back to the capital, to the workhouse. Another horrifying thought struck me, that, perhaps, I was considered a suspect in the murder of my mother, father and little brother. It would surely seem suspicious, that they'd died the very same night that I had taken off with Dante. I closed my eyes and summoned the courage. Once I was ready, I slunk my way through the darkened backstage area and took to spying on the person. Not being all that big, not much over five foot, it wasn't much of a task to stay hidden. Sometimes I'm grateful for my dark skin—that it gives me an advantage in the night-time, working like a natural ally.

As I stole closer, watching the figure fish through various aspects of the backstage area, tug on ropes here or inspect bags of sand there, I felt my foot slip and come down with an impossibly loud *crunch* on something or other. I stopped dead but I knew that the damage had already been done.

The person tilted their head in my direction, hands still clutching a sandbag before them. I could sense their eyes twitching through the darkness, attempting to make out the source of the sound, and then, all at once, I detected their glare fall upon me and linger there for several seconds.

It took my mind a moment or two to process the fact that the person had taken off running, that they were beating their way out of the backstage area. And another few seconds before my brain screamed for me to follow, which I did.

The person wore a long coat which flapped out behind them, a hat pressed down tight upon their head. I tried my best to keep up the pace, keeping track of the obstacles that the person before me dodged, but however hard I pushed myself I could feel that the person was leaving me behind. A strong scent of honey pervaded the person's trail and it took me back to sitting in that field that morning, eating my first breakfast in the countryside, and—at the same time—stripping me of my edge. I tripped over a loose rope and fell, with a *thud*, grazing my knee along the edge of a discarded piece of brick.

Pain flashed through me but I tried my best to put it out of mind, forcing myself back onto my feet and after the intruder. I could only limp now as I felt the gooey slime of blood slicking the side of my leg. I winced to myself out of pain and limped onward, with every step hearing the *splatter* as another drop of blood landed on the floor.

A fresh breeze blew through the woody, dusky smell of the backstage and I knew that the person had managed to reach the door, had managed to get out into the night. This only incensed me and I pushed myself harder, telling myself that I wasn't prepared to be a deadweight—to simply sit about and soak up the food and water Dante gave me. I needed to make a positive contribution, and this being the one job Dante had assigned me I was determined not to fail.

I pushed myself harder and soared out through the alley door, which hung open on its hinges. I emerged into the alleyway and eyed the carriage, Old Billy and Silver, both waiting patiently for Dante's rapid escape following the show. And then I saw him. The person. He ripped around the corner, into the main street, the road which featured the entrance to the theatre. I blazed after him.

It was easier now, here in the twilight world, the gas lamps edging back the night from the town centre. The person, who I was now certain to be a man, from their gait, the long overcoat, and the wide-brimmed hat they kept pressed to their skull with a leather-gloved hand. I dodged through the sporadic traffic: a rag and bone man, a couple of waiting taxicabs, no more, certainly nothing to be compared with traffic in the capital, and I arrived on the other side of the road, just in time to watch the man disappear into a nearby alleyway opposite the theatre. I hesitated a moment and then rounded the corner. Only to come face to face with nothing. Complete emptiness. The alleyway was a dead end. Just a brick wall reaching up several storeys.

CHAPTER SIX

I STOOD THERE in the alley for a little while longer, trying to work out exactly where the man had gone. But there wasn't a clue. I started to doubt my perception of him slipping into the alleyway at all. Had I really seen him? I plodded back out, crossed the road and returned to the backstage of the theatre.

When I arrived back at my lookout spot I noted that Dante had already waved away the conjuring. Now he stood back on the stage with Jessica for company, doing another of his tricks, while the white-faced audience just watched on, no doubt still attempting to digest that being they had seen conjured before them. When the act finished there was a smattering of applause. It grew louder and louder as the audience realised the show had reached its end in such subtle fashion.

Again, I thought, *what an anti-climax*.

Dante helped Jessica off the stage and she returned to her seat a couple of rows back. He gave a bow to the audience, snatched up his coat and top hat, both of which had returned to the stool, and then the curtain dropped. As Dante replaced his top hat on his head and draped his coat over his arm, I considered what I was going to tell him. I had to tell the truth, but it was so disappointing that the first thing he had trusted me with I had failed at. I felt like a disgrace, a deadweight.

He whizzed by me, placing his arm around my shoulders as he went. He gave me a slightly tired grin. His face remained drawn, his expression gaunt. That conjuring had taken a lot out of him, like the one the night before, and I reached the decision that I should just put off telling him about the man. What would it hurt to tell him in the morning? Now he needed to rest and he could only do that if he wasn't stressing about someone sneaking around backstage. I know it sounds a flimsy piece of logic, but I recalled how he had reacted to the stage manager earlier on in the evening—that anger which had flushed through him, and I was afraid that he might subject me to that same irate stare.

So I did my best to look worry-free as we headed on to his dressing room, where Farol remained prostrate, snores reverberating in his throat, arms splayed in all directions. Dante slumped into his chair, allowed his arms to dangle over the sides. He looked more exhausted than he had the night before. He was sweating profusely, damp patches showing up at his armpits. Slowly, he turned his head to me. "Why don't you go and see what Jessica's doing, out in the lobby?"

"What?" I said, hardly able to understand.

"Out in the lobby." He waved his hand vaguely. "I don't know, pretend to be her handmaid, or something. See what you can learn from her."

My heart thumped against my chest. I told myself that it was now or never. If I didn't tell him about the man then it would be just as bad as lying—was it possible to lie without ever saying a word?

"Go," he said, and this time I obeyed him, startled a little by his abruptness.

I hadn't thought of how I might feel out in the lobby, between all those upper class people, wearing only my tunic and trousers. I dodged out of the way of elbows, side-stepped spilling drinks and covered my ears when the thunderous laughter broke out—sounding so strange and alien after what had just been witnessed. I noticed a couple of weary glances in the direction of any laughter. If I had to pick a word to describe the tone, that looming atmosphere of the lobby it would have been 'funereal.'

I picked out Jessica, just across the lobby, standing alongside three gentlemen—all of whom, judging by their fresh faces, were bachelors. Tonight she wore her brunette hair in tumbling ringlets, which brushed at her shoulders. Every time she would tilt her head back to laugh, she would flick her hair behind her ear, before dropping her hand back down to her side. It took me a couple of viewings of this routine to notice that, each time she completed such a motion, her hand swooped into one of the gentlemen's pockets and snatched something from inside. I caught them quickly as she turned her palm: a pocket watch, a purse, and then, more daringly, what looked like a pair of emerald rings she'd slipped right off one of their fingers. I looked around and noticed a middle-aged lady, with sleek blond hair staring right at me from behind a fan. I decided that I either needed to make my connection with Jessica known or get out of there. One thing I've learnt is that it's better not to hang around somewhere you don't belong for too long. If something goes wrong the blame will always—*always*—fall at your feet. And so I darted through the crowd, brushing up against the silky fabrics of ladies' dresses, the coarser materials of men's suits, before arriving at Jessica's elbow.

Jessica noted me out of the corner of the eye but made no other reaction. She broke out into a smile again, following another of one of the bachelors' quips. "Yes," she said. "It's rather unbecoming that style of the farmers, isn't it? That portly gut over-spilling their trousers. One might think that they don't scrape together enough for a piece of twine to keep their waistbands raised."

This triggered a riotous reaction from the men, each of them falling about, slapping their thighs, cheeks rosy from drink. One of them spilled a little whisky on my tunic and I couldn't help but say, "Watch out, won't you?"

The bachelor flashed his eyebrows at me, took a final swig of his whisky, finishing it off before rapping it down on the bar behind him with the *slap* of glass on wood. "And what on Earth are you doing here?"

Keeping up with the developing situation, Jessica broke out and said, "Oh her," she said, "she's my handmaid."

I wondered whether she and Dante had run this kind of routine before with another girl, and, if so, what had become of that girl?

The bachelor paused a moment, lips parted and then broke out into a grin. He gestured to the barman behind him for another drink then turned back to Jessica. "How very quaint," he said.

Another of the bachelors, literally crossed eyed with drink, leant forward, outstretched his index finger and stroked my nose

—as if he might be able to rub the colour of my skin off. Seeing that it wouldn't, he appeared to stumble back a step.

The bachelor who'd spilled his drink chortled and said, "What's the matter, Percy, never seen a native before?"

"No," Percy said, still wide-eyed, sipping at his drink once again. "Never up this close. Not in a theatre, anyway."

Jessica looked to me again. I could tell by the way her eyes were skittering about the lobby that she was looking for a means to escape these men. She'd got what she'd wanted and now she was ready to leave. Her smile faltered a second then she caught herself and beamed full-heartedly. "If you'll excuse me, gentlemen, I'm afraid that I'm feeling a little faint following all the excitement this evening. You wouldn't begrudge me an early night, would you?"

The bachelor who'd spilled his drink spoke for all of them. "Of course not, my dear." He picked up the fresh drink the barman set down for him and held it up. "That is," he said, letting the words linger in the air, "on the condition that you allow me to escort you to your carriage. I know that, to a city dweller like yourself, this place might seem like something of a cultural backwater, but I can assure you that our thieves are just as impertinent."

"No," Jessica said. "Really, it's no trouble."

The bachelor seemed to take offense at this. His two friends chuckled away. He puffed up his chest, held his drink at his navel and tilted his chin back. "Now, now," he said. "I *must* insist, my dear. You see that I am a gentleman, it's an instinct which has been bred into me, generations strong it is. I simply cannot take no as an answer, if you'll accept my apologies."

I decided that this might be a good moment for me to make myself useful, so I piped up. "Ma'am, I thought you wished to go round and meet the magician, he did extend you the invitation, if you'll remember?"

Jessica didn't miss a beat. She brought back her easy smile. "Yes," she said, as I watched her tip away her drink behind the bar—something I guess she'd done throughout this encounter, "that's quite right. It slipped my mind completely."

But the bachelor remained unswayed. "What a marvellous idea. Yes, that sounds like just a perfect proposition. I'd be delighted to make the acquaintance of this fellow."

I could see the panic enter Jessica' s eyes, but she cast it off, like the professional conwoman she was. "All right," she said, shifting her glance back at me. "We'll all go to meet him, then."

The bachelor knocked back his fresh drink and set the glass down on the bar. He looked over his two friends and smirked, before offering his arm to Jessica, which she took without a second's hesitation. As we strutted past the pair of ushers guarding the entrance back into the theatre, the bachelor glanced back over his shoulder at me and said, to Jessica, "So aren't you going to introduce me to your little slave?"

That word panged in my mind. I felt my whole body heating up. I ground my teeth together and looked straight ahead. Although, at the time, I'm not sure I fully understood the ramifications of the word, I did know that whenever my father heard that word in his presence he was sure to introduce said person to his fist. In our house it became a taboo, something which wasn't even discussed—merely neglected into submission. And so I found myself left half-confused, knowing only vaguely that it was a horrific term said out of deeply held hatred.

Jessica, however, didn't bat an eyelid. I hoped it was because of the act she was holding up, rather than out of agreement or acceptance of the term. "That's Sara," she said. "She's been with me ever since she was little."

"Yes," he said, glancing at me out of the corner of his eye. "That's the best time to get them, like dogs, really, train them up before they learn any bad habits. Let them know who the master is, that's what Father always says." He stopped walking and tipped his hat to me. "My name is Gerald Forsneer, by the way. Pleased to make your acquaintance."

Try as I might, I couldn't raise even a fake smile to him.

He gave me a smirk and then continued his march forward, toward the stage, supporting Jessica on her way. As they climbed the steps, I listened in to Gerald telling Jessica about his father's plantations, in the colonies, and how one of his younger brothers —apparently something of a tearaway—had been sent there as punishment, made to 'learn some manners.'

I tried to imagine a field full of people just like me but my mind boggled. I'd spent so long being different from everyone else that I just couldn't summon the image into my mind's eye. It seemed like a mental mirage—too unwieldy to get my head around.

We arrived into the backstage area which now—I supposed according to some compromise struck between Dante and the stage manager—was well lit and buzzing with life. Stagehands thumped about all over, tidying things away, preparing other things for the next day's performance.

Gerald stopped one of the stagehands and asked him for the location of Dante Gobornik's dressing room. The stagehand looked to be on the point of asking him on whose authority he was standing there backstage, but at the last—following a subtle wink from Jessica—he backed down and pointed off in the correct direction. Gerald thanked him and jerked Jessica after him.

As we stood outside the door to Dante's dressing room, I felt a thrill of anticipation pass through me, some unholy sense telling me that something horrible was going to happen. It was like an itch before a gigantic gas explosion—only afterwards does that itch make any sense.

Gerald rapped his knuckles smartly against the door and waited back, patiently, doing his ridiculous peacock posture again, puffing his chest out as if he was about to cackle the farm awake.

A sleepy-eyed Farol answered the door. He looked to me, then Jessica, before—with a touch of bemusement—taking in Gerald. However, utilising the understanding and unquestioning trust which surely flowed between himself and Jessica, their years of working together, he stepped aside and allowed us all into the dressing room.

It was as if Dante had been given advance warning of our visit, because he was already on his feet, standing, looking fresh-eyed. Sure he looked a little dressed down, much like his stage appearance, wearing his white shirt with the sleeves rolled back to the elbows—workmanlike—as he accepted Gerald's handshake.

Gerald grinned to himself, Jessica forgotten for the time being, as he hungrily took in the whole of the dressing room, right down to the battered trunk. He returned his attention to Dante and said, "What an extraordinary show. I must say that I've never seen anything quite like it."

Dante smiled back, keeping up that faux accent—I thought of it as a mirror image, as if he was using Gerald as some sort of a model for his expressions, his mannerisms, a yardstick for his shrewd impression. "I'm glad you enjoyed it," Dante said.

"Not sure 'enjoyed' is quite the right word, but it will certainly live long in the memory, I don't mind telling you that."

"You are too kind."

Gerald slipped into silence for a moment, as if judging a careful proposition, scouting out all the angles, all the possible scenarios that might result from it passing his lips. "I say," he began, "you don't happen to do private shows at all, do you? It's just, my father, he's celebrating his fiftieth birthday next weekend and he'd be just *fascinated* by this sort of thing—really would love this."

Dante seemed a little thrown by this proposal for a second and then he rebounded, shaking his head. "No," he said. "I'm afraid I don't do private shows."

Gerald exchanged glances with Jessica—I could see what was happening, he saw this as being a great opportunity to demonstrate his worth to her, show what an expert negotiator he was. He allowed himself a bemused grin. "Come on, man, I'm sure we could work something out. Tell me, how much do they pay you for a show—something like the one you've put on tonight?"

Dante muttered something under his breath.

Gerald cupped his hand to his ear and stooped forward. "Didn't quite get that, what did you say?"

Farol took a step forward. "He said that he doesn't do private shows."

Still smiling to himself, Gerald rolled his eyes. "All right, then. How about ten pounds?"

That did seem to get Dante's interest—he stuck out his lower lip and thought about it before shaking his head, and attempting to remain distant from the whole proposal.

"Fifteen?" he said.

Again, a shake of the head from Dante.

This time, Farol trod over to Dante and whispered something in his ear. I overheard him berating him—saying something about that being enough to pay a month's expenses. I was sure that Gerald didn't hear as much, since he seemed more enraptured in his own private, drunken auction than genuinely trying to sniff out unfair advantage.

"Twenty!" Gerald said, with a note of finality about it.

Farol continued consulting with Dante, clearly trying to talk sense into him, trying to convince him that it would be worth their while to accept this fool's money. In the end it was Farol who turned away from the conversation and said, scratching his nose, "Fine, we'll take it."

Gerald clapped his hands together and his grin widened. "Marvellous! Father will be just thrilled." He rifled through the inside pocket of his jacket and produced a scattering of notes, which he passed over to Farol. "There you are, there's five pounds there, take it as a deposit, I'll pay you the rest on the completion of the show."

Farol took the notes and flipped through them, checking that they were genuine, then, without another word, he carted them over to the trunk in the corner, glanced back at Gerald a little suspiciously, then went to work on the padlock to the upper compartment.

Gerald turned his attention back to Dante—who was looking stone-faced. "Come on," he said. "Cheer up. Can't have you moping about. Or have you got another show in the next couple of days? If you do, I would have no qualms in compensating you for any lost revenue, to keep you around town until Father's party."

"No," Dante said. "It's fine. We've got a few days off."

"Then that's just splendid." He looked to Jessica with a drunken hunger in his eyes, his tongue just prodding out over his bottom lip. "There is just one condition, though, an additional thing I wish to ask for."

"What's that?" Dante said.

"This lovely creature here, I wish you to bring her along to the party. It would be such a shame for her not to come along. I think we might well get better acquainted at the party."

I noted the panic in Jessica's eyes, that he had so easily seen through her act, that she was indeed in league with Dante.

"Oh please," Gerald said, batting his hand in recognition of the startled looks surrounding him. "You may have something really spectacular at the centre of your show—what with all that conjuring business—but that rubbish, that pretence with this lovely girl, anyone could see through that. Just stock illusionist garbage."

My heart rapped a little faster. So it wasn't just me who saw through that shoddy opening, and closing, act.

He eyed Jessica again, reached out and brushed away a rogue ringlet at her neck.

She flinched at his touch.

"And you'd better be on your best behaviour at Father's party, my dear. All that thieving won't serve you at all—in fact it would be the grossest of insults to the invitees." He noted Jessica rising in protest, open-mouthed, no doubt about to attempt to make a joke of the situation—paint it as some kind of a misunderstanding—and he waved her away. "Please," he said. "Mere trinkets. Keep them, I shan't tell my friends if they inquire as to the whereabouts of their personal items. But here's a suggestion, you know, for the future. Why not keep that

Gypsy blood in check, channel it into those winning looks of yours, hmm?"

Once more, the whole room chilled. I was too afraid to look up from my feet—to look to see how Jessica was reacting to this. Gerald had played her, all of us.

"I think that's enough—" Farol started, before being cut off by Dante.

"Listen here, sir, we'll take your money, we'll put on a show, but you're to leave my people alone, is that clear?"

For the first time in the whole encounter, Gerald's smile slipped from his lips. "How about you 'listen here,' *foreigner*? My family holds a great amount of sway in this county, so I'd be *extremely* careful about making demands of me—just remember that if I were to so much as raise my voice right now, a dozen officers would come scarpering." He nodded to Jessica. "I'll have her arrested for a start, and we'll see where we can get with the rest of you. Accomplices, at the very least, or perhaps," he paused for effect, allowing the word to fill the room, "there's some dirty secret in your past, something that could quite easily be dug up." He broke into a slimy smile again. "Everyone's got their secrets."

The whole room sank into bitter silence. I thought I could hear Dante muttering curses under his breath, Jessica sobbing quietly. I noticed that Farol had frozen at the trunk, in the process of putting the deposit money away in the padlocked compartment.

"Right, then," Gerald said, casting a glare around the room. "I suppose the time has come to take my leave. You have my wishes. I shall have a servant meet you here later on tonight and escort you to a convenient spot on my estate—somewhere cosy you can bide your time, getting prepared before the party. I want to keep it a surprise, so I'll make sure you're not bothered and"—he shot a glance at Jessica—"kept well out of the way of the main house. Any questions?"

Silence reverberated about the room.

He flashed a light smile and took Jessica's hand in his own, planting a kiss on the back of it. "I shall say *adieu* to you, my lady." He cast a glance around the room. "And I will see the rest of you this weekend." He lingered at the threshold of the dressing room. "Goodbye," he said, before slipping out into the backstage area.

When I brought my head up to inspect Dante's reaction I expected to see him there, fit to burst, but instead he looked pensive, head tilted to one side, a neutral expression marking his lips. I wondered if he might be so exhausted from his display tonight that he just couldn't feel any more. Or perhaps he was plotting—working out how he might bite back against Gerald. As is always the case with Dante, it's almost impossible to ascertain, to second guess his thoughts. And, in the end, he just slumped back into the chair at his dressing room table and glared at himself in the mirror.

Jessica tapped me on the shoulder and gestured for me to follow her outside. I shot Dante a final glance then went with her. Outside it felt much better, to get out into the light backstage area. There was something about Dante, something about being with him that was akin to being below storm clouds, an electricity in the air, an unpredictability. It was something I'd only notice being away from him.

She led me out into the alleyway, to the waiting carriage, then she sat up on the backend of it, fished her cigarette case from her bag and snapped it open. She withdrew one and slipped it between her lips, lighting it with a match then sucking in the smoke. She shook her head and I realised all at once that she was close to tears. It sounded in her voice. "Dante's going to kill me," she said.

"What, why?"

"The stealing."

"He doesn't know that's what you do?"

She smirked then sucked at the cigarette again. "Oh he knows, but it's strictly prohibited. He tells me that it could bring the whole legitimacy of his act into question."

"He seemed to take it fine, back there."

"Yeah? Well that's because he was facing down a whole roomful of people—when he gets me alone, that's when I'll hear about it."

I let the air between us thaw a touch before daring to ask a question of my own. "I thought that Dante did pretty well out of his act, so why do you do it?"

She sucked at the cigarette a moment, pensive. Then she yanked it away from her mouth and tapped the ash onto the dirty ground. "I don't know, it's just a compulsion. It's so easy being out there in the lobby after shows with all those drunk, posh twits, I can't help myself. I see the opportunities and something just takes over, some deeper feeling, and I snatch whatever I can get away with." She sucked the cigarette all the way to the filter and then dropped it on the ground, crushing it below her towering heel. She met my eye and I felt something pass between us—at least I felt a twinge in my gut, a profound sensation that our relationship had just gone up a notch, that the frostiness that had marked our earlier interactions had thawed to an extent. She leant into me as if telling me a secret—little did I know that she was. "There is something else," she said. "The stealing, it's not just compulsion, at least that's how it started out, but it's not that anymore. I . . . and you can't tell anyone this, okay? This is just between the two of us?"

I nodded.

"I'm saving everything I steal, keeping my own money to myself."

"But why?"

"So that I can run away."

I had no idea how to respond to that statement. I guess I wanted to ask her why, but that seemed a touch impertinent, so I didn't. I held back, listening for anything else that she might want to unburden herself of. But that seemed to be my lot, for now. We stood there in silence while she smoked her way through another cigarette.

During this whole fallout, this whole affair with Gerald, I'd almost forgotten about the intruder backstage. I examined Jessica and decided, based on her own situation—what she'd just told me, confiding in me with a dark secret—that my own issue paled in comparison. So I rocked back on my heels and held forth.

She listened to me with dead eyes, staring at the glowing tip of her cigarette. When I finished she looked up, a serious note taking over her whole face. "You've seen them too?"

"What do you mean?"

She let loose a sigh then said, "There's a whole lot you don't know about Dante yet."

"Well, aren't you going to let me in on it?"

She shook her head. "Not just yet. The time's not right. You couldn't take it in at the moment I wouldn't worry about it, though. There was no one there, not really."

I felt a little cheated, that she had seen fit to tell me her own problems, and yet when mine surfaced she shut up completely.

But I thought that I was already doing a good job myself of putting the pieces together, beginning to see the shape that this puzzle was taking on. "Was it . . . was it a ghost?"

She examined me seriously again, no sign of the joviality she had faked back in the lobby, and then, sternly and evenly, she nodded in reply.

My heart felt like a block of ice, like it would freeze my whole body.

CHAPTER SEVEN

W E STAYED AROUND the theatre for a long while, waiting for Gerald's servant to arrive, each of us in our own worlds. As for myself, I dragged myself off back into the theatre and sat on the edge of the stage where I dangled my feet down and mashed my heels against the sturdy wood there. I thought about all that had happened that night: the 'ghost' I had seen skulking about backstage, Jessica fishing through the upper class men's wallets—and her telling me that she wanted to flee. And then there was the show itself. Everything was so overwhelming it was almost an afterthought that I found myself thinking about my parents, their dead bodies lying on the floor of what had been my home. It was hard to believe, it had been so sudden. But that was how it was. I noticed the steady footfall passing behind me, coming closer all the time, and I turned my head. It was Dante.

Dante had replaced his top hat and coat, and he looked all ready to go, whenever this servant showed up. He looked better now—his complexion was darker and his eyes steadier, or maybe he had just slopped on a load of makeup. He approached me, taking great care to set the heel of his shoe down first as he took his steps, as if he was wary of making too much noise. I followed him with my gaze. Finally, when he drew alongside me, he crouched and then sat down next to me, kicking his heels against the wooden slats of the stage in the same childish way I did. He stared out into the seats—the empty gallery. I wondered what might've been passing through his mind and, as it turned out, I didn't have long to wait before I discovered what it was. Still facing forward, he said, "You must be feeling thoroughly wretched."

I noticed he was still speaking with that infuriating upper class accent. To my horror I noted that it had taken an extra edge to it—become more refined, I thought, after having shared the company of Gerald. He had turned that knife-edge encounter into a learning experience. How had he found the capacity of mind?

I rolled his question about my mind, trying to work out how I felt. I really had no idea myself.

He slipped me a sidelong glance. "You know, with your parents—losing them, I mean."

I studied his tone, trying to work out if there was any humour to it. Looking back, it must've been infuriating—which is to say that it still infuriates me—the way that he trivially brushed aside my parents' demise as if it were nothing at all. And yet I didn't blow up, I didn't shout and scream at him, I just sat there, still clattering the backs of my heels into the stage, thinking it over, trying to force myself to believe that it was real —that my parents had really gone.

He brushed at some dust on his coat sleeve and then said, "I lost my parents about your age." He studied me closely. "How old are you anyway?"

"Fourteen."

"Fourteen? Hmm, yes, I remember fourteen. In that case I was a little younger than you were, then."

This time he sent a flutter through my heart, caught my attention, made me believe that we might be kindred spirits after all—even with only this tragic connection in common.

"I was in . . . back home when they died."

I wanted to ask where home was, but I got the impression that it wasn't information that would be forthcoming and, in any case, I felt my throat constricting and tears threatening to come. And if there was one thing that my upbringing had taught me it was to be strong, to never ever show weakness.

"Maybe I was twelve, thirteen years old, I never knew my birthday so it's hard to say, but I remember—yes, I do remember a quite deafening roar, the way that it just ceased hold of me, made me want to scream out loud at the injustice." He glanced at me again. "No doubt you're feeling something similar?"

Funnily enough I just felt numb. There wasn't anger, not really. Who could I have to blame? I hadn't even stuck around long enough to find out how they'd died. I speculated as to whether they might've each had a stab wound in their backs, blows to the backs of their heads or maybe a gas leak had done for them. And then I got to wondering what might've happened if I'd been there with them—if I hadn't been at *Smartsbridge Theatre* that night, with Dante.

"Hmm," Dante said, still studying me. "Ever since they died I just felt this weight on my shoulders, this responsibility for myself I'd never felt before—I knew that if anything happened to me it would be all my own fault, no one else's, and while it was shocking, horrific even, it was also liberating, freeing for me."

I have to admit I was having a hard time trying to figure out what he was saying, or trying to say to me. If these were supposed to be words of condolence then they came out awfully strangely.

"That was how I learnt that I had to find some means, a way to provide for myself—and that was when I decided that I would become a magician."

Again, it seemed like he had done a full circle, coming back to himself at the end, asking a question that I was sure I hadn't asked. Was he seriously insinuating that I needed to work out what to do now my parents were out of the way? The day after I'd stumbled across them dead? Didn't he think that I knew that, that soon it would be a consideration once I'd gone through the grieving process? I guess that, since I had a hard time believing, processing the fact that they were really gone, I hadn't yet the capacity to think to any sort of future—to imagine any sort of future—without them.

With the two of us alone, I decided that now was the time to confront him with that strange figure who'd been lurking around backstage—no matter what Jessica had told me. It had been my job after all to keep a look out for any strange happenings. Why shouldn't I tell him? I tucked my knees up to my chest and said, "Dante? While I was backstage I saw someone—a man, I think. He was wearing a wide-brimmed hat and a long coat." I met his eye to gauge his reaction, but Dante continued to stare before him. "I . . . I chased him from the theatre, into the alleyway, through the street. But somehow he got away from me. He seemed to disappear into thin air."

I wondered for a long time whether or not Dante had heard

me, since he continued to stare out at the seats, his eyes occasionally flickering about in their sockets as if considering an invisible book before him. "Yes," he said, his answer taking me off guard, seeming to come to me out of a void, "there are lots of them after my secrets."

I absorbed those words, scanned them for meaning, and found them vague, impenetrable. "Who?" I said. "Who's after your secrets?"

He seemed puzzled a moment and then broke into a smile, as if he had forgotten I was there and he was just recalling who I was. "Just . . . they just *bother* me, that's all."

I don't know what it was about his reply, perhaps it was the delivery—the tinge of anger in his voice—but the hair stood up on my skin and I felt my veins tingle with the blood seeping through them. Again, I felt the eerie cold which had descended over me while watching Dante's show—it was back again, just as fierce.

Farol appeared behind us, at the side of the stage. "Sir? The servant's arrived."

Dante shuffled to his feet, helping me up after him. Then he blazed a smile in my direction and took off, at a march, after Farol to meet the servant.

I just stood on that stage, looking out into that great empty space, thinking over what I had witnessed that evening and what it had meant. I knew that there was something different, something special about Dante. But I felt no closer to the answers. I wished he would just give up his vague disguise and come clean with me. And then I wondered whether he had ever come clean with anyone—'ghosts' was what Jessica had said, but was that the truth? Could I really trust her? After all, she had freely admitted that she wished to get away.

It was a cold and jerky journey, up through winding hills, stony paths, nothing like the journey to *Ditchfurth* from the capital—which had been smooth road the whole way. Gerald's servant rode a horse before us, guiding Farol, Old Billy and Silver on their way. I found myself—again—crammed into the carriage between Jessica and Dante, both of them gazing out their respective windows.

Rain lashed the windows about half an hour out of *Ditchfurth* and I felt the temperature drop another couple of degrees. I clutched myself tight, trying to preserve whatever warmth my body could give out. We finally arrived in our designated spot sometime after midnight, where the servant pointed out a field complete with a wash house and reiterated Gerald's strict instructions that we weren't to go travelling about the estate lest we bring Gerald's father's attention to our presence and ruin the surprise for the party. In fact, the servant was so obstinate that he repeated the importance of not ruining the party twice, as if we were some sort of party-ruining extraordinaires. I breathed a sigh of relief when he padded off on his horse into the unpleasant rain-whipped night, leaving us—my family—alone at last.

Farol rubbed his hands together and grinned, his cheeks rosy from the gusts of wind, apparently enjoying this weather. With Dante's help, while me and Jessica returned to the carriage to wait, he produced a canvas from the back of the carriage. The two of them set about putting the thing up—as they did so, Jessica turned to me and explained. "Whenever we've nowhere to go for a few days we simply pitch a tent. It's nice sometimes, you know, to be in one place for a while. When I was a little girl we would move around a great deal."

I cocked my head. "Was it true when Gerald called you a Gypsy?"

She coloured a little. "Yes, well, I guess there are some aspects of our lives that will never leave us behind." She straightened in her seat, eyeing the progress on the canvas—Dante and Farol had it spread between them, already beginning to resemble a sizeable tent. "No," she said. "That's not right. I'll always be proud. It's who I am." Then, out of nothing, she lurched forward in her seat and clasped hold of my hands.

Her skin was freezing cold and a little damp.

"Promise me, Sara, that you'll never be ashamed. Your past is just as much a part of you as your future, and I'm proud of my heritage, just as you must be proud of yours."

I managed to extricate myself from her grip then glance out the window. "Or as proud as Dante is of his?"

Her glad expression shrivelled up. "Yes," she said. "Just like that."

***

All things considered it was a fairly comfortable arrangement. The tent was divided into four separate compartments, all easily large enough to place bedding and lay out personal effects—not that I had any. When Jessica had remarked that I didn't have any clothes of my own with me, she had given me a dress she claimed to have grown out of—a faded red dress, quite lovely and flowing—along with some underwear and a nightie. I thanked her for all of them, even though everything was a couple of sizes too large for me. She claimed that I would grow into them. As I lay there, curled up in my bedding, feeling quite snug in the tent—our four bodies in close contact forming quite an effective radiator—I considered that I'd never had this amount of privacy at night before, never had this space to myself. I looked around me and savoured it for a while, before slipping off into a well-deserved sleep.

When I woke I knew that it was still night without even opening my eyes. I could tell that it was the dead of night, that time when not a sound disturbs anything—all the creatures are sleeping or else trying to be invisible. I've always found that I wake at that exact time of night, perhaps it's that absolute silence which is communicated to my body, a time when I need to be wary. Maybe I'd awoken thousands of times before at that time of night, only to rock off back to sleep, seeing that there was nothing around—nothing to worry myself with. But, that night, I sensed things were different. That there was, almost certainly, something which required my attention.

Before I had quite got my thoughts together I found myself on my feet, rubbing the sleep out of my eyes. I yanked on my shoes—the same ones seeing as Jessica hadn't a pair going spare —and I snuck out beneath the canvas.

I stood outside the tent, savouring the night air, sticking out my tongue to taste its freshness—a freshness I had never before experienced back in the capital. I examined the dew gleaming off the long blades of grass in the moonlight and looked over to the carriage, the horses tied up to a post nearby, each of them lightly swaying in their sleep, tails occasionally flicking about them.

I waited with bated breath. And then, out there, on the fringe of the field, I saw a stirring—a stirring in the shadows. A figure. A person. Watching me.

My heart missed a beat. I felt faint, still shrugging off the veil of sleep. I stood stock still, trying to work out whether this was just my mind playing tricks on me—the shadow of a tree, just the way a tuft of grass happened to grow . . . I even extended my imagination to an escaped animal: a cow or pig, maybe even another horse, that had got away from one of the endless fields on the estate. And then the figure shuffled to one side, adjusted its gait, and I was positive that it was human.

A thousand thoughts sparked in my mind in that moment. I considered returning to the tent, getting back below the blankets, closing my eyes and attempting to sleep—I thought of raising the alarm, shouting for the others to wake. And yet, I knew that neither or those options would bring me the answers I searched for. If I slept the figure would surely be gone in the morning and if I raised the alarm then I was just as sure that Dante would wave this away as another episode, while Jessica would hand me some half-intelligible muttering. This time I had to go after them, and track them down so that I could speak freely, understand for myself who or what the hell that figure back at the theatre had been.

And so, feeling the soggy grass *swish* against my nightie, I jogged across the field, in the direction of the figure, taking care not to let them out of my sight. I had learnt my lesson from earlier, with the alleyway, and I was certain that if I could just keep up then all the answers would come clear—I would have some sort of clarification as to what exactly I was involved with in being part of Dante Gobornik's troupe.

The figure appeared to take no evasive action until I was about ten paces away, and then they took off running, swinging over the fence and soaring between the trees on the other side. I steeled myself before grasping hold of the splintered wood and hurling myself over, after the figure.

The moonlight proved a worthy ally in my pursuit, like a spotlight it flagged up the figure's location. I caught every one of those zigzags, those double-backs, those crossovers, and, best of all, felt like I was gaining on them, coming closer and closer with every one of my strides. And then, out of nowhere, a root sprung up from the ground and I caught my foot in it and flew forward. The last image that raced through my mind before I collided with the enormous, oak trunk ahead of me—that extremely solid tree—was Dante's dishevelled features, how he had looked draped in his chair following the show. As the silver, impossibly white flash blew right through my skull I had the horrible, gut-wrenching feeling that the man I was seeing in my mind's eye—Dante Gobornik—was a dead man.

Birdsong brought me round. The merry twittering and the rustling of twigs and branches. Sunlight shone on the backs of my eyelids, a crimson blaze. In the distance I made out heavier sounds. Footfalls. My head pounded with my beating heart. My mind felt shredded, torn into a thousand misfitting pieces. I was lying on soft ground. I reached out and touched the area around my body. Soft earth. Long grass. Soggy. As I attempted to open my eyes a sharp pain ripped through the centre of my skull and I closed them again. I realised that I was lying in the sun—the morning sun shining down where I lay. I had passed out and slept through the night.

I sucked in air through gritted teeth and tried to open my eyes again. This time I managed to get them open—two narrow slits, looking out at the foliage surrounding me: the muddy browns, ivy greens, and the scurvy yellows. The voices drew closer. I thought of Gerald's warning—that we were to stay hidden. I had to get out of here, and fast.

I thought I could make out the distinct speakers now, if not their exact words. If I had to guess I would've said that there were at least half a dozen of them. Lying in that tall grass I felt like a small animal, in danger of falling beneath the tread of their boots. And I think it was that dread which stirred me into action finally.

Before I knew it myself, felt fully back in control of my capacities, I was already on my two feet and running, away from those voices. As I slipped past a tree trunk I halted and listened out for the voices. They had descended into silence. And then, listening in closer, I heard a hushed whisper—no more than twenty, thirty paces away—and the words, "There. Shoot for goodness sake, man!"

A rifle shot cracked through the still morning air and I heard the *whistle* of a bullet headed right for me.

CHAPTER EIGHT

I WATCHED ON, beleaguered, as the bullet pounded into the tree beside me and sent up a cloud of bark dust. I glanced back over my shoulder and made out the forms, through the dust, and I sprinted onward, not interested in pushing my luck any further. I knew that I was balancing precariously between life and death at that very moment.

I just continued to rush through the trees, dodging the roots which jutted out, trying to trip me up again, and barrelling out of the way of the tree trunks. I ducked to avoid several low-hanging branches and then, all at once, I was out into a field— the towering, golden wheat crops swaying lightly in the breeze.

I looked around me, taking in the forest as it descended the slope behind, down into a valley. After I'd rushed off from the camp the night before, I'd become disorientated—I'd never seen the estate in the day and so it was unfamiliar to me. But there was on thing that I clung to, and that was a sensation in my gut that the night before I had chased that figure downhill, and so to get back to my camp I needed to go uphill now. And that would mean crossing the field.

The voices got louder behind me, an excited tone rippling among them. Their boots pounded against the ground and I was sure that I could feel every step vibrate through me, rattle my bones, like a warning . . . or a death bell.

I dived forward into the field and smoothed my way through the wheat, glad to see that it went far above my head, enough to keep myself hidden from the men. As I continued on my way, a horrible thought struck me—the thought that as I proceeded further and further through the field the men might be able to make me out, if they stood right on the edge. In short, this wheat would only keep me hidden when the men were relatively close. That might've been fine if they'd only been hunting with spears, bows and arrows, but they had guns.

As if confirming my worst fears, a twin pair of rifle shots cracked and two more bullets zipped above me. They had seen me, I knew that now. I dropped flat on my face and waited, praying that they weren't close, that they wouldn't fire off another shot to make sure they'd killed me dead.

On the light breeze which carried above me, I caught snatches of their conversation. "I say, I think you might just of hit him there, sonny-boy."

It was an older gentleman, but his tone reminded me a little of Gerald, as if—

Another man spoke up, this time I recognised the voice. Gerald. "Can never be too careful," he said. "Never seem to pass a week these days without hearing about a goring—blighters play dead till you're right over them before sticking you with their antlers."

Now I knew that they were hunting deer. And, at least on

the face of it, that was what they believed me to be. Terror gripped hold of me and I scrabbled my way along beneath the line of wheat, using my elbows to get purchase on the rugged terrain, to propel myself along, moving at a snail's pace in the direction of my destination.

The two men had at least given up their running now—they trod firmly and steadily. I heard the man I believed, now, to be Gerald's father address the group. "That's it, boys, spread yourselves. Don't give this blighter any easy way out. Any of you see it so much as rear its head don't hesitate to shoot it back down."

That added an extra element of desperation to my movements. I listened to the sound of the crops scrubbing against my nightie—the whispering, brushing sound, like terrified spectators. The footsteps got louder. And louder. I told myself that I had to hurry, but I couldn't poke my head up. I was sure that I'd made it most of the way across the field before they'd shot at me, so I couldn't be all that far from emerging on the other side, to hurling my way down into the ditch and to the safety of the campsite. Surely Gerald, having warned us off exploring the estate, would bring his party to a halt around there, and I would have nothing to fear. And then, in my ears, seemingly *far* too close, I heard, "There! Saw some movement!"

There was a chorus of muttering and I felt all my muscles seize tight, my blood warm my cheeks. I increased my pace, feeling a rock snag at my nightie and hearing the rip of material. I could worry about my clothes later. Right now I had to stay alive. And then, finally, I got to the other side. The wheat just ceased to be before me. The hedgerow filled my vision.

"Anyone seen any blood yet?"

"Nah, nothing."

"How odd, could've sworn you shot it right down about here."

"And no sound, either. Slick bugger, eh?"

"Who's got the flask of whisky?"

I lurked there, on the border of the field, planning my next move. But before I could assemble any great masterstrokes, another shot rang out.

"Over there! That's the bastard!"

I urged myself forward, out of cover, surely exposing myself to the men, though I didn't dare look back. I shoved myself through a thorn bush and then thudded down into the ditch, beneath the undergrowth, certain that I would be hidden from now on. I thought I could hear the clanging of pans back at the campsite—someone preparing breakfast. Surely I would be safe now?

The voices got closer, the *trudge* of boots. I listened as someone patrolled the area above the ditch, then turned back and addressed the others. Again, it was Gerald who spoke. "Nah, it's no good. Made off through the ditch, bloody blazed off the other side, hasn't it?"

There was what I can only describe as a group jabbering—a joint declaration of disappointment. One of the men fired his rifle into the air out of despair, I suppose. Still, it sent a shudder all around the collar of my nightie and I almost felt urine seep out, a panicked reaction to this extreme, possibly deadly, situation. I craned my neck upward to try and make out the men above me, feeling the thorns embedded in my skin starting to sting.

I could only see a pair of boots through the thicket. Gerald, I supposed. Another pair joined him. And another. Gerald's father spoke once more. "And you don't think that we should pursue

A SLEIGHT OF HAND

the blighter through there? Surely he can't have got too far, he's been shot for goodness' sake."

Gerald played the situation well, keeping any anxiety out of his voice that might've been there, that his big birthday surprise for his father could be on the point of being ruined. "I'm not so sure I got him, Pa. I mean if we consider the evidence: no blood, moving quickly, out of sight already, then I'd reach the conclusion that he's given us the slip. You know how it always ends when we go off chasing a rogue stag—bloody better off traipsing our way back to the house, getting on for mid-morning coffee, isn't it?"

There was a murmur of agreement from the other men, but Gerald's father remained obstinate for the time being—clearly Gerald had inherited this quality from his father.

"Oh, come now, Gerald, there's always time for coffee. This isn't a ladies' perambulation society, this is a hunt, dammit. We came out here to sack ourselves a deer—and you tell us that this might well be a stag. I say we keep on going after him, we'll track him down. Blood or no blood, I'm sure you got him back in the forest. It would be a grand waste."

"Still," Gerald said, again without emotion, despite the situation, "I think we'd best be getting back, must I remind you that you promised Mother you would attend the mid-morning coffees to decide on the final decorations for your party."

Gerald's father let loose a long sigh, as if his son had delivered the *coup de grace*. He could only respond with a series of uttered swearwords and a few middle-aged grumbles. He got over himself after a moment or two. "All right, all right, let's head on back. He's right. Gerald's always right."

I thought that Gerald's father expressed a degree of pride in that remark, in placing his trust in his son's judgement. Something which I'd never before noticed a parent acknowledge in their child—although I suppose the children I'd known had grown up in a world far different from that of the Forsneers. I filed that particular titbit away for later use, that Gerald held a measure of control, counsel over his father.

I listened in to the men retreating, making their way back across the field. Someone passed the flask of whisky to Gerald's father and I listened to the *slosh* of liquid as he knocked it back and took a swig. One pair of boots, however, lingered at the ditch. Gerald stayed there.

I decided that now was the time to make my move. It would be better for me to get back to the campsite, before Gerald got suspicious—assuming that he wasn't already. I crawled my way up the bank, to the other side of the ditch. As I peeked through the undergrowth, the thicket, I could make out Dante's carriage standing at the other side of the fallow field, Old Billy and Silver resting there, leaning against the fence posts. I watched white smoke circle up into the sky on the other side of the carriage, where the camp awaited me. Just as I was on the point of stepping out of the thicket, of resting foot back in safety, I heard a distinct, swift *click* over my shoulder and found myself pivoting around to see what it was.

From where I stood, in the field, I could make out nothing but foliage—there was no way of seeing to the other side. Or so I thought, because, just then, I picked out a bare patch which no leaves covered. I stood there, eye to eye with Gerald Forsneer. Or, should I say, staring down the barrel of his rifle.

"You," Gerald said. "Did you not understand what it was that I said?"

All my muscles clenched tight and I felt my throat dry up. Those two twin pits of soot—the barrels of the gun—only a slight twitch of the finger and a bullet would be racing right through my brain. I couldn't take my eyes off those holes.

"Well?" he said. "They ever teach you to speak in the colonies, or what?"

Again, I felt that familiar twinge in the depths of my guts, that reminder that I was different to them all. Still, I found myself frozen.

"No one would care, you know, if I just put a bullet through your skull. I'd dump you right here, in this ditch, cover you with some leaves. The wolves would do away with you before daybreak tomorrow. What do you say to that?"

My whole body chilled.

I watched on as his muscles all rippled tight, he closed his right eye and seemed to tighten his grip on the rifle. For a horrible second I was sure that he was going to shoot me, do just what he'd threatened. And then, just as I shut my eyes and sank my teeth into my lower lip, I heard light footsteps behind me. I had no need to look around. I knew who it was. There was a sense of him, an unmistakable rising of hair on my arms. Dante.

"Put the gun down," Dante said, this time his slightly cracked accent coming out, no trace of that upper class one he turned on for performances.

For a moment it appeared that Gerald was shaping to shoot, his finger twitched on the trigger and his eyes narrowed even further. Then, without a word, he allowed the gun to drop down at his side, he allowed it to dangle from his arm and an easy smile played out on his lips. "Just a bit of sport," he said. "No harm done."

I felt Dante's sure touch on my shoulder, his fingers gripping my skin, and I felt lighter—the tension melted away from me. It was a fatherly touch. He stood at my shoulder, not making any movement toward Gerald, simply staring back at him.

Gerald glanced about himself. "Well," he said, still smiling, "looks like I've lost my hunting group, eh? No doubt they'll be a touch vexed about me, what I've got myself up to." He reached up and doffed the peak of his faded, plaid hunting cap. "With your kind permission, I take my leave."

I locked eyes on the back of Gerald's neck, that downy hair skirting the reddened skin there. He trudged his way back across the field, rifle hoisted over his shoulder, gait free and easy, swaying slightly from side to side. I wondered whether he might've been a little drunk. They'd clearly been at the whisky, after all, but I traced my mind back to the night at the theatre when he'd seemed completely shitfaced and yet he'd come across all lucid and free-speaking once we'd got into Dante's dressing room—maintained enough clarity of mind to make threats, secure his bargaining position.

"Come on," Dante said, leading me away from the thicket. "Servant came by this morning and gave us some duck eggs." A smile broke out on his face, his white teeth like cinderblocks, as he spread his arms. "Should see the size of them."

I took a final glance at Gerald retreating across the field, and that carefree walk of his. I couldn't help but feel in great danger whenever he was around.

I don't know what I was expecting from Dante—I guess that I thought he was going to punish me somehow, reprimand me for having broken Gerald's ground rules. But, as I was beginning to find out, Dante really didn't have that many rules himself, and he certainly had very little respect for the rules of others. In fact, if I had to make some comment on that day I would say that he was a lot smilier than usual, and I started to think that, perhaps, he was quite glad that I'd wound up Gerald, just a little. I wondered if he'd have been so joyful, so light-footed, if he'd known exactly why I'd run off from the camp the previous night.

That afternoon the sun shone down strong on the whole camp, drying us out after the storm. Silver galloped about the field, head held high, mane buffeting in the wind. He looked a fine horse, and he knew it too. Old Billy, on the other hand, took to waddling about at the fringes of the field, occasionally dipping his head to chomp away at a particularly delicious-looking patch of grass.

After my broken night's sleep, I lay for most of the afternoon on my side, watching Dante and Jessica rehearsing, going through those all-too-painful routines—Dante demanding that they practise the cold readings and mentalist trickery till they had it by rote, all the feigning that by no means did they know one another. I overheard Dante proclaiming that Jessica would go up to the house much earlier than the rest of us, that she was to come up with some sort of story for Gerald and his friends, so that she wouldn't be discovered. Gerald's friends had never seen that Jessica and Dante had known each other beforehand, only Gerald knew of Jessica's connection to Dante. Still, I wondered why Dante bothered to go through with this whole warm-up routine at all. It just seemed so tacky, so below what he was really capable of. Then again, I suppose he could do whatever he wanted. He was Dante Gobornik after all.

As I lay there, soaking up the sun, I felt an indescribable cocktail of emotions. There was my parents, always there, at the back of mind—I knew that they would always linger in my mind, like shadows at midday—but, at the same time, I felt a great positivity ripping through my body, tweaking my spirits, making me feel strangely positive about my future. This was far better than my life in the capital, even with these ghosts, or whatever they were, thrown into the mix. I had fresh air, a travelling life where I got to see the country I had been born in but never fully understood or truly felt part of. On reflection, I can say that that was the turning point for me, the time when Dante, Jessica, even Farol, began to feel like family. How naïve I was, though, because all that tranquillity, that thin veneer of comfort, was about to be shattered absolutely.

CHAPTER NINE

THE MORNING of the show rolled around. I noted how uptight Dante was, unusual for him. After breakfast, when I slipped off down to the stream with Jessica to wash the dishes, I noticed him wringing his hands and muttering to himself. I asked Jessica whether something in particular was bothering him.

Jessica dipped the plate into the stream and gave it a scrub with a blotchy sponge. "He's been having trouble sleeping," she said. "The usual things, the nightmares, the cold sweats, you know, just stress, I suppose."

I reflected on Jessica and Dante, those faint murmurs I would hear in the tent at night. At first I had understood that we each had our own compartment, and we did, but I'd soon realised that Dante and Jessica slept together. I recalled the heavy breathing and the *rustle* of blankets carrying through the canvas walls, lying awake, staring up into the darkness feeling hot and bothered, unable to keep my limbs still while I listened to them. I knew what they were doing, at least I'd heard kids talking about it—back in the capital, in the playground. But, for some reason, I'd just never thought of it as something truly real, something that took place in anything other than imagination. I suppose my mother and father had done the same, they must've done, while I'd slept hunched up against that wall. And yet I'd never noticed. The worst part of lying there, feeling the sweat slippery on my skin was that I felt a stirring jealousy—no, stronger, *hatred*—for Jessica, as if she were stealing Dante away from me, because she'd said that she wanted to run away. I was sure that she would leave us alone: just me, Dante and Farol. It just seemed . . . natural. But with each rustle of blanket, each sucking kiss, each stifled breath, I felt that fantasy slip further from me.

I dunked the cups in the stream, watching the coffee grounds float away on the crystal-clear water, drift around the bend and out of sight. I decided that I couldn't keep the figures—the ghosts—bottled up like this. I had to tell someone, and since I'd already told Jessica about the other night—the one who had skulked about backstage at the theatre—I thought of her as a worthy *confidante*. I turned my head slowly, dragging the cups from the stream and setting them, upside down, to dry on the grassy bank. "Dante told you about me getting caught by Gerald and his hunting pack, didn't he?"

Jessica continued to focus on the dish she was currently washing. She gave it a final, harsh scrub and then set it beside my drying mugs. "I think he might've mentioned it." She turned to me. "Why?"

The words stuck in my throat for a moment as I attempted to get them clear in my mind, before speaking. Already I was having doubts about speaking to Jessica about this—she had told me that it would be better to talk directly to Dante. "I saw another of them," I said. "Another of those 'ghosts.'"

"And that was why you ran off?"

"Yeah."

Jessica slipped into silence. I thought she had put the conversation out of her mind as she continued to wash away at the cutlery—marked with egg yolk—then she said, "How did you see it? I mean, what prompted you awake?"

"I . . . I don't know. It was just, you know, a sensation. Like I felt someone was watching me. I had this urge to get out of the tent and look around. And there"—I pointed behind me, in the vague direction in which I'd seen the figure appear—"they just appeared, and I had to give chase."

Jessica just nodded to herself, now taking a tea towel and folding it upon her lap, turning the damp fabric over and over until it was so tightly folded that it would have fit in the palm of her hand.

Seeing that I wasn't going to get any sort of response from her without further prompting, I said, "What do you think about it?"

"About what?"

"The ghosts."

"Oh, yes, well," she said, again seeming to lose her train of thought, her mind appearing to drift into blank as if there were something blocking her from moving forward. "I really can't think of anything to say, Sara, and I'd prefer that you didn't bring up such a subject with me again."

The words burnt me. They were delivered so nonchalantly, so deadpan, as if she were scolding me for having slighted something deeply shameful in her past—made fun of her heritage. I just stared down at the still-dirty plates, slipped one off the top and set about washing it, resigned to having dropped the theme. Maybe it *would* be better for me to speak with Dante, even though he had so readily brushed me off last time. Not today, though, his mind was occupied with the show. I'd need to wait until tomorrow, at the very least. Some time when he wasn't tired, when his mind was free. Already, I could see it might be tricky to pick my moment.

Soon after, Jessica disappeared into the tent to go and get changed into her evening wear, all ready for her blending-in routine, in a way doing just what Dante did—faking that upper class manner and accent. Acting.

If Dante had been bothered by my flouting Gerald's rules, he overlooked them now, leaving camp, taking a long walk along the side of the field before disappearing into a thicket, crossing a ditch and slipping from view. I found myself alone. Well, almost. There was Farol, doing some maintenance to the carriage, a pot of scarlet paint before him that he had acquired from a member of Gerald's house staff, dabbing at various features of the design, giving a dab of colour to the tongue of a dragon, the tail of a tropical fish, adding heat to the flames which lapped at the carriage door. I loomed over him, fascinated by the design, coming back to life from beneath the caked on dust and muck.

Farol cocked his head back, a little irritated. "Do you mind?" he said. "You're standing in my light."

"Sorry," I said, stepping aside.

His quick, blue eyes found mine for a second and then drifted back to his work at hand. He dipped the brush into the tin of paint and tidied up a dog's collar on the design. A few more strokes later and he peered at me over his shoulder, a look of thunder on his face. "You just gonna stand there, or what? Haven't you got anything useful to be getting on with?"

"No, not really," I said, feeling a little useless at that moment. "Have you got any jobs for me to do?"

He exhaled a long sigh then set the paintbrush back in its pot. He scratched his thinning hair, his fingernails scraping at the exposed scalp the size of an orange in the centre of his cranium. "Dante not given you anything to be getting on with?"

"Nope."

"Right, well. . ." He glanced from side to side, finally his attention fell on the set of paint pots which awaited beneath the carriage, staying out of the sunlight. He flattened himself to the ground and reached for one of the pots, groaning as he did so. He passed me a pot of aqua-marine coloured paint. "Use this for the grass."

I prised off the lid and examined the contents. "This looks like a strange colour for grass, don't you think?"

He shook his head. "Gives it a more magical quality—reminds you of the sea, don't it?"

"What do you mean?"

"Well, what we're doing here, with this carriage, it's not exactly a realistic interpretation of the world, is it, now? This is a magical fantasy land, all painted on the side here. You could just as well say that dragons don't exist—which as far as I've been able to establish they don't—but that's not the point of this design, is it?"

"Then what *is* the point of the design?"

He thought about it for a long moment, then shrugged and said, "I'll be damned if I know. If you've got a problem with it, take it up with Jessica. She's the one that got it from us—it's a family heirloom as I understand it."

Just the mention of Jessica's name sent a chill through me. I shuddered. I didn't want to think about *her* for a while. It felt like she had betrayed me, pretended to be my friend only to back off when I really needed her.

"Here," Farol said, shoving a ruffled, old brush into my chest.

It might've been old, well-used, but at least it was clean.

"Do the grass—any bits you think should be green."

"Like the dragon scales?"

"Yeah," he said, resuming his own licks of scarlet paint.

I sank to my knees and observed the design before me. It was just about possible to make out what colours the various decorations had been before, but only just. In another way it would've been foolish to try and recapture *exactly* how it had looked before—using the exact colour tones. And I decided, like Farol had suggested, that I just needed to embrace that this would be different, a living breathing, not-necessarily-real-world-representative, piece of artwork. I remember my breath hitching in my throat as I brought my sodden brush to the first patch of grass, a hillside, terrified that I might make a mistake—that Farol might shout at me. But I painted, thin strokes, and he stayed quiet. We remained like that for a long time, neither of us speaking, feeling the sun on our backs, a quiet ease passing between the two of us. And then a thought flashed in my mind. Why didn't I ask Farol about the ghosts?

Almost as soon as I'd thought of it, I declared it insane—a stupid idea. I hardly knew Farol at all and it wouldn't be a great start for me to give him the impression that, at best, I was a frightened little schoolgirl or, at worst, I was some delusional psychotic that needed to be dispensed with. Still, I couldn't shake the urge. Not one little bit. And it was as I turned my attention to a lake set between a pair of towering mountaintops that I found my lips moving, my tongue stoppering sounds, caressing and nudging the words from my mouth.

I didn't quite realise what I'd said till I saw the expression on Farol's face—the scrunched up features, the light scowl, those bushy eyebrows almost brushing his eyelids. I expected him to reprimand me, the way he was looking, but he just stayed quiet. And then, just as I thought the whole matter had been forgotten, he glanced around—looked twice to the tent where Jessica was changing out of sight—and then leant into me, voice dropped to a harsh whisper. "What you . . ." He paused and looked around again, ". . . seen exactly?"

I scoured my mind trying to work out just how I would put it, so that there would be no confusion. I was satisfied that I had Farol's attention and also that this was something that was better kept secret—between the two of us. "A couple of figures. The first was backstage, at *Ditchfurth Theatre*, and then, that night, when I ran off, here." I pointed in the general direction in which the figure had appeared. "That was it. The figure was over there. And I ran after her—him, but just couldn't catch up. Then I bumped my head and fainted. Next thing I knew I woke up with Gerald and those hunters stomping through the forests."

Farol held his brush before him, it was dripping paint onto the ground, but he either didn't care or didn't notice. He leant in still closer. "And . . . and did you get a good look at them?"

I shook my head.

"Shame," he said.

"Why's that?"

He seemed to remember the brush, looked to it dripping everywhere and then dunked it back in the paint pot. He rested his hands on his hips while he knelt, focussing on some detail of the carriage's design. "Myself," he said. "I never managed to catch them up."

My heart beat faster. "So, you've seen them too?"

"Oh, aye, I have. They . . . I don't know. I used to do what you did, following them, trying to chase them down. Soon enough though I just twigged that it was a waste of time—a waste of breath too. Never did manage to get a good look of one of their faces, let alone catch one."

"And . . . and you're not frightened at all?"

"I guess I was at the start, who wouldn't be? I mean, they're not like those ghosts you read about in books, too human for that, right?"

I nodded.

"Yeah, that's it. Too human."

I waited for him to fill in more gaps for me, but he resumed his painting without another word about it. I decided that I had to know more—or, at the very least, one thing more. "The ghosts," I said. "Have they got anything to do with Dante? Is that the reason I'm seeing them?"

"We shouldn't talk too much about this, you know—don't like speaking behind the boss's back, bit disrespectful, don't you think?"

My cheeks burnt out of embarrassment, but I was determined. "But you *know* about them. Don't you think that's unfair? Shouldn't we all be on an even keel? I want to know what these ghosts are, and what they want, if I'm going to be seeing them all the time from now on."

Farol gave me a nauseous smile then said, dabbing scarlet about the sun's rays beaming down on the scene. "Listen, don't you think that I've asked Dante about them from time to time?

He doesn't want to open up about it, about them, and I think we just have to respect that. He pays my livelihood, haven't you heard the old saying, 'If it don't scare the cows, who cares?'"

"No, what does it mean?"

"It's means, if there's no trouble from something then what's the point of worrying about it?"

I considered this point of view and then said, "But, aren't you curious? Maybe it's not dangerous right at the moment, but what about if it becomes so?"

Farol ran his brush along a long wooden part jutting out, his tongue poking out between his lips. "I guess we can cross that bridge when we come to it." He paused then eyed me. "Look at it this way—I've been touring with Dante for the past five years and none of those *things* has ever done me any harm whatsoever. If they could harm us in some way why wouldn't they have done it by now?"

That was a difficult argument to fight against, especially considering that Farol had the upper hand of experience, that unquestionable quality of maturity—his word was far more powerful than mine, as a fourteen-year-old girl.

We painted on in absolute silence. I felt that I had reached the end of the line with Farol—as far as he was concerned he'd put the issue of all these ghosts to one side, and I suppose that I decided, for the moment, it was wise to do the same.

A few minutes later Jessica emerged from the tent. My breath stuck in my chest. Really, she was ravishing. I took a second just to absorb her appearance. She wore a dark red dress which just brushed her knees. Her shoulders were bare, only a pair of thin straps holding the dress up against her supple breasts. Her hair flowed down her face, curling in on itself at her cheeks, so as to set her face in a kind of heart-shape. On her feet she had a pair of stodgy boots, while she dangled her high heels from her fingertips. She tiptoed her way through the tall grass and over to us. Her face looked flushed, and I supposed it was because of the tent—it must've been pretty warm in there considering the blazing sun. She looked to Farol and then to me before saying, "You're not planning on going in that, are you?"

A little confused, seeing as I'd imagined I would be staying here during Dante's performance up at the house—and I was quite glad about it, secretly, not all that keen to run into Gerald again. "What do you mean?" I said.

She rolled her eyes. A light smile hung to her lips, and I judged that our uncomfortable conversation down at the stream had been forgotten . . . for the moment. "You have to come with me," she said. "It's all part of the act—I already said you're my handmaid in front of Gerald's friends, if you don't come they'll think something's wrong, smell a rat."

I wanted to tell her that the opening and closing acts were so turgid, so utterly forced and like every other magician that had ever existed that the audience—anyone in the audience—would take it for granted that she was a stooge, so the whole point of putting on any kind of show seemed a little ridiculous. But I wasn't about to rock the boat. After all I was a new addition to Dante's troupe, there were established elements of the act already and I had no authority in attempting to change anything. Not yet anyway.

"Come on," she said, taking hold of my hand and leading me back toward the tent. "I think I've got just the thing for you."

About twenty minutes later I stood with Jessica scrutinising me from top to bottom, an eyebrow arched as she did so, hand on her chin. She'd put me in a light yellow dress which she'd long grown out of—sometimes I wondered how many clothes she lugged around that she'd long grown out of. With her head tilted to one side, she took a step forward and adjusted the bow she'd looped into my hair, through my thickly tangled curls. She cracked a smile. "There," she said. "That's just right, I think."

And that was the last chance I got to make any comment on my outfit for the evening.

Of course it would have looked odd for us to roll up at the house in the carriage, Old Billy and Silver pulling us, Farol driving us. As Jessica put it, "They'd spot the Gypsy a mile off." So, through the same servant who had brought us to this field, Jessica had a message sent up to the house—to Gerald—asking for a horse drawn carriage to pick us up.

Farol had squeezed himself into his tuxedo while Jessica had been getting me prepared in the tent. Already he was sweating profusely, it was literally leaking from his pores, pooling on the peaks of his chubby cheeks before rolling down his neckline. I did wonder what posh men did on hot evenings such as this. It couldn't have been all that comfortable. I guessed that tonight I was going to find out.

The horse and carriage rolled up a little while later, the same servant driving. The horses were both greys, like Silver. These two horses had gold-leaf-brushed bridles and their coats were kept in immaculate condition. When they drew to a halt they snorted and raked their hooves in the dried mud, waiting for us to get on. I looked over to Old Billy and Silver, neither of whom knew what to do with these intruders—so they just stared on, Old Billy still munching on a mouthful of grass.

We clambered up into our seats, Farol looking uncomfortable

to be sitting in the open-topped carriage rather than driving the horses. Still, without any further delay, we buckled out of the camp, and up the long, driving slope, toward the house.

———

As we made our way up the drive the sun was setting and a series of gas lamps blinked on, along the path, to guide us on the way. In the fading twilight, the house itself seemed to be a part of the natural landscape. It rose up from the ground, made out of brown stone, its walls crawling with climbing plants. Trees lined the drive leading up to the steps of the house. Everything looked so beautifully well-kept. No sign of any dead leaves or fallen branches. This was a slickly run estate —but with people like the Forsneers in charge it was little wonder. As we drew closer and closer to the house I only began to absorb how enormous it really was. Only when the carriage bucked to a stop at the steps and a footman strutted up to the door and opened it for us, did I realise how it towered over me, seeming to reach right up to the sky. When I looked along it lengthwise I couldn't make out where it ended, just non-stop windows, brickwork and wild plants growing. I recall wondering how many people lived there and began to resent the fact that Gerald had made us sleep out in a field. Surely he could've tucked us away in a long-forgotten bedroom somewhere.

The footman wore a white wig. I remember staring at it for a long time. The way that it elongated his face, made him seem sickly and thin. Of course I knew that some of the upper classes liked their servants to dress up like that. But it just seemed so— so silly. I did my best not to stare as I followed on Jessica's heels, keeping myself level with Farol, whose sweat patches now showed through his black jacket.

The entrance hall was done up with bouquet upon bouquet of flowers. The smell was a little overpowering and I felt my nose twitch. Their colours were so vibrant, the purples, the creams, the reds, and—like the dress I was wearing—the yellows. The interior of the hall was all wooden, the staircases, the carvings on the walls, and the frames of the several portraits of stately-looking gentlemen looking down on me as I proceeded onward, still guided by Jessica.

Finally we were greeted by a grinning Gerald. He was wearing a tuxedo, like Farol, however, unlike Farol, his fit him like a glove, his trousers showing of his muscular thighs, even his bulky calves, while the upper half betrayed his bulging pectoral muscles and his flat abdomen. Strangely, knowing all I did about him, how he had treated me out on the estate, I felt a flutter of butterflies in my stomach. And if that was how I was feeling then I couldn't imagine how Jessica might've felt at that moment.

Gerald clutched a flute of champagne in his left hand, keeping it level with his solar plexus, as if it were something truly dear to him. His complexion was already rosy from the alcohol and he was slurring his words slightly—as I'd remembered him doing back at *Ditchfurth County Theatre*, but then he had suddenly become so lucid. I wondered whether this might all just be an act, that he was playing the alcoholic, fun-loving son to catch people unawares, so that he would get their defences down, see who they really were. That had worked with Jessica, so why shouldn't it work with the rest of the world?

As Jessica looped her arm through Gerald's, he half-whispered in her ear, "Remember, my dear, keep those curious hands to yourself tonight. I'll have you know the local constable's here tonight if he's required and I'll have no hesitation having you, and your ilk"—he flashed me and Farol a glance over his shoulder—"thrown into a cell for the night. Do I make myself clear?"

I watched as Jessica's ears glowed red, colouring with shame. If there was something that I'd noted about Jessica's disguises or, rather, people seeing through them, it was that it turned her into a little girl—made her look vulnerable, caught red-handed. And I almost believed her when she claimed that she could hardly help herself, that stealing was just a part of who she was, something compulsive and uncontrollable. I started to believe that, perhaps, that story about her running away was just a means of justifying what she did to me.

Gerald led us through a series of corridors, all done out with eye-catching wooden adornments, the swirling cornices and sleek skirting boards. Everything looked like it had been polished within an inch of its life, and I guess that it put me into some sort of a stupor, because I'd never experienced anything this . . . *refined* before.

We emerged into a room full of activity. A chandelier hung from the ceiling, sparkling glass. One of the lights caught my eye and burnt. I turned away, back to the focus of attention—Jessica and Gerald. Up ahead there was an older man, with grey whiskers, and a balding head of hair. He wore the collar of his shirt popped upward in a way that made me think of him as birdlike. Only when Gerald stepped forward and the man spoke, did I recognise the voice as being that of Gerald's father. "Charmed," he said. "All of you. You're most welcome." He turned to Jessica. "Especially charmed to meet you, my dear.

Yes," he said, flashing his son a glance, "Gerald has told me all about you."

Jessica played her part well, blushing a little as she allowed him to kiss the back of her hand. "I *am* honoured Lord Forsneer, I've never seen such a beautiful estate in all my life."

He smiled, his eyes twinkling just a touch as he did so. He was carrying a flute of champagne too—I supposed that Gerald had inherited his drinking habits from his father. He gave her a nod, allowing us all past. As I walked by him I noted his mouth curling a little at the edges, as if he had swallowed something bitter, but as quickly as I tried to get a second look he'd moved right onto the next guest—a lady with a frilly turquoise hat and lurid orange dress. Something didn't sit right with me about this family. Something that I couldn't put my finger on.

As we lost ourselves mingling in the crowd, I found my attention drawn away from Gerald and Jessica's flirting and to the interior balcony which overlooked the whole room, because, up there, staring down at me, was another of those figures. Nothing more than a dark shadow, expressionless, featureless, but definitely there. And then, just for a second, I saw something in the face, something unmistakable. It took me so off guard that I felt my mouth latch open and I exclaimed, "Mum?"

CHAPTER TEN

M Y HEART RAPPED against my ribcage. I sank my teeth into my tongue and tasted the rusty, bloody flavour in my mouth. I continued to stare up at the balcony. There was no mistaking it now—it was my mother.

I got caught up in a panic, looking around me. Of course I wanted to chase the figure, find out where it was, because I was sure that *this time* I really could catch them and find out what they wanted. I glanced at Farol to see if he had noticed, but he seemed more interested in examining a portly lady beside us, more specifically her ample bosom almost bursting out of the top of her corset dress. Jessica and Gerald were caught up in one another's company, of course. And it seemed that Jessica was putting her back into this impression of her being a respectable, high class *lady*. I glanced about me and decided to take my chances.

Not being too tall had its advantages here. I could skirt the crowds of people, weaving in and out between them. I got a few stares—but that was inevitable even if I'd merely stood still on the fringe of Jessica and Gerald's group. Before I knew it, I'd managed to slink from the hall and got out into the corridor.

I recognised the change in tone of my shoes and I looked below me, to the lush carpet which was more like walking on thick grass. I heard voices drifting along the corridor, more guests arriving, making their way toward the main hall. I picked the opposite direction, hoping that it might lead to a staircase. It did, and I climbed up, clutching the banister as I went, my eyes watchful for any questioning glances. But there was no one around. For now.

I emerged on the first floor landing. The carpet sat snugly against the floorboards, worming its way around the curves of the house. I headed in the direction of the hall, hoping that it would bring me to that same balcony. When I came across the doorway leading out onto the balcony, I glanced around the doorframe, only to find no one there—the figure, my mother, had simply disappeared. I cursed to myself and turned back, heading along the hall, back toward the stairs. As I rounded the stairwell, heading back down, I was already castigating myself, telling myself that it had been a big error, dangerous, for me to go off alone in the mansion. It could quite easily get us all into big trouble. And just as I got down onto the halfway point of the staircase I ran into one of the bachelors from the night at *Ditchfurth Theatre*. Percy.

He seemed to stumble backward, to grasp at the wall. He was drunk, of course, just like all the other 'noblemen' at this party. I attempted to round him, but as I did so he snatched hold of my forearm. I thought he might roar out, call for a servant—or the constable Gerald had mentioned in passing—but, on the contrary, he dropped his voice to a low tone, to that tone which to a drunk person is the quietest-ever whisper, and to a sober person a little below a shout, and said, "I remember you. You, you from that . . . theatre," he finally added, having obviously had a little difficulty making the whole connection.

I looked to his grip on my forearm and judged the situation. I knew that he could easily overpower me if he wished. Even though he wasn't the biggest of men, or particularly well-built, I knew that he would have easily enough power to overwhelm me.

He closed an eye and squinted. "I say," he said, swaying a little, "what do you think you're doing up here. This, this is off limits to guests, you should know that. Everyone else, they're down in the hall."

"Yes," I said, subtly trying to squirm from his grip, but failing, "I was just on my way now."

"Where's your, your—"

I arched an eyebrow. "Mistress?"

"Yes," he said, with a light grin that grated with his physical hold on me, "that's the word I was looking for. Just right. *Mistress*," he said, testing the word as if it were the first time he'd spoken it and he wished to memorise it.

"Well, I'd better go to her. You know, she'll be waiting for me."

He continued that drunken grin for a few moments and then shook his head resolutely. "No, no, no, *no*." He added the last 'no' with a degree of finality. "Not yet, just stay a bit. Talk to Percy."

Now, I might not have known an awful lot about drunk men at that point in my life, but I knew enough that once they started speaking in that creepy, childish way—in the third person—it was time to make one's excuses and leave. Again, I attempted to extradite myself, with no luck.

"What's the . . . rush?"

"I have to go," I said, realising that I was repeating myself, that I couldn't think logically. I had just seen my dead mother up on the balcony and I really wasn't in the mood for thinking myself out of any problems. I simply wanted to get myself back by Jessica's side, back into my assumed role.

Then, to my horror, Percy puckered his lips and closed his eyes. "Just a kissy-wissy, just a little peck on the lips, go on." He leant into me and his sticky, warm alcohol-soaked breath wafted all over me. "Please. Ever so quick. I promise."

I backed up, now twirling myself around in his grip. I yanked my arm but I couldn't shift from his sure grip. He was too strong for me. His lips drew closer and closer, his breath growing more and more rancid. I felt a churning in my stomach and bile stung the back of my throat. I would vomit, that was what I'd do. Now consciously trying to get up the meagre contents of my stomach, I attempted to bring him closer. But then, just as I was on the point of spewing my guts all over the hideous creature, I heard that same, assured, familiar voice carry up the stairs. "I say, Percy, what on *Earth* do you think you're doing?"

The voice was like a shot to the buttock. Percy flinched and drew himself up straight, stroking the wrinkles out of the front of his tuxedo. He tilted his chin back and eyed Gerald, who was climbing the stairs. Jessica emerged behind him, her fingers intertwined with his.

"Percy?" Gerald said, with an extra degree of sternness. "I asked you a question."

Percy folded his hands at his cummerbund, like a scolded child. He peered at clasped hands and puffed out his cheeks. "I," he started, "I was just looking for the lavatory, got a bit side tracked, speaking to Miss . . . Miss—"

"Blind," I said, filling him in and immediately regretting it, having enjoyed watching him squirm, having his friend reprimand him.

"That's it," Percy said, with a slight smile. "I was just *speaking* with Miss Blind, here, that's right, we were having an awfully good chinwag at that. She was just telling me about her times, her families' times in—"

Gerald narrowed his eyes, but his voice remained the same—flat and even, as if he were speaking to a dog, that's right, as if he were disciplining a hound. "There are lavatories on the ground floor, and I'll thank you to use those."

"Oh," Percy said, flashing his eyebrows, "yes, of course there are, Gerry. Silly me! It's just, well, I think that I might've just had a drop or two of that champagne and you know how it is, a little bit of an overindulgence, if you'll allow me to leave it at that."

Gerald continued to stare down his friend. I wondered why he was helping me out—what he'd seen in his friend that had called him to my aid. Then I got to thinking whether, deep down, he really wanted to impress Jessica in some way, despite all that stuff he said about her being a *Gypsy*, and his jibing of her stealing habits. Or maybe he just liked to have things under control. If anyone was going to take a step on the cruel side it would be him, and he would crush those that thought otherwise.

Percy smiled weakly, cleared his throat and then brushed by Jessica and Gerald. I listened to the soft *thud* of his shoes on the stairway carpet.

Gerald looked to me, his expression grey, devoid of life. "What *do* you think you're doing up here, sneaking about my house?"

"I . . . I'm sorry," I said.

Gerald glowered at me and then, clasping Jessica's hand tighter, he yanked her behind him, down the staircase, after

Percy. I caught Jessica's eye as he tugged her behind him. Her eyes were wide with fright, her rosy lips parted slightly. I guess that she knew, then, exactly what it was that had brought me up to the first floor of the Forsneer mansion, and she was chilled to her bones.

I lingered there, in the stairwell a few more seconds before descending, going after them. But not without a quick peep over my shoulder, back onto that shadowy landing where I had seen my mother.

Back in the hall, I noticed the frantic motion, the excitement twanging through the air. Guests were shuffling toward a narrow corridor at the other end of the room, champagne glasses crooked in their fingers, laugh lines brandishing their cheeks. The stench of perfume and aftershave wormed up my nostrils, making me feel a little giddy—sending my mind spiralling around. The faces of my family: my mother, my father, my little brother—the babbie—all scarred there, embossed images on the backs of my eyelids, every time I blinked. I took deep breaths, telling myself that whatever happened they would always be with me. Whatever these shadows were, theses figures, they were not my mother, or anyone else, while my family would always be with me, they were gone—they had departed this world, perhaps gone onto the next. Hadn't they?

I located Jessica and Gerald, canoodling as they ventured along with the stream of people, following the crowd. I shimmied my way through the dresses and suits, knocking an elbow here and there, sending a few drops of champagne plopping to the ground as I went. Finally I caught up with them. I focussed all my attention onto the tail of her dark red dress, the flimsy material which showed off the curve of her buttocks—firm yet womanly, soft as a parted peach. And I watched as Gerald's hand descended to that spot, lingered there for a moment, and then, following a jerk from Jessica, floated back upward, to her lower back.

I crunched my teeth together to ward off the spinning snatching hold of me, those waves upon waves of nauseas ripping through me. While laughter and the *tinkle* of glasses sounded all around me, I found myself scouting out every nook and cranny of our surroundings, finding shadows, examining them, turning them over in my mind, trying to work out whether or not they were more of the same figures.

The corridor bent this way and that, and it was a bit of a crush getting through it. Finally, though, we emerged in a gigantic room, nothing less than a fully-fledged theatre, here in the centre of the mansion. I craned my neck back and took in my surroundings, the beautifully rounded, dome ceiling, the maroon drapes hanging from the walls, and then there was the stage, set before us. It was set in darkness, just as Dante liked it.

I felt a hand brush my own and when I looked down I saw it was Jessica's. Her fingers danced over the backs of my hands before finding my own fingers, and intertwining themselves around mine, in the same way she had held onto Gerald's hand. I felt my stomach ease, the tension seep from my shoulders, the nausea subside, just for a moment. And only then did I realise that I would be facing up to another of Dante's shows this time, for the first time, as an audience member, sitting here in the gallery. A spectator like all the rest.

I listened to all the sounds of the other guests descending into their seats, their chatter to their neighbours, more sloshing of wine waiters pouring out more champagne. And then, the chatter slowly descended into a lull, as I heard the doors at the back of the theatre swing to a shut with a meaty *slap*. Jessica clung tighter to my hand, squeezing so hard that I felt my heart throbbing through it. After a minute or so I had to tap her on the shoulder to ask her to relinquish her grasp a notch.

The houselights dropped the gallery into total darkness. There was a murmur of excitement and then guests began to shush each other. Soon enough there was almost total silence in the theatre, only the shuffling of guests getting comfortable in their seats or the rustle of women adjusting the lie of their dresses. Thick footsteps sounded on the stage and it could only be one man. Dante.

A spotlight sparked up and illuminated a monochrome circle where Dante stood, steeping his face in a fleet of shadows—each of those high cheekbones leaving a sooty trace down the side of his face. His black eyes caught the spotlight and they reflected the white light like a pair of well-polished mirrors from within his dug-out eye sockets which betrayed the sleepless nights Jessica had told me about.

I heard someone whispering behind me, in hushed tones. "They say that no one's been able to work it out yet, not even the magicians they've had following him—no one knows how he does it. I can't imagine—"

There was a sharp "*Shhh*" from behind the person and they stopped speaking.

This time was different somehow. Was it because this was a private function? Did it put Dante ill at ease? There was no attempt to address the audience, none of those sparky introductions, that *faux* accent which marked his speech early on in the act and drew more and more tired as he went on. His clothes, too, he was simply wearing his shirt sleeves rolled up to the elbow, his waistcoat over the top. I noticed there were several buttons undone, revealing a tuft of obsidian chest hair poking out. He just stayed silent, drawing all attention to each of his movements. He clasped his hands together before him, about stomach height, and stared down at them, as if he had caught some insect there.

My throat welled up. That same energy crackled through the air. I could feel people shifting in their seats so I knew they felt it too. I wondered what had happened to the opening act, the act featuring Jessica. I looked to her, but she was transfixed on the stage. She must've been equally taken off guard. He had decided to skip right to the meat of the show, no more of that beating around the bush. I recall thinking, quite clearly, that that was a good thing.

Dante held his hands before him and I noted the shimmer of a smile pass over his lips, his eyes illuminating just for a moment, and then, all of a sudden, he tore his hands apart. Light scattered from within, bright white shards of light. They bobbed and bounced about the theatre. Woman shrieked, leaping up from their seats and batting at their hair, as if the shards of light might've got themselves stuck there. Men drew deep breaths, attempting to stay calm before joining their wives and companions in standing and waving their arms all about. But, as this wildness spread through the hall, I just sat there in my seat, pressing myself down into the material, wishing for it to end. I had never imagined him capable of something like this—something so devastating, such a spectacle.

The shards of light continued to whip around the theatre, causing carnage wherever they went. It was similar to what had happened in the previous performances. Some members of the audience took their leave, women running in their high heels for the exits while men, sheltering their glasses of champagne, hurried out after them.

Several of the shards of light skirted my cheeks, before soaring off to bother someone else. After the initial shock, the first time I had seen them appear, I began to think about what they were—where they had come from. And I started to look around, to gauge other people's reactions. The first face I caught sight of was Gerald's. Unlike the rest of the theatre, he seemed almost entirely unmoved by the event, his eyes slunk back in their sockets—if I hadn't known better I might've said that he looked a touch bored. He continued to watch the show as if out of a sense of curiosity, rather than the profound wonder that seemed to have struck everyone else—myself included—in the theatre. Despite all those shards of light bobbing about, some just missing the very eyeballs he stared with, he remained focussed on one thing and one thing only. Or one person. Dante, up there on the stage, arm outstretched, palm open toward the audience, peering out through the slits of his eyelids, with the very bottom, the whites of his eyes.

As the shards of light gradually grew dim and petered out, some landed in clothing, flashed a couple more times—like dying sparks—then went away for good, leaving no traces. Some guests returned to their seats, smiles pinned to their lips, others—as before—had had enough and had retired to the hall for the evening, no doubt to douse themselves with yet more champagne and to laugh about the folly of their reaction, while behind those smiles, that self-effacement, their nerves were shredded into tinsy, tiny pieces and this night would live on, forever, in their minds.

I sat there, in my chair, gripping the arms, and I remember

thinking to myself that Dante had turned a corner, that this was a different act—a better act. He had done away with those cheap mentalist routines and decided to do what he did best, because it was the only part of his act that was *real*: the conjurings. And at the same time I wondered why it had taken him so long to get to this point, to be willing to throw away the old part of the act, to realise that he did in fact have a great talent, a great power, which was less than uncommon. It was magical.

As the panic following the shards of light died down I heard the beginnings of scattered applause, and pretty soon, just as loud as the clapping I had heard following one of Dante's main acts—the conjurings of the shadows, the figures. I looked around the delighted faces, half fright, half pure, unadulterated, pleasure. They reminded me of those faces on children in my neighbourhood, when the fair would come to town and we'd be queuing up for the haunted house, everyone with their tickets clutched in their fists, never knowing quite what to expect. This, though, was completely different from that haunted house—because I knew that, whatever Dante was doing, it was real.

Dante stooped over himself, hands clasped once more in that familiar position at his waist. The audience stilled. No little gestures, everyone, very literally, right on the edge of their seats, holding their collective breath, waiting to see what would happen. Minutes passed, maybe ten minutes, with everyone just staring at Dante. I would never have believed that people had attention spans which could hold out as long as they did, let alone upper class people who had never spent a day chopping wood, or an afternoon wringing clothes dry or a midnight shift digging sludge out of storm gutters with their bare hands. But I was witnessing it now. They couldn't have unlocked their gazes if they'd wanted to.

I started to make out a faint *hum* in the air, coming from Dante, resounding from somewhere deep in the pit of his chest. And then I grew to wondering whether it was him making that sound at all, or whether it was coming from somewhere else— from all around me. I glanced about but could see no logical source for the sound. Again, I cast a glare at Gerald, who now rested his chin on his hands, as before refusing to break eye contact with Dante. And then, much to my surprise, as I looked back to the stage, I saw Dante standing there, glaring downward at Gerald—quite unmistakably, the two of them having some sort of a stand off.

I squirmed in my seat, looked around me to see if anyone else had noticed this silent battle. But the rest of the audience seemed unflustered, unmoved if they did. They were more inter- ested in what Dante might do next, of course.

Gradually, I watched as Dante's eyelids fluttered downward as if he were falling, involuntarily, into a gradual and gentle sleep. I had to blink rapidly, strain my vision, through the grim dark- ness all about me, to work out whether or not he continued to look out at us through a narrow gap in his eyelids. Finally, I was satisfied that he had, indeed, shut his eyes and, to all appear- ances, he was sleeping on his feet, standing right before us.

I felt Jessica squirm slightly beside me and then I saw that Gerald's lingering hand, ever curious, had drifted to her thigh, was worming its way, slowly, upward, beneath the hem of her dress. Jessica continued to face forward, though, no other reac- tion present on her face. I wished there was something I might be able to do to help her, but I told myself that she was a big girl —a fully-grown woman—if she wished I had no reason to think that she couldn't snap one of Gerald's fingers off.

For the first time during Dante's meditation, his apparent

sleeping before us, I noticed the tell-tale signs of people growing restless, the shuffling of feet, that familiar rustle of women straightening their dresses again, and even, as the wait lengthened and lengthened, quiet conversations batting back and forth. I closed my eyes and waited it out, feeling the tension wafting over me from the stage, willing Dante to do something —*anything*—to impress these people. With my eyes shut I could make out Gerald's warm breaths, that slight *click* as he drew in each inhalation, unquestionably savouring Jessica's featherlike skin, drinking her in with his fingertips. And then, all at once, the spell was broken.

A single shrill, high-pitched *scream* totally shattered the waiting room, and everything just descended into chaos.

CHAPTER ELEVEN

THRILLS TREMBLED through my body. I didn't need to open my eyes, there was no need. I knew what would be in the hall—had seen it better. I . . . *felt* their presence all around. If I opened my eyes I would only confirm it. I found myself gripping tight to Jessica's hand, my fingernails digging into her skin. It felt wet, warm, sticky. And only when that rusty scent stung my nostrils did I dare open my eyes and look down to see that I had drawn blood. I recoiled, tearing my grip from hers, appalled at the damage I had inflicted.

Jessica, however, remained unmoved. Like Gerald, she continued to stare at the stage, while the whole theatre seemed to be coming down all around us. I sucked in a handful more breaths and then allowed myself to gaze around the hall, to take in the utter madness sending tremors through the place.

Shadows, more than I'd ever seen before, ten, twenty, thirty . . . many more than that, all skipped their way along the aisles. They reminded me of young children—the kids under ten—

when they'd get out of school, and come bounding out with that unbreakable enthusiasm, skipping ropes, balls, crudely crafted wooden swords, flying all over the place. There was a youthful energy about the shadows tonight, as if they had some reason to be cheerful. I just stayed in my seat watching them go by, those ever-changing, ever-melting faces pulling tricks on my mind.

Then I saw her again. My mother.

My heart stuck in my throat. I tipped myself out to the edge of my seat and stared. There she was, unmistakable. Her winding, coiled hair drawn up into a headscarf, her hands trailing down by her sides. I knew those underfed, yet fudgy cheeks anywhere—it was as familiar to me as any landscape. It was her, of that there was no doubt. And she was standing there, glaring at me, waiting.

I cast a glance at Jessica and Gerald to see if they had noticed. Jessica now squeezed her eyes shut and I observed that Gerald's hand had now completely disappeared up her dress—that he was touching her, and it was causing her pain. And all the while he never so much as looked at her, he just kept on staring at Dante, there on the stage, lost in his private world of spirits, apparently unaware of the kerfuffle in the theatre, the women bellowing at the tops of their lungs, and the men roaring out in fear. I wanted this to stop. Wished for it to stop.

I pressed my fingers into my eyes and waited, feeling the throb of my pulse in my skull. I counted the seconds and then looked again, to the aisle. There she was, my mother, still waiting for me. I glanced around at the ensuing madness, the shadows skipping on their way. None of the others had fleshed out features, as my mother did. In a blaze of queasiness, I slipped along the row, tapping the guests with besieged faces to move their legs for me, to let me out. And just like that I was standing before my mother, her empty face staring at me.

It felt like my body might break apart at any second from the tension. It was like someone had tied a invisible string around my waist and they were proceeding to pull it tight, squeezing all the air out of me, suffocating me.

My mother, the shadowy figure, turned on her heel and trod on down the aisle, heading toward the exit of the theatre. I chanced a look back at Gerald and Jessica. Neither of them noticed me, seemingly hadn't registered that I'd left at all. I could see that Jessica's eyes were sealed shut, Gerald's still fixed on Dante, on the stage.

My mother led me out of the theatre and along a corridor marked with various hunting oil paintings. Soon we emerged outside, on balcony, carved from light grey stone, lit by several candles on sticks, covered from the light breeze by glass sheathes. The view looked out on the garden down below and I was a little surprised that no one else was out here tonight—that none of those who had stormed out of Dante's performance had thought to come out here for some fresh air. It was so beautiful, just the sort of place that I had always dreamt about, and never quite believed existed.

I turned my attention to my mother, or whatever this shadowy representation of her was, and waited for her to speak. But she just kept on staring, apparently waiting for me to make the first move with eternal patience. My throat constricted and I felt the swell of tears gripping hold of me. Was she angry because I'd forgotten her, my previous life, in such a short time? What must she have thought of her daughter, storming out that night with no explanation, and never coming home? I decided that I needed to reason with her, to get my words in first—to try and make some sense. "Mum?" I said. "That night, the night you . . . you and Dad, and the babbie, the night you died, I didn't come back home because I was looking for a job—something to help out with the house. I . . . I just thought," I said, just about getting it out without spilling a tear, "that if only I could find something, anything, then things wouldn't have been so bad—we wouldn't have had to leave our home."

I examined her, not sure whether or not I was going completely crazy, if—to anyone else that might've happened to be watching on from some hidden position—I might've looked like a mad person speaking to thin air. If anyone said anything I could always claim that Dante's show had got my mind all wobbly, made me see things that weren't there. It would be excuse enough for me to slip away, to slink back into the house and find Jessica once more, where I was supposed to be.

"Well?" I said, growing increasingly uncomfortable from my mother's stare. "What do you say?"

Her mouth seemed to form out of nothing, like an invisible fist had punched a slab of clay and left an indentation. But there were no words. I leant closer, sure that I was choosing not to hear. But no, she simply wasn't saying anything at all to me. Her mouth was moving without any meaning.

I waited a little longer and she seemed to realise that I didn't understand. Her mouth slipped back into her head, becoming indistinguishable from the rest of her blankness. I decided that I had to try again. It seemed that she could understand me, so at least that would be a start. I began again. "Mum? I'm sorry that I left you all behind, but I had no idea what happened to you—I was scared, going with Dante seemed like the best thing for me to do, he's kind and he's looked after me"—I thought of Farol's words—"given me a *livelihood*, it's much better than any life I would've had back in the capital, begging off the posh folks, sleeping in rags in an alleyway, underneath a ventilation vent if I'd been lucky. Really," I said, "I'm going to be all right."

This time my mother made no attempt to speak, her mouth didn't reappear. She simply tilted her head to one side and looked at me. It was a beautiful gesture, somewhere between an air of pride and love. At least that was how I interpreted it. I had no other way of knowing what she thought—of hearing her responses. With the dawning realisation that the end of our interaction might be drawing near, that Dante would soon return all these shadows—these souls—to whence they had come—I decided I had to reassure her, attempt to give her some peace, wasn't that what all wandering souls strode the Earth looking for? I gave up on chewing my tongue and then said, "He's a good man, Dante, I want you to believe that."

This time I read the fear in her eyes, the way that her eye sockets appeared to expand. Her mouth lilting open a touch. Even her cheeks seemed to retreat into her face.

"What . . . ," I said, seeing that something was wrong. "I don't . . . are you frightened?"

The only response my mother gave me was in her ever-widening eyes and mouth.

"Dante?" I said.

My mother's eyes opened in a full-on glare and then, all of a sudden, she loomed above me, growing several feet in height and then, in a fell swoop, drifted right through me as if I wasn't even there.

My heart chilled and my whole body got caught with trembles. I pivoted around and watched her go, back along the corridor, in the direction of the theatre. She didn't turn to look back at me. In that moment I felt so empty and helpless, so alone in the world. I had been sure that I had found my mother again, that—in some capacity—she and I would be able to set things straight, to work out any lingering issues, that I would be able to make her see that, really, I was getting on fine—I was going to be fine. And the net result of the meeting had been precisely the opposite and quite the contrary, now I was afraid that I had riled whatever remained of my mother, stoked her out of her rest.

I thought on that for a while, staring out into the empty garden, those tea lanterns all burning out, making it seem fantastical—it was truly beautiful at night. And then I heard the roar of applause drift along the corridor, out onto the balcony, and I reminded myself that I was supposed to be back there, sitting beside Jessica.

Thankfully it seemed that, in all the excitement, my slipping out hadn't been noted. I took advantage of the audience, all on their feet, clapping and whooping outrageously—the joint effect of the relief from fear and a light soaking in alcohol having worked its magic. I sidled back along our row and eyed Gerald and Jessica, afraid that the former might have noticed my absence and have more questions for me this time around—perhaps he would be shameless enough to have me searched to see if I'd stolen any of the family silver. But, to my great delight, he just stood there with the rest of the audience, clapping pugnaciously at about half the tempo of the rest of the crowd. His eyes, as they had been throughout the whole show, were set on Dante, never moving, never shifting, not even to cast a glance at Jessica or me.

Dante held up his hands, still refusing to speak at all, and he gave the audience a heady bow, bending right over, his fingertips almost brushing the tops of his shoes. When he straightened back up, he puffed out his cheeks, gave a final wave, then made his way off stage. That, I supposed, was the end of the performance.

Finally, Gerald did turn his attention away from the stage, to Jessica. He spoke in his gravely tone now, no sign of any slurring. I knew this was the time we had to take care—when he was at his most dangerous. I realised that whatever game he was playing it was reaching its end stages and he was preparing the killing stroke. What he had in mind I couldn't have said. Not until the words had passed his lips.

"Terrific show," he said.

Jessica loosened her shoulders—I noticed that she'd sat with them hunched up for much of the performance. She pinned on a smile as she clapped along with the fading applause. "Oh yes," she said, "quite spectacular, didn't you think?"

"I was surprised that he didn't ask you up onto the stage. What happened there?"

Her fake smile got more intense—I knew it to be inversely proportional to how she was feeling. "Earlier this afternoon Dante thought it might be a better idea to drop the whole act completely. You see, I think quite a few of your friends saw the show back in Ditchfurth." She nodded in the direction of Percy, who was waggling his head around, laughing outrageously while he near enough stuffed his nose between the bulging breasts of the woman beside him. "Dante believed," Jessica continued, "that the illusion would be broken, so we decided to cut that part of the show."

"A good decision, I feel."

"Yes," Jessica said, her voice growing fainter, weaker.

Gerald seemed to produce a full flute of champagne from somewhere. He held the glass up to Jessica. "This is to you, my dear."

Jessica again feigned a grin.

He knocked back the contents of the glass in one then dropped it down at his feet. "Servant will get that," he said, trailing his arm around Jessica's shoulders and forcing us to make our exit from the row, to join the exodus no doubt headed for the garden for the post-show drinks. "We should mingle for a while," Gerald said. "Then, well, we shall see where the evening takes us, shall we?"

Jessica didn't respond, but her compliance was clear. What was she supposed to do now? He had her all wrapped up in a box with a ribbon on top. If she refused to bend to his whim, he would have her arrested, imprisoned—perhaps even sent to the workhouse. And I got the feeling that he would work it so that I would go with her. He would get the ultimate joy of a complete package, sweeping a Gypsy and a black girl from the streets of England in one, single shot.

As I followed on their heels, I listened to Gerald and Jessica's one-way conversation. "Yes," Gerald continued, "quite a remarkable spectacle, and I have to admit that I'm really quite beaten as to how he does it. Oh, I know just how that opening act worked—with you as the stooge, a quite lovely stooge I may add, but a *stooge* nonetheless—I've seen that sort of performance ever since I was a boy. But, tonight, all the *conjuring*, those shadows. Tell me, my dear, how does he do it?"

If I hadn't been listening till that point, Gerald's question would've caught my ear. I listened in intently, sure that now Jessica would have to give him some sort of a satisfactory answer.

Jessica stumbled and almost fell to the ground. If it hadn't been for Gerald's sure hand, bringing her back to her feet, she might well have cracked her head on the solid, marble floor. Once Gerald had her back upright he glanced about, as if looking for someone to blame. Not finding anyone in the immediate vicinity, his hand found its way to the small of Jessica's back once more. "I'd take more care to watch where you're going, my dear. There're all sorts of jagged bits in this house—comes with the age, I suppose."

Jessica murmured something inaudible and they carried on.

I followed in their wake, feeling a little put out that she had not only managed to avoid Gerald's question—but left my curiosity unquenched also.

We emerged outside, on the balcony and, once more, I looked down on the garden before us, the tea lights illuminating various parts of foliage. Gerald helped Jessica down each of the stone steps, taking special care with her now—afraid that she might fall again and hurt herself, thus having an excuse to turn in early, to return to our camp out on the estate, I thought.

A waiter cropped up before us and offered Gerald another flute of champagne, which he accepted with glee. Jessica took her own too. The waiter dipped to offer me a glass and then, apparently thinking better of it, straightened up and carried onto the next guest. I should've been used to that treatment by then, but it still sat badly with me.

I spotted Farol across the room. It was funny, he almost disappeared into the crowd, what with wearing that tuxedo, and being well into his sixties. He could easily have been mistaken for a nobleman. And that got me to thinking what it was exactly that made a nobleman. Money? Title? Success? I supposed it was some lucky combination of all of those.

Farol was still enraptured in conversation with the portly lady from earlier, the one dressed in the corset. Both of them stood on the balcony—Farol booming with laughter and slapping his thigh every time she appeared to crack a joke. It gave me pause for thought, made me wonder whether he had some sort of an escape route too, if this whole deal with Dante went turnip-shaped. Maybe he was planning on getting cosy with some rich widow. I had to admit, from his perspective, that it wouldn't be a half bad retirement.

Finding myself alone, or at least with no one to talk to, I took in the garden, the various drinkers, the ladies and gentlemen, all of them having seemingly recovered from the ordeal of Dante's show. I wished that he had given me the same order as the last show, for me to wait for him backstage. On reflection, I'd felt much better in the wings, in the darkness, watching from there, than down with the rest of the audience. I knew I didn't belong and I had no intention really to try. It was too late now, though, because I'd have to follow Gerald and Jessica, and Gerald's curious hands, around for the rest of the evening. Lucky me.

Just when I thought that things couldn't get much worse, or at least any more tedious, I noticed that Percy was staring at me from the circle of friends he stood inside. He shot me a smile, as if this were the first time we'd ever interacted—as if he were testing the waters. Immediately, of course, I looked away, hoping that he would give up whatever sad game he was trying to play with me. I knew that as long as I stuck near to Jessica and Gerald I would be okay, he surely wouldn't risk invoking Gerald's wrath for a second time in the evening. Then again, I hadn't bargained for outright stupidity.

As I turned away and tried to focus on one of the flowers

which was illuminated in the uneven orange glow, I noticed, out of the corner of my eye, the unmistakable sensation of movement. He was coming over. Again. Really, I could not believe this man. He was ridiculous.

"Miss Blind?" Percy muttered to me, surprisingly crisply, soberly.

With my back to him, I closed my eyes, wished him away, then seeing that it wasn't going to work—that I just didn't have the capacity for *that* kind of magic—I reluctantly turned around to meet him face on.

Percy grinned at me. I made out his dilated pupils and the sharp, warm odour of champagne clung to him as if he had bathed himself, suit and all, in it.

I shot a glance to Jessica and Gerald but they seemed to be engrossed in some conversation or other and then, impossibly, they turned away from us, Gerald leading Jessica to some place or other, deeper in the garden. I found myself trapped, wanting to follow them, and yet reading the subtext, that they—or at least Gerald—wanted to be alone together. It looked like I would have to face down Percy for myself. I could do it. I was a big girl after all.

Percy jabbed his tongue into the corner of his mouth and followed my gaze. "I *wonder* where they're off to, those two." He looked back to me, a sleazy grin on his face. "That friend of mine, old Gerald, he really is something of a fox, don't you think so?"

"Yes," I said, "I suppose he is."

Despite my worries early on in our interaction, not without reason, Percy turned out to be okay after all. He was just so childlike, so open-eyed with wonder at everything. I decided to put our exchange on the stairs down to this facet of his personality. When he got hold of something his instinct was not to let go —like a frightened child. And unlike his 'foxy' friend he didn't really try anything physical, seeming afraid to touch me, more than anything. I was glad at that.

He told me about his own family, how he and Gerald had grown up together, attended some posh school that I couldn't pronounce the name of, let alone spell, and then, finally, set up business together. He got a touch vague when I asked him for further details of this, grumbling something about imports and exports, and I drew the conclusion that, perhaps, he wasn't quite the brains of the operation—that he was little more than a glorified plaything for Gerald to keep around the office, someone to pat him on the back and to accompany him when he went off drinking. That made me feel better around Percy too. Below the surface he was harmless.

During one of Percy's many monologues—I guess he didn't get much chance to hold forth while Gerald was around—I tuned out and listened in to a few sample conversations milling around the guests. It seemed that everyone was hanging on, that was no one was making to leave, because they were waiting patiently for the appearance of Dante. They all wanted to know, where was that man who could conjure such delights, apparently without any recognisable explanation? And, I had to admit, I was eager myself to see Dante. But for other reasons.

Just as Percy threatened to tell me yet another story of 'high spirits' and 'scandal' I was relieved to hear the *tinkle* of a teaspoon on a champagne glass, and the calling of a throaty voice for everyone to come to order—to pay attention. I didn't need to incline my head to know that it was Lord Forsneer, just as commanding as his offspring, the prospect of crossing him just as terrifying as the prospect of crossing his son.

"Now, now!" Forsneer bellowed above the simmering conversations. "I'd like to thank you all for coming tonight, and especially for putting a much-needed dent in the Forsneer Estate wine cellar."

There were guffaws at this remark.

To myself I thought that, if his drinking on the hunt was anything to go by, then he did a pretty smart job of getting through the wine cellar all by himself.

Someone sparked up a song in Forsneer's honour and, soon enough, the whole garden was singing along. I'd never heard the song before and, to be honest, at that time found the words unwieldy, difficult to remember—nothing like those songs which Dad would sing down the pubs on a Friday night, come piling in through the door early in the morning still singing.

Once the song had come to an end, and there had been a toast in the host's honour, Forsneer continued, "What we've witnessed tonight is nothing short of remarkable, as I'm sure all of you shall agree."

There were, indeed, murmurs of agreement.

"And I believe I'm right in saying that you're just as anxious to meet this dear fellow, this performer who has put on such a terrific show."

Shouts of agreement this time.

"However," Forsneer said, taking his time over the statement, allowing it to take on a little gravity, "it seems that he cannot be located, not in any place whatsoever. He appears to have gone missing. Which is bloody typical, just after I'd paid the blighter!"

There was a resounding laughter, another toast to Forsneer's health. As the ruckus died down I listened to the reaction of the guests. No more than a few remarks along the lines of it being a pity, but not really venturing much more than that. I supposed this was just another *entertainment* to these people. Another light distraction giving them an excuse to get drunk.

Forsneer cast his gaze down to his shoes, his champagne flute sagging in his hand. "Well, even if he has fled the premises, I don't see why we shouldn't give him a toast in any case." He raised his glass and the assembled guests copied their host. "To Dante Gobornik, the finest magician I have *ever* had the pleasure of witnessing."

"Here, here!" called out several of the men.

Everyone drank.

I took that opportunity to sneak away from Percy's side. It was quite funny. I'd already got myself two or three groups away from him before I took a chance on a glance back over my shoulder to see him only just then bringing his drained champagne flute down from his lips, and looking around, thoroughly confused at finding me gone.

I was decided. If Dante had seen fit to get away from this depravity then I saw no reason why I should linger. Jessica and Farol could quite clearly take care of themselves. As I made my way back into the house—the servants only looking down their noses at me, but not taking any further action—the foliage running along the side of the house caught my eye. Movement again. That same mechanism which had allowed me to see Percy approaching. And then, I was certain, there was another of those shadows, lurking there, in the gloom.

I looked around. No one was watching me now, all the waiters now distracted, pouring out more champagne for the increasingly drunken guests—some were being served whisky now. And so I sidled around the corner of the house and stared into the darkness, unsure at what I might see there. Perhaps my mother again, or another member of my family. But, no, it wasn't anyone that I recognised. It was a gentleman, dressed in a completely black suit, a black tie, and black trousers. His eyes too, were black, and that should've given it away to me, but, before I could work it out for myself, he spoke. "Sara?"

It was Dante.

CHAPTER TWELVE

J UBILATION SHOOK ME. Everything would be all right now. Dante was here, and he would help me find the way back to the camp. I looked to him, waiting for his signal to help me sneak away. Taking in his appearance once more I realised how different he looked—how he was dressed in a disguise—I'd never seen him wearing this suit before.

His lips crinkled in a smile, doing that damn minding-reading trick of his again. "This is just something I pick out when I don't want to be recognised." He eyed me closely. "You're a clever girl, I remember that it took both Jess and Farol a good two or three weeks before they realised who the man in the black suit was."

I wanted to tell him that I hadn't *quite* worked it out—that he had rather given the game away by calling my name, speaking in his familiar voice. But I wasn't all that worried about him pinning me as a 'clever' girl. In fact I quite liked it.

"So, it's kind of like that beggar disguise you wore, on the night we met?"

"Something like that."

Although I had more questions for him, that I wanted to probe him for the reason why he saw the need to disguise himself, and, following that, wanting to tell him about seeing my mother—I knew that it was different. Hadn't Farol said that the entire time he had seen those shadows, being a member of Dante's troupe, he had never been able to make out their identities. It made me uneasy and I wished to have the matter cleared up as soon as possible.

The babble of conversation and the tinkling of glasses drifted down to where we lurked, on the fringes of the party. I looked to Dante, eyes wide. "What now?"

Dante stuffed his hands into his pockets and slouched—again something I had *never* seen him do before. Despite his lax posture, his eyes were as sharp as ever, prying through the crowd, scanning faces and discarding them just as quickly. I knew what he was going to say before he spoke the words. "Where's Jessica?" he said.

"Oh, she . . . I saw her going off with Gerald, toward the back of the garden."

I'm not sure what I expected his reaction to be, perhaps some *machismo*-afflicted rush through the crowd, batting people aside, before muscling back his girl. But he just stood, still slouching slightly, watching the crowd with intense care. "It's time for us to go," he said, seemingly half to himself, and then, turning to me, "Go get Farol."

There was a sternness, a lack of humour in his voice that I had never sensed before. It sent a shiver up my spine and I felt just as afraid as I had back in the theatre, watching him summon up those shadows. I lingered a moment, unsure what to do next, and then I burst into action, scuttling through the waiters, dipping beneath their outstretched arms, the trays they carried, and over to Farol, who continued to stand at the balcony with the voluptuous lady. Although I'd hardly run five seconds, I found myself out of breath and sweating profusely.

Farol seemed to grasp my panic since, even through those rosy cheeks and jolly composure, his chubby cheeks vibrating with laughter, I saw the serious note in his eye. We didn't need to speak at all. He turned, still smiling, to the lady, reached out for her hand and planted a kiss on the back of it, bowing as he did so. I watched on as the lady blushed slightly and brought her own chubby hand up to her cheek. Farol wheeled himself around, so that he backed away from her, still speaking as he went. The lady gave him a pincer-like wave, moving only her fingers, leaving her wrist completely stiff. And then, with a final word of departure, Farol turned to face me, grave-faced. "We're off then?" he said.

I nodded in reply.

"What about Dante?"

"He's gone off to get Jessica."

Farol stayed silent and then said, "He . . . how was he dressed?"

"All in black."

Farol's complexion seemed to chill a little, his eyes wandered about their sockets. "He didn't say whether or not he needed some help, did he?"

"No, he didn't specify."

"Ah, good, good," he said, gazing over the crowd, as if looking for someone—Dante, I supposed.

Together we returned to the side of the house. Dante was gone, as I'd half-expected. Farol took a final glance back over his shoulder before jiggling onward, moving away from the garden scene, leaving it behind him forever. I struggled to keep up with him, already feeling weariness weighing down my bones.

A couple of coachmen offered us a ride back home, but Farol turned them down, saying something along the lines of wanting to get some fresh air. I supposed it was some kind of inset pride, since there was no sign of the servant who had brought us up to the house, these coachmen would discover that we were staying on the estate, camped out in a field. Farol's pace didn't slow down until we'd reached the end of the well-lit drive when fatigue claimed him. He stopped dead, doubled over and breathing heavily—quickly drawn breaths punctuated by grunts. He reminded me of an exasperated pig in a tuxedo, like one I'd seen once on a postcard, when I'd gone down to the pub with Dad. I didn't tell Farol that, though, obviously.

"You think he'll be all right?" I said.

"Yes," Farol said, a little too hurriedly to be convincing. "Fine."

We continued on our way, our shoes crunching over the gravel path. I stumbled a couple of times in the ruts left by carriage wheels, but caught myself before I took a tumble. I felt the weight between us, some sort of a murk hanging over the conversation. There was an assumption and I got the impression that this situation—this situation involving Jessica and Dante—had taken place before, and, from Farol's reaction, I judged that it hadn't gone all that well. I decided to break through the thick mist between us by bringing up what I had experienced that night—Farol would be a good test, before I'd take it to Dante. "I need to tell you something."

The moonlight set Farol's face in a silvery glow, making him seem much older, more haggard, harder worked. He continued to face forward, focussed on the track ahead of us, probably still preoccupied as to what was going on back at the house.

I took his silence as an invitation to continue. "It's about the shadows—ghosts, whatever."

Still he faced forward.

"You see, tonight, I think I saw the face of my mother in one of them."

I was sure that this would stop him in his tracks, but, if anything, he increased his pace, as if determined to leave the house behind as soon as he could—for us to escape this place as soon as possible. I wondered what the rush was about. Finally, Farol spoke up. "Sometimes I think I see people in their faces."

I thought back to what he'd told me before, that he had never been able to identify them. Had he been lying to me?

"Sometimes," he said, looking back over his shoulder with a neat flick of his neck, "you can see things where there's really nothing at all." He tapped his temple. "Mind has a habit of making sense out of a load of nonsense sometimes."

"No, but that's not it. I'm certain that I saw her. In fact, I saw her in the theatre and followed her outside—to the balcony —while the performance was still taking place. She was trying to speak to me, she had a mouth and"—I felt myself welling up a little—"I just couldn't understand a word. Her words were silent. Or, maybe, I just couldn't understand them."

The next thing I knew, Farol's steady hand descended on my shoulder and he gave me a strong squeeze. I looked to his face and he was giving me that doughy smile of his—what I decided was a sort of grandpa grin, a grin which spoke of extensive life experience, that I was still a mere, naïve child just seeing things in the darkness.

I suppose the first moment that I caught drift of there being something wrong, that there was something up with the whole situation, was as we drew closer to the campsite. Farol suddenly got more fidgety, something which seemed strange considering the amount I presumed he'd drunk that night—drunk people didn't get anxious. And then I wondered how much of what Farol had done tonight had been an act. Perhaps he had the same gift Gerald had, that ability to play the fool, make himself *seem* drunk so as to bring down others' defences. In any case, there was a marked shift as we approached, his strides grew longer and more determined, his gaze firmly fixed on the carriage ahead of us.

Without any further explanation, he began to bark orders at me, telling me to help him pack up the tent. Between us, we rummaged through the items inside, tossing everything into a few trunks. I noticed that Dante had already packed up. His trunk already sat on the top of the carriage, all ready to go. Whatever he had in mind it was premeditated—and Farol had seen this all before.

I had no time to ask questions as we brought the tent down between us and then hauled it up onto the roof of the carriage. Next was Jessica and Farol's trunks, which we hoisted between us up beside Dante's. I presumed that sometime in the future I would have a trunk of my own. Together we brought a tarpaulin down over the trunks to make them waterproof and to add a degree of safety to the journey, so that if our hurried roping of the trunks failed they might not fall straight off into the road.

Within no time at all the whole camp was packed up. All we left behind was a smouldering brown patch, ashen ground, where we'd built our fires, and the flattened grass where we'd pitched the tent. I looked out over the field for the last time, picking out that hole in the hedgerow where I had crawled through while escaping Gerald's hunt. It all seemed such a long time ago now, like it had happened years ago, and not mere days.

Farol jogged up to the carriage holding both horses by their bridles and attaching them to the carriage with swiftness that's only earned after hundreds, thousands, of iterations of a task. Then he hoiked himself up onto the front of the carriage and growled at me over his shoulder. "Get in!"

I did as he said, hardly getting the carriage door shut before we lurched off, passing over the field, heading up the dirt road, taking the now-familiar route up to the house. As I listened to the heavy breaths of the horses, the crunching and occasional sliding of their hooves over the loose ground, I got another of those tingling sensations. One of those bad feelings. That we were about to find ourselves in deep, deep trouble.

I leant up against the window of the carriage, pressing my nose against the cold glass. Up ahead the house looked much as it had before, lurking there on the hillside, more an extension of the landscape than a human addition. Just as we arrived at the end of the drive, however, I began to see that things weren't quite as we'd left them.

For a start, all the tea lights, and I mean every last one of them, that had previously marked the drive—glowing away to give some semblance of order in the night—had been extinguished. At first I thought they might simply have burnt down, expired. But all at once? Then I floated the possibility of a strong wind. Sure, they were protected by that thin film of glass, but it wouldn't stand up to something so robust as a gust. However, all the time, in the pit of my guts, I knew that there was only one explanation. Dante.

Farol slowed the carriage as we creaked our way up the driveway. I knew that he was worried of raising suspicions, because this carriage, what with its fantastical paintings and rugged construction, would stand out like a sore thumb pulling up outside the Forsneer mansion. And then, up there, behind the mansion, I saw them. A blaze of white light, clawing at the sky, snatching at the stars, like elongated human limbs, determined to extinguish life. As we pulled up to the front of the house, I noted that there was no one there—that the coachmen had disappeared off inside the house, I supposed, to check what on Earth was going on.

I clicked open my door and stepped down, staring in awe at those lights passing above us. That familiar chill was more than simply an inconvenience now, it was whipping around, stinging my skin.

Farol, in a gruff voice I had never before heard, said, "Back in the carriage. Now!"

I lingered a second, taking in the lights, feeling that cold, and then I did as he said, planting myself back onto the cushions and peering out at the mansion, heart pounding against my tongue, wondering just when Dante, and Jessica, would emerge.

The horses grew a touch restless at the scene. Silver bent his neck back, snorted, and rubbed his head up against his companion. Old Billy, on the other hand, stood proud, unmoved, as if this were something which he had witnessed on countless occasions. I listened to Farol whispering to them from the driver's seat, and how it reassured Silver, how he seemed to get a grip of himself—although he refused to look back at the mansion, preferring to stare off down the driveway.

And then I saw the pair of them, Dante and Jessica, hurrying out through the front door of the mansion. Jessica's whole face was contorted in panic, her cheeks rosy and her dress—I noticed as they drew closer—torn at the hem. On the other hand, Dante remained unmoved, focussed. One thing did mark his face, though, that background joviality, that touch of humour which he often displayed just wasn't there. I wondered whether it might have been a facet of that *Man-in-Black* persona, or maybe it was the gravity of the situation coming home to him.

I snatched at the latch to the carriage door, opening it wide in anticipation of both of them. I heard the door *slap* against the freshly-painted exterior and winced a little, thinking of all the work Farol had put into it. And then I got a hold of myself, told myself that this was a serious situation—that from the looks of things we were all in grave peril.

The two of them were about ten, fifteen, strides away from us, almost at the carriage, when I observed that all-too-familiar figure darken the doorway of the mansion. And almost as quickly as I identified him as Gerald, I took in that long, thin object he held in his hands. A hunting rifle.

I opened my mouth to cry out, but it was too late, and my call was lost to the *crack* of the shot. It ripped through the air and pounded into the side of the carriage, sending up woodchip. My ears rang turning my skull into an echo chamber. I could only think to throw myself down into the carriage, into the foot space. Another shot, and a brief *grunt* of grief. Moments later, Jessica hurled herself into the carriage, not stopping to find her footing before reaching out and taking Dante's hand, lugging him in behind her. I took it upon myself, seeing Gerald's arm raised again, readying yet another shot, to slam the carriage door shut behind us. As that final shot *whistled* overhead, I heard the stirring of the horses and then the rapid *clip-clop* as they broke into a gallop, dragging us, fishtailing horribly, down the driveway and away from the Forsneer mansion. Out into the endless, inky-black night.

CHAPTER THIRTEEN

T HE CARRIAGE was a flurry with panic and I found myself pinned up against one of the sides as Jessica busied herself attending Dante. Pressed up there, against the cool glass, I watched on with trembling eyes as I saw the extent of his wound. Gerald's bullet had struck him in his flank and blood was drooling out all over the place. Without a moment's hesitation, Jessica tore free a fistful of material from her dress and pressed it to the wound. Dante's blood turned the dark red material a black colour almost immediately.

In my terror-struck state, I recall leaning back, looking out that window, back to the mansion. And then, all of a sudden, I saw a flame erupt upward, at the top of the house. The white lights had gone now, and it was clear to see that the Forsneer mansion was on fire.

At first Jessica's words were muted, like someone had stuffed a damp rag into my ears. And then they came to me, and I heard what she was saying. "Sara! Sara! Help me, Sara!"

I turned my head and took in the scene.

Dante had his head back against the seat, eyes screwed up in pain and his feet stamping the floor. His hands were balled into fists, smacking down on the cushion every couple of seconds.

I was lost in that image for a while, this totally calm, austere presence, and here he was going almost berserk, submitting so freely to his emotions. It was almost more than I could stand. And yet, I still managed to bring Jessica back into focus, to concentrate on her instructions.

"Sara, your dress, we need your dress too!"

For a fuzzy second I was sure that she meant me to pull it off, over my head and hand it to her, so that I would have been naked save for my knickers. And then I absorbed what she herself had done and twigged that she only needed a scrap, just *something* to stem the bleeding. So I tore a shred off my dress and passed it to her.

Jessica pressed down on the wound, but I could still see the blood seeping out the edges of the makeshift bandage. The carriage bounced over a dip in the road and she lost her grip on the spot. When she got herself back into an upright position, the wound was bare again, the blood flowing relentlessly.

When I spoke it was like my words came back to me in the form of an echo. "Shouldn't we go to a hospital?" I said.

Not looking over her shoulder, trying to refind her grip on the bandages, she said, "Do you really think we're in a good position to find a hospital?"

I suppose that I just spoke without thinking. But, it was fair to say, I had been pretty much left out of the loop as to what exactly had happened back at the Forsneers' mansion. Why was it on fire? What had Dante done back there? Right now, rushing along the road, almost tipping over as we went, wasn't the time to raise such questions, though.

Beyond the rickety *thumps* and *creaks* of our own carriage, I thought I could hear the approach of horse hooves, battering along the dirt road at our hind. Indeed, when I dared look through the window I saw them—dozens—all on horseback and closing in fast. To my distain I saw that they each carried a gun. Already I could see their plan, to draw level with us and let off all the shots they could. And with Jessica occupied in patching up Dante, Dante being patched up, and Farol needing all his attention to drive us forth into the night, I knew that it would fall to me to stop them. But how? How was a frightened little fourteen-year-old girl supposed to stop these rampaging drunken toffs? And that was when I felt her presence. I felt her with me. My mother. This time I had no need to see her face. I just *felt*.

It's hard to explain. That same chill just descended over me, but this time it was totally different. It was nothing like the sensation that Dante conjured forth when he brought out the shadows because I knew that I—*myself*—was producing it. I wanted to wish her away from me, to bid her farewell at such a vital juncture, I had work to do if I was going to see off our pursuers. And that was the last conscious thought I recall having at that time because, after that, my whole mind went blank as a clean sheet of paper—a bright, bright light, too bright to comprehend—and I felt my whole body descend, down toward the ground. I knew that I was a vessel and they were passing through me. Out of whatever depths they scrounged and coming to me of their own volition. And, more than that, they wished to help me.

I don't remember much more of the next moments, save for the sensory details. The horses' *shrieks*, the firing of rifles, the stench of Dante's blood mingled with gun powder thick in the air, and the taste of vomit on the back of my tongue, the rough-feeling fabric which I sat on, digging my fingernails into, attempting to get purchase, trying with all my might not to fall through this world and into the next. And, after that, the descending calm. That feeling in my solar plexus, like a gale-force wind hitting me right there, passing through my skin. Then, just like that, it was all over. When I opened my eyes I wondered whether I had escaped the tornado or if I was merely stuck in the eye of the storm.

I looked to my side and saw Jessica, sitting quite upright, staring blankly at me. Her hand continued to rest on Dante's side, stopping the free flow of blood. The snippet of my yellow dress now turned brown with his blood. Then I realised that Dante too was no longer enraptured in pain, but looking at me too, his mouth a thin line, something between confusion and outright joy at our escape from our pursuers. There was some-thing else there, too. I felt his invisible touch, like a guiding hand, keeping my steady, not letting me get away. It brought forth a memory, when I'd been a little girl—no more than seven or eight—and when I'd waded too far into a river, on the outskirts of our neighbourhood. Dad, he'd grabbed me, just as sure as the sensation I felt now—kept me from being sucked out by the current.

Unable to completely believe what had just happened, I looked back out the window, only to see nothing. Just the cool night air behind us, gravel kicking up from the backs of the wheels of the carriage. No one was coming after us. For now.

We steamed on through the night, Farol not letting up on either Silver or Old Billy. I listened to those relentless hooves, pawing and tilling at the road. I guessed that they must've been packed full of energy, the both of them, considering that they'd spent the best part of a week in a field—a kind of horse's holiday.

Once we'd got clear of our pursuers, Jessica had become more measured in her approach of treating Dante, taking care with his wound. She got the bleeding under control, improvising a fresh bandage from yet more dress and the elastic from a garter she acquired from somewhere. The crushing panic within the carriage ceased and we wheeled on in comparable peace. Total silence.

Throughout the entire night I remained up at the window, peering out into the ever-lightening landscape around us. The trees on the horizon soon took form, like a theatre backdrop, slowly being lit from above. It had an element of unreality to it: the dawn.

In the course of the past hour I'd noticed that Farol had been going easier on the horses, not driving them so hard along the road. I guessed that he assumed we were safe from immediate danger. I looked over to Dante and Jessica.

Jessica sat slouched, her head resting against Dante's shoulder, her eyes open a fraction. Dante slept on, uneasily, his eyeballs gyrating behind his eyelids, every couple of moments he twitched, the violence of his actions threatening to jerk him awake.

As the day dawned further, so much so that I could make out the various shades of green and brown in the foliage at my side of the carriage, I noted that Farol was bringing us to a halt, and speaking in a hushed tone. At first I wondered whether he might be speaking with the horses, easing them past some obstacle or other. However, when we reached a complete stop, I was sure I could make out another man's voice. Sure that we were stopped for the time being, I shifted out of my seat, unbuckled the door and stepped out into the new day.

Beyond Silver and Old Billy, both of them with their heads bowed, breathing profoundly, I made out a cabin, nothing more than a few wooden planks hammered together, sticking out at all angles, with a space for someone—a guard?—to look out from. As I rounded the carriage, I made out the uniformed man conversing with Farol.

To say that he was uniformed might be to give him a little more of a sense of looming authority than his appearance truly deserved. In short, the man was about Farol's age—at least in his middle sixties—although he was thin as a beanpole. He wore a dark blue uniform which was frayed all over the place. While he talked he would stick his finger in his ear and waggle it about, and that was what he was doing now.

I remained there, out of sight, hidden by Old Billy's sizeable flanks. I peered out through the gap at the two men.

Farol was speaking. "Look, I don't see what the problem is, you know, we're just on the move, getting onto our next destination."

The uniformed man removed his finger from his ear, wiping it on the side of his trousers as he did so, then said, "That might well be, but I'm under strict orders only to let those with the right authority past on *this* road."

"And why's that?"

"Well, sir, this road just happens to be the property of the Forsneers, and they charge a fee for the passage of any such carriage, like the one you yourself are commandeering. Need to pay for road maintenance, don't you know?"

"Fine," Farol said. "So where do I pay?"

"*Pay*, sir?"

"Yes, who's going to suck my blood?"

The uniformed man flashed his eyebrows at him and took up a more rigid posture. "I'll have you know, sir, I'm only doing my job." He wiggled his cap up a degree then said, "You should've sought the correct permit from the Grounds Keeper's office beforehand."

"And where's the Grounds Keeper's office?"

"Oh, that'd be a good ten miles back, sir."

Farol swore and kicked at the ground.

The uniformed man cocked his head to one side and gasped. "If you'd please, sir, I don't make the rules around here. If you've a problem with the system then I'd suggest you take it up with Lord Forsneer himself."

Farol looked back over the carriage, back over his shoulder at the road and then, right at me where I stood hidden behind Old Billy—I don't think he saw me. Now more focussed on overcoming this issue, Farol dug into the inside pocket of his tuxedo jacket—which he'd had no time to jettison in the rush—and produced a purse. He glanced up at the man. "How much, then?"

"*Sir!*" the uniformed man said, holding his hands up to him and backing away slowly. "Please, I've told you how the process works, I'll take no money here."

"How much?" Farol said, his tone a touch more irate.

"It's not a question of how much, sir, it's a matter of principle. You know the rules just as well as I."

Farol clinked out a handful of change from the purse and shot the man a sidelong glance.

The uniformed man coloured a little and then pressed his lips together. "I take it as an insult to my honour that you even float the proposition. Just what sort of man do you think me to be?"

Farol shook out the rest of the change from his purse and offered it to the man. "If you feel that way inclined then you could always take our money and pay the Grounds Keeper yourself, I'm not making any slight on your honour. However, the fact of the matter is that we're in a great rush, and so would be extremely grateful if you'd see to allowing us past your station and onto the public roads."

The uniformed man shook his head vigorously. "Out of the question, sir, I'm afraid. You'd be better striking me down than attempting to flout the rules, it's people like you that have this country in such a blooming mess, and another thing—"

In a flash of flesh and the *crack* of bone, I watched Farol punch the man, right in his left cheek. He fell to the ground like a lumbering pine, twisting slightly in mid-air before striking the ground, unconscious.

I felt my breath flush into my lungs and my whole body shook with the shock.

Farol hovered over his adversary for several moments, perhaps to check if he was still breathing. Next he glanced around then picked him up beneath his armpits, dragging him over to the man's guard post.

I remained there, beside Old Billy for several seconds before realising that I had to move. I had to get back into the carriage. So I shifted back around and let myself in through the door. I took up my seat beside Dante and Jessica, both of whom were now fast asleep. I guess that the night had really taken its toll on all of us.

From then on I noted the pace of our travel slowing noticeably. There was little doubt that Farol wanted to give the horses a rest, and maybe give us a better chance at some sleep. Still, I felt on edge, more affected, I found, by that brief encounter with the guard on the road than by anything that had happened the night before. I just hadn't pinned Farol as that sort of a man before, possessing that kind of hidden strength. Why, he'd simply throttled him right in the face. And although the man had been old, I didn't imagine the age between them to be much of a factor, since Farol wasn't any spring chicken either. I tried to reason with myself, to tell myself that he had done it for our protection, so that we would be safe, and somehow that made it feel a bit better, if not totally okay. Pretty soon after I found my eyelids drooping of their own volition and the woozy tug of sleep dragging me down into its abyss.

I dreamt of those shadows, all around me, circling. In my dream I was spinning around in my place, attempting to identify each of them, and failing. Every time I recognised some detail or other the face would change. I saw them all, all the members of my family: my mother, my father, the babbie, all together at once, and then they'd simply slip from my memory just as if they'd never been there at all.

I woke with a jerk, afraid that something horrible was happening. But we were moving on just as before, going at a light trot, the countryside passing us by on all sides, the fields swishing with caramel-coloured crops, fruits on the trees ripe for plucking. This place was so indifferent to any human toil—had no interest in where and what we'd done the previous night. And I was glad.

Jessica stirred at some time in the afternoon, blinking herself around. She looked lost for a long while, staring around herself, as if hardly able to believe where she was—that she'd somehow been transported here, to the carriage, and that she was leaving the Forsneer mansion behind. And then she locked eyes on me. At first she gave me a light smile, and she did her best to keep it up. But I could see, beyond the sheen in her eyes, the fear dwelling there, sitting in the shadows, ready to rise up and come to the surface. And so it took me off guard when she spoke. "You," she said. "You're just like *him*."

I had no idea how to respond to that. "Wha . . . what do you mean?"

The smile slipped from her lips. "You know what I mean."

I turned this over in my mind—thought back to our pursuers. I had a twinge in my gut, this wasn't the reaction I'd been expecting at all. I had thought that she would be thanking me for helping us get away. If it hadn't been for me, with whatever I did, then we'd all be sitting in a prison cell at that very moment. Or worse.

Dante sucked air through his teeth, sighing gently, and then he came around. He rubbed his eyelids and then peered out through narrow slits, as if he were fighting off a mean hangover. He tried to prop himself into a sitting position, but Jessica prevented him, laying her gentle touch on his abdomen, forcing him back down to rest. Content, to just lie there, he peered about him and said, "Where are we?"

"Out of trouble," I said.

He nodded weakly and then inspected his flank. Overnight the improvised bandage had turned manky, gone a dirty brown-red colour. He brushed the bandage but stopped short of peeling it back to have a look. Then he turned his attention to Jessica. "Is it bad?" he said.

"You need some antiseptic. A surgeon, really. There's no telling whether the bullet's still in the wound."

"Have we got time?"

"We'll make time."

I felt a little left out of this conversation and so I decided that moment was the appropriate one to butt in. "Excuse me," I said. "Where are we going exactly?"

Without turning around, Jessica said, "Abroad."

"What?"

She tilted her head in my direction so I could make out her face in profile. "That's the only safe place for us now. We'll have a few days, a week at the most for the news to travel around the country. Our only hope is to get a boat and head to France."

The idea set a fire inside my chest, made it flicker and burn inside me. *Abroad. France.* Those were words that I'd only ever heard salesmen utter in the capital, on their way between houses, selling 'exotic' produce. I had a neighbour who once had some French perfume, and didn't she let the neighbourhood know it. But this was real. So real that I could almost reach out and touch it. There was something else bothering me though, and I decided to raise it. "Will we ever be able to come back here, to England?"

Jessica and Dante exchanged glances, but it was Jessica who replied. "Who's to say? But for the time being we cannot afford to hang around here—it's too dangerous."

"But what about the shows you've booked?"

She shook her head. "They're lost. But when, *if*, we return then I'm sure they'll oblige us, be understanding about things. This wouldn't be the first time that a performer has been forced from this island due to some uncouth circumstance. In any case," she said, turning back to Dante, "we have more than enough money to be getting by with, enough for a month or two, anyway."

"And what about the surgeon?" I said, knowing somewhere from something someone had told me once, that they could be expensive. There were always stories floating about town where men who worked in the factories had died because they couldn't afford the surgeon's fees, and his family would die of hunger soon after, if they didn't swallow their pride and resort themselves to begging or thieving.

Jessica gave me a cold glare, and I saw that—perhaps—she hadn't factored that into her sums. She looked away from me and said, without much conviction, "I'm sure we'll manage."

It was getting dark before anyone spoke again. And it was Dante, who propped himself up on his elbows and peered out through window at the sign passing us by. He mouthed the word to himself several times before managing to build up the strength to utter it out loud. "Girth," he said. "*Girth*."

"What about it?" Jessica said, looking out the window with a dreary expression.

"Here, we'll stop here," he said.

"Dear," Jessica said, the first time that I had ever heard her refer to Dante in an endearing way in company, "we should continue travelling tonight. We might make the coast by morning. It'd be better for us to take the boat, get the wound looked at in Calais."

Dante shook his head and when he spoke again, he seemed to be twice as emboldened as before. "Here," he said. "I have friends in Girth."

Jessica sat on this for a while, obviously not yet wanting to feed this order onto Farol. I wondered if she was enjoying this little power trip, for once being the one to filter and sort the great Dante Gobornik's requests. Then, with the merest glance at me, she poked her head out of the carriage and passed the news onto Farol.

I overheard a shouted discussion between the two of them. It seemed that Farol was just as reluctant for us to stop in Girth, but, in the end, it was Dante who won out. And soon after we were climbing a steep slope, through a forested patch and making our way along cobbled streets, a rare flat patch of ground, to where the town of Girth awaited us.

The first thing that struck me about Girth was its peace and quiet. As I disembarked the carriage I felt at home, somehow, in this sleepy village. It seemed just the right tonic following our encounter with the Forsneers. This would be a place where we could recharge ourselves before heading off, onto the continent, in search of yet more adventure. Despite everything that had happened, I felt wildly positive.

While Jessica and Dante went searching for a surgeon friend of Dante's, and Farol saw to the horses, finding a local blacksmith to see to the horrific state of their hooves, I set off on my own exploration into the town.

The houses were squat constructions, most of them still with thatched roofs. The windows were webbed with lead and women bobbed in and out of front doors, baskets of washing in hand or to chase after their children, calling them in to bed. There was a chapel and a pub at the centre of the town, each of them looking in at the fine stone-carved fountain which sent up a fine spray, carried in loose waves on the breeze. I sat on the edge of the fountain, my feet resting on the cobbles before me, and I watched the world go by.

It was a fine summer's evening, just the trace of cloud on the horizon, in the direction from which we'd come. I wondered whether we'd narrowly escaped a storm. Might the party at the Forsneers have been a different affair if only it had rained? There wouldn't have been a garden party, but I wasn't so sure that would've stopped Gerald and his curious hands.

I sniffed at the air, savouring the apple blossom, the light smell of cow dung and the freshness—which I still couldn't get quite over—the straight, unpolluted air. It was quite easy to imagine that nothing at all had happened to us, and that we were, as we appeared, nothing more than weary travellers looking for a brief stop.

A large figure caught the corner of my eye, rushing toward me. I turned my head to look. Saw that it was Farol. But why was he running? To begin with I thought it was a joke, that he was showing off his light-hearted side once more—putting that brutality he had shown back on the Forsneers estate into shadow, into the past. And then I heard his voice, between his percussive breathing.

"Dante . . . he's . . . dying."

CHAPTER FOURTEEN

I LAUNCHED MYSELF off the rim of the fountain and felt the hard cobblestones beneath my feet. Together we bounded off across town. Several times I stopped to allow Farol to catch up. He mopped his brow as he went. He had peeled off his jacket but still wore his dress shirt, and I made out the dark sweet patches at his armpits, collecting at his chest. I remember giddily hoping that he might get his suit cleaned during our stay in Girth. That was probably the start of the psychosis setting in.

We reached the surgeon's office, a quiet townhouse, much like all the others around it, marked out only by its wooden sign with the gold lettering which read: *Trevor Finely Practitioner of Medicine*. I felt my stomach pushing against my skin, oozing its way about, and I realised I was truly frightened for Dante— that, perhaps, our acquaintance would end so soon after we had met. There were other worries there too. What would I do if he left us behind? I knew not to expect anything of Jessica and most likely of Farol. They would have enough trouble making their own ends meet without an adolescent girl to care for.

A kind lady, who I took to be Finely's wife, showed us to the sitting room and handed each myself and Farol a cup of steaming tea. From the looks of things it seemed that Finely practised medicine from his home. From some indistinct point in the house I could hear the *scrape* of metal on metal, and the occasional *moan*. I caught Farol's eye, sitting opposite me as he held the tea between his hands, staring down into the mulch.

"What," I started, "what have they told you?"

Farol paled a little at this question and took a long glug of his piping-hot tea before answering. "That he's lost a lot of blood. The surgeon, he got the bullet out, there were several fragments wedged in there, but . . . but, it seems that there was some complication, that he might've hit a vessel, an artery." He shook his head and then repeated, "He's lost a lot of blood."

We waited there, in silence, each of us with our cup of tea. Those sounds . . . those sounds, almost too faint to hear, but just loud enough so that they were there, in the room with us. Every second I was anticipating Jessica coming into the room, sobbing into a handkerchief to serve us with the grim news. But as time stretched onward she never appeared and my hope grew. Perhaps it wasn't as bad as previously thought.

Outside night set in and the glow of gas lamps shone in through the windows. Finely's wife appeared once more, smiling as she shut the curtains and took our cups of tea. Now, with the curtains closed, I felt like I was secreted in some unknown chamber of the world—kept apart from the rest of humanity, in some state of flux. I tried to catch Farol's eye, but he was now reclined in the chair, feet spread before him, mouth parted, eyes closed, lightly snoring. I guess that there was a limit to how much stress he could take in one day—or had it been a couple of days? As for me, there was something greater tying me to the outcome of Dante's operation. I feared that, if he did pass away, I would never know about this power which I appeared to share with him. And I could never know what it meant. I was sure that I could drag out what had happened back at the mansion from Jessica, once she had got over the worst of her grief. But my power, that was what really bothered me. I simply had to know.

A large clock in the hallway chimed midnight. I straightened up in my armchair. My back ached and my arms felt stiff, unwieldy. Farol slept on. I thought I could hear the light tread of footsteps approaching. Perhaps it would be Finely's wife, come to bring us a snack or, maybe, to turf us out of her house for the night. However, it wasn't her.

A well-built man with wide, proud shoulders appeared before us. He wore a white apron which had long been stained with Dante's blood. Although his hands were clean I could make out the patches further up his arms which still remained bloodied. He wore a pair of wiry spectacles which had the effect of making him seem older than he was—at least in his fifties, rather than the early forties I would have guessed him to be. This was Finely, the surgeon, I supposed.

Farol stirred from across me and gazed upward, expectantly, at the doctor.

Finely had a thick regional accent and spoke quickly, in a series of isolated statements rather than sentences so I had a little trouble deciphering his words. But I think that I got the general idea. "He's up there, resting up, a real mess, challenging procedure. Shouldn't be long now, before we know."

"Know what?" I said, more out of shock than lack of understanding.

He just peered at me and puffed out his lips. "I've known Dante a long while, a friend, a good old friend."

Seeing as Dante couldn't have been much older than in his late twenties, early thirties, I wondered exactly what constituted an 'old friend' around there. Still, I suppose that Dante would've been glad for anyone who might've been able to help him in such a perilous situation.

"Long time since he's come here, to visit us I mean, good to see him again, I just hope . . ."

And his words trailed off before us, his voice fraught with exhaustion.

I made out the wrinkles ingrained on his forehead and I wondered how many lives those represented—how many sleepless nights Finely had spent thinking of *what ifs* and *should haves*, lives that had slipped through his fingers. Would another line etch itself there should Dante pass on in the night?

I raised my voice. "Can we visit him?"

Finely seemed to consider this, then he looked across to Farol. "If you'd like."

I shot Farol a glance and he seemed to send a message to me through his eyes—that it would be better if we stayed where we were. I knew why, that he was worried of invoking Jessica's wrath. But who cared? He was *our* friend too, not just *her* lover.

I rose from my seat before Farol could say anything and looked to the doctor expectantly. In turn, he examined Farol, who finally gave in any resistance. And we were trudging through the house, to a back room, kept shut with a flimsy wooden door. Finely paused at the door, hand on the latch, thoughtful— perhaps wondering whether this was such a good idea after all. Then, having passed through this moment, he depressed the latch and allowed us inside.

Rubbing alcohol sizzled through the stale air, that stench I'd always associated with death—or those about to die, I'd witnessed people being trodden over by horse and carts in the streets of the capital, among other horrific scenes. In the bright light the all-white room seemed to become almost too much for my eyes to absorb—burning my retinas. Once I got over the initial uncomfortable sensation, I made out the pair of figures, first Jessica, propped up in a chair, Dante lying on a raised bed, head slumped over on a pillow, apparently sleeping.

Finely looked over me and Farol. "I've given him something for the pain, he'll be out for a while, he can't hear you for the moment."

I looked to Jessica, who stared at the both of us with a piercing, icy stare. My stomach knotted and I wondered whether I'd made a big mistake in coming to visit. We were stomping all over her territory, that was surely how she felt about the thing. Again, I reminded myself that Dante didn't *belong* to anyone. And in any case she seemed to be resorting to silent protest as her only means of resistance.

I trod up to Dante, reclining on that bed. I looked at his face —he was pale, his complexion almost blue. His cheeks seemed puffy and I wondered if it might be some side effect from the drugs the doctor had administered. I looked down his body, to the wound in his thigh. Finely had bandaged it up, the wound looked much healthier now, from my non-expert perspective, but I could see—by the way Finely lingered at my heels—that he was ready to step in at any urgent moment if he noticed any sign that Dante was in trouble. I glanced sideward to Farol, who fiddled with his hands, generally looking greatly uncomfortable at the whole situation, having to watch his boss in this state.

Jessica spoke, her voice nothing less than a *hiss*. "All this," she said, focussing on me, pointing at Dante's wound. "This is *your* fault."

I was so taken aback by this accusation that I could hardly get enough breath to reply. "I'm . . . I'm sorry?"

She continued, "If you'd told him that I'd gone—that I was back at the campsite, or better, that I'd run away, then he never would've done what he did."

Despite the wild accusations, which seemed to me nothing more than spiteful hitting out at the nearest target—somewhere for her to channel her anger at Dante's condition—I thought this a good opportunity to get more information on what *had* happened last night.

I curled back my lips, in imitation of a spiteful reply, wanting to egg her onto giving me a complete explanation. "And what did happen last night?"

She rolled her eyes, as if this were the most obvious thing in the world.

I felt one of Farol's chubby fingers on my forearm. I shrugged him away, staring Jessica down. "Enlighten me. I'm just a stupid child after all."

"He lost it," she said.

"Yes, I'd gathered that much, but why did the mansion end up burning to the ground?"

Jessica rose her eyebrows to indicate Finely, standing right at my side.

A welt formed in my throat. Oops.

Finely, however, busied himself with the details of his patient, inspecting his leg with a long, flat tool. He seemed to have overlooked that minor mention of mine. Perhaps I'd been wrong, that this wouldn't be the best time to fill in the gaps of exactly what happened. Maybe it was best just to leave Jessica to her spiteful mood and wait till she was ready to speak in a normal tone of voice, calmer. But if Dante were to pass away that night, I knew that I would never find out what had happened. I had no doubt that Jessica would excommunicate me. So now I thought this a good time to go.

I nodded to Farol, who looked relieved that I'd finally put us all out of this tense situation, and together we made for the door. I didn't have to look around to know that Jessica was burning holes in my back with her stare, and I got the feeling that our relationship—ever since I'd seen off our pursuers during our escape from the mansion—had altered inextricably. The reason was quite simple: Dante and I had a deep connection, shared a special power, that she simply could never have—and thus would never fully comprehend. And I have to admit that I felt more than a little smug at that realisation. Walking out of that room I felt like the bigger of the two of us.

Finely was kind enough to lead me and Farol to a pair a guest rooms, one each, for the duration of the night. He told us that he would inform us as soon as there was any change with Dante —if he woke up from his drug-induced sleep or if there were any further complications. For me, having my own room—for the first time in my life—was just magical. Never before had I ever imagined that I might have a *bed*, let alone a door to shut, and— never in my wildest dreams—a window looking down into a beautiful town at the crooked street which ran past the house. I could even make out the fountain from the view I had.

I tossed myself back onto the bed, which was almost too soft to believe—almost too soft to be comfortable—and then I allowed my head to fall onto the pillow. It was like resting my head against a great, big fit-to-burst raincloud. I felt like a princess.

There was a *knock* at the door and, without me saying a word, Finely's wife wandered into the bedroom. She carried a tray, which steamed away. On it I saw that it contained a fresh mug of tea, along with a plate replete with sliced ham and a parted bread roll. Not having eaten since the night before, it was like a feast to me. Finely's wife left me alone and I took full advantage to gorge myself. After I'd finished, not knowing what to do with the tray, I placed it on my bedside table and then lay back in bed, staring at the ceiling. Despite all my fatigue, my bones feeling weary and my muscles stretched beyond breaking point, I just couldn't sleep. My brain wouldn't switch off.

I listened to the gentle pad of footsteps coming along the landing, the gentle *knock* again at my door. Finely's wife appeared once more. I glanced at her feet—those slippers woven out of what-looked-like the finest wool. It was the type of wool I'd see in those fine shops, where all the servants for the rich types would go shopping, to knit their employers something special. She made to cross the room, for the tray, and then thought better of it, instead plumping herself down on the edge of my bed. "What's your name?" she said.

So, I told her. "Sara White."

She crossed her legs. "Well, Sara, and what do you happen to be doing with Dante Gobornik, conjurer extraordinaire?"

The way she spoke that word 'extraordinaire' had more than a touch of distain to it, as if she were implying he was some kind of a fakery, nothing more than the average cheap parlour trick-ster. If that was how she felt then I had no intention in changing her mind. If only she would come to a show—if Dante might put on a show when, *if*, he got better—then I was sure she would think differently.

I racked my brains, thinking of some explanation, and I decided on the truth. She may have talked in less than glowing tones about Dante, but she'd been good to me and Farol, treated us with great hospitality. I owed her the truth. "Well," I said, "I just saw an advertisement at the local pub, he was looking for an assistant—and I decided to go along and try out." I shrugged. "He seemed happy to take me on."

"And"—she paused briefly—"what does your family make of it?"

I felt a light pang in my breast. "Family? Oh . . . they're all dead."

"Dead?"

"That's right."

"How terrible."

I gave her a steely nod, trying not to show off any of the emotion surging through me, that overwhelming urge to cry. Sometimes it felt like I'd dealt with it, knowing that my family were gone, and then other times it just rushed back to me, like a frothing, out-of-control torrent. And then there was that whole issue of them cropping up in shadow form, as ghosts. So there was the question as to whether they were really gone at all. And if they hadn't really gone at all then what did I have to feel sad about?

"You're an orphan, then," she said, phrasing it as a statement rather than a question."

Again, I nodded.

"And don't you think that someone, a girl of your age, should be in school?"

I considered it and then said, "I don't know. Most of my

friends had left. I didn't like most of the kids that were left—almost all of them were boys."

"And . . . and did they pick on you, because of the colour of your skin?"

That question knocked me back, seemed to come out of nowhere. But still, I kept my emotions in check and answered it the most truthfully I could. "No, not really."

She folded her hands on her lap and squeezed a little closer to me. "But you *were* different, weren't you?"

"Yeah, I suppose."

She gave me a firm smile as if she were digging up some deeply inset psychological demons—as if she might trawl up some painful aspect of my past. Unlucky for her, but there really wasn't anything all that painful, discounting the deaths of my parents, of course. Until then I'd had a pretty much normal childhood. In fact I'd even stretch to say that I'd had a *happy* childhood.

I awaited her next question, and it wasn't long in coming.

"Don't you find it hard, travelling from place to place, you know, not having a home to go back to?"

"I don't really know, to tell the truth I haven't been part of Dante's group for all that long, so I'm not really sure whether or not I like it."

"What will you do if you decide you don't?"

I turned the question over and over, examining it from all angles. What *would* I do? I guess that the prospect just hadn't even occurred to me, not even in theory. There was simply so much that I didn't know, so much more left to be discovered that I'd had no reason to explore it. As I thought it over I wondered what this lady had at stake with all these questions.

Before I got to formulate my own reply to her previous question, she put that on the table.

"Sara, I'd like to ask you something—and I hope that you won't take it the wrong way, you can feel quite fine saying 'no' if you feel it to be impertinent or out of line."

"Okay," I said, growing nervous, as I always do when someone prefaces a question with a disclaimer.

"I'd like to know . . . I mean, I'd like to offer to . . . take you in with us."

I can honestly say that I wasn't expecting that. Not even a little. Hadn't even crossed my mind. I cast a glance around me, unsure how to respond, what sort of implications it might have for my near future. If Dante did die then what options would I really have? I came to a decision surprisingly quickly. "Can I think about it?" I said.

She nodded, a little glumly and rose up. She stepped over to my bedside table and picked up the tray. On her way to the door, she turned on her heel and looked me over a final time. "You will let us know what you decide, won't you?"

"Yes," I said, the word coming out all whiny.

She gave me a gentle smile and then disappeared out of the door.

I lay back in my bed, knowing that there was no way I would get any sleep that night. Not with all the gears turning in my mind. Not with Dante knocking on death's door.

I watched the dawn illuminate the fog which descended on the town, turning the streets into veiled crevices, making it seem like I was the last person on Earth. Although I felt an overpowering weariness tugging me downward, I just couldn't find the peace to drift away into sleep. Any sound in the house was like a pinch. Every *scuffle* I interpreted as shoes on carpet, every *creak* as a footstep—Finely, or his wife, coming to inform me that, unfortunately, Dante was gone. In the end, I decided to sit on the floor. The bed was so soft that it made my back ache, my neck stiff.

Slowly, the sun peeked up over the rooftops, melting the fog away, leaving the cobblestones glistening like blocks of ice. A few people ventured out from their homes—I noticed a group of miners, trudging their way, silently, pickaxes slung over their shoulders, iron helmets perched on their heads, through the village. Women too bobbed along the streets, making their way to the market, to get the freshest produce for their husbands' breakfasts. I watched as a man led dozens of donkeys right past our window, en route to some place or other. And then, downstairs, in the house, I heard those unmistakable noises of Finely's wife preparing breakfast: first the *shuffle* of slippered feet on carpet, then the *clanking* of pots and pans, and the piercing *whistle* of a kettle on a stove. I sat on the edge of my bed, staring at the door, waiting to be called. My stomach felt like water and I was hoping that a little food would ease its unpleasant groaning.

And then, through all that stillness, the nothingness spread throughout the house, I heard a loud and distinct, blood-curdling *scream*.

CHAPTER FIFTEEN

T HE SCREAM ripped through the walls of the house, sent my bones rattling. I stood, stumbling as I did so, stricken almost lame with dizziness. My brain tried to make sense of it, to work out what it might be. But there was only one situation, one person that it could be. It was Jessica who was screaming. And Dante was dead.

I flew out the door, bumping into Farol's flabby chest. Judging from his tired eyes, his unusually gaunt, joyless face, he hadn't slept either. Together, me first leading the way, we barrelled down the stairs, and through the house, almost knocking Finely's wife down as went. I glanced at her—aproned, wearing oven gloves, and a look of extreme concern spread across her cheeks—and couldn't find the words to excuse our panic. Surely she had heard the scream too, so no explanation was necessary.

I sprinted off, through the house, toward the doctor's

surgery. When I arrived there, to the wide open doorway, the first thing I noticed was Finely standing, back straight, pressed against the opposite wall to the patient's bed, white-faced and eyes wide with fear. Slowly, I turned my gaze onto Dante—or was it merely Dante's body?—lying prostrate on the bed, apparently lifeless. Seeing nothing out of the ordinary or, at least, nothing I hadn't grimly expected, I turned my attention to Jessica, who was similarly panicked, a mirror image of Finely, pushing her own body up against the wall, as if to attempt escape.

Farol arrived at my side, out of breath, face flushed. "What . . . what's happened here?"

Neither Jessica or Finely responded. Both still completely absorbed by shock.

"Is he . . ." Farol began, and then he simply took a step forward, over to Dante's bedside and touched his fingers to his wrists, taking his pulse. He flinched once, twice, and then gazed back at Finely and Jessica, then his gaze fell on me. "He's . . . *alive*," he said.

Finely seemed to get a bit of a grip on his fright. He muttered something under his breath and then said, a little louder—loud enough for us to hear in any case, "Impossible."

"What's impossible?" Farol said, leaning back, his eyes darting between us all. "What're you talking about?"

"He . . . I . . ." Finely's eyes fell to Dante once more, as if he were reluctant to look back at his patient. "We left him, fell asleep, for a while. Both of us. I . . . we, just woke up, now. He . . . well, he was *dead*."

"Are you sure?" Farol said. "Maybe you just couldn't find his pulse."

Finely shook his head. "No, no, you don't understand. He was"—his voice cracked—"*stiff*. Stiff as a board."

My mind swam and I stared at Dante, trying to comprehend exactly what Finely was saying. Only later would I clarify what happened to people when they died, that they went all stiff, that was the moment when they definitely couldn't be saved. For someone to come back from a condition like that it was . . . well, unheard of—akin to raising the dead.

It was Finely's wife who broke the silence crushing the room. When she spoke it was clear that she was just as steeped in shock as the rest of us, unable to believe what her husband had just recounted. "I made breakfast."

It was decided that we should all clear out of the surgery so that Finely could see to his patient, run some tests on him to check all that had appeared to happen had actually occurred. As I crunched my way through rashers of bacon and consumed piece after piece of toast, I kept an ear out to the rest of the house, hoping to hear another of those cries, this time one declaring that Dante had got up from the bed—that he was all better now.

During breakfast, I attempted to make eye contact with Jessica, who Finely's wife had somehow managed to extricate from Dante's bedside. But, of course, she remained ostensibly focussed on her own eating, with no intention at having any sort of contact with me. And I guessed that to be a watershed moment in our relationship, the time when our communication truly broke down—when it appeared that under no circumstance, no imaginable scenario, could we be cajoled to act in a civil manner with one another.

As it turned out, Dante didn't get up from bed. And as our second day's stay in Girth drew to a close it seemed highly unlikely that we would be within 'a few days' of setting off, continuing our journey, crossing the Channel into France. I started to worry about it, to think that we would surely get caught. It wouldn't be long before the locals began to talk among themselves, of the news spreading about the magician—the *wizard*—who had somehow burnt down the mansion of a respected, if not respectable, nobleman.

I was sitting up in my room, staring out the window and thinking, when Farol knocked on my door and asked for my help. I followed him through the house and then out into the street. He led me to the carriage which awaited a few doors down in an empty lot, overgrown with grass and sprinkled with various pieces of rubbish: cut-off leather, discarded metal and broken wooden chairs and tables—stuff for the rag and bone man when he came around. Old Billy and Silver grazed away, contentedly enough, in the lot, taking care not to munch on any of the rubbish among the miniature glade.

Farol bridled both horses and then led them over to the carriage, which he harnessed them to. Then, without uttering a word to me, he hauled himself up onto the driver's seat. Not wanting to be alone inside that still-blood-stained carriage, counting the bullet holes in the outer design, watching the road pass through them, I climbed up onto the seat beside Farol. Although he shot me a sidelong glance, as if I had somehow invaded his territory, made him a little uncomfortable, he said nothing as he brought the reins down on the horses' backs and the sound of *clopping* hooves danced through the air, echoing back at us as we went on our way, heading out of the village, away from Girth.

We rode on for five or ten minutes, before Farol slowed the horses and had them turn into a large, seemingly unremarkable field. The path through the field was nothing more than a muddy path, half-rutted by wheels. We continued on our way. I clung to the driver's seat, afraid that I might be hurled off at any given moment. I wondered how Farol had got the knack of staying perched on top the driver's seat, hours on end, without ever toppling off. I guessed that his weight helped him some, in the same way that it's difficult to toss a boulder off a cliff top.

I guessed that we passed about half an hour on that path, heading away, deeper into the countryside. I wanted to ask Farol where we were going, what we were doing, but the air was so pregnant between us, so filled with mystery and apprehension—both our lives would change forever depending on the outcome of Dante's health, and we were just *doing* until that time came, filling up the hours. Or, at least I thought that was the function of the ride.

A hillside loomed before us, almost invisible in the mounting darkness. The path grew yet more rugged. It dipped down low and rose steep, both the horses hissing breaths through their grinding teeth. We drew up to the hillside, apparently having reached the end of the path. Again, without a word to me, Farol clambered down the side of the carriage, leaving me up in the driver's seat—where I supposed I was meant to remain.

Only then, after Farol had taken several steps into the night, did I notice that cabin—a tiny, one-roomed, haphazard structure. I noted the light smell of smoke on the wind and realised that it had a chimney, a wood burning stove inside its shabby frame. Farol waited outside until the door creaked open and light spilled out from within. A figure darkened the doorway and, for one horrible second, I was sure that it was another of those shadows—that Farol knew more about them than he was letting on, that he had brought me here to meet with one of them. But that horrible, tension-fraught moment passed and the man returned inside, into his shack, only to come back out with a heavy coat draped around his shoulders, prowling his way forward, apparently showing Farol the way to some unknown location.

Both of the men disappeared, leaving me sitting there, up on the driver's seat. I shuddered to myself thinking that I only had the horses for company. It wasn't only the supernatural which sent twinges up my spine but the natural predators. What if something came out of the bushes and spooked the horses? I had no idea how to steer the damn carriage after all, so I wouldn't be much good at getting the situation back under control.

As it turned out, Farol and the man returned a little later. Farol leapt back up to the driver's seat and took the reins once again. The man waddled before us, hands stuffed into his coat pockets. He led us right up to the hillside and, just when I thought it was a dead end, I noticed the lantern the man had placed inside. It was a cave, half-hidden by a grass tuft dangling down over the opening. Farol took the carriage inside and stepped off, landing with a *thump* on the other side. I mimicked him, still unsure exactly what it was that we were doing. Farol strode up to the two horses and detached them from the carriage. He attached a lead rope to each of them and, standing in between the two horses, led them back out of the cave, past the man lingering at the entrance, and back out into the night.

I glanced back at the carriage, realising that the top rack—where we'd stowed the trunks—had been emptied already. I supposed that during the day Farol had lugged them into Finely's house all by himself, not that me or Jessica would've been much use in helping out anyway. Still dumbstruck, I stepped out of the cave and went after Farol.

The man trailed at our heels, his lantern providing a modicum of light, just enough so that I wouldn't trip over the larger rocks in our path. Farol reached a wooden gate, the entrance to a field surrounded by a fence. He unlatched and let the horses inside, keeping them alongside himself. And then, giving each a tender stroke of the nose, he undid their bridles, gave them a *slap* on the flank, and they cantered off into the field, clearly delighted to have been given this much free rein after having had to make do with the dishevelled old lot back in Girth. Now, suddenly, it all made sense. Since it seemed that we weren't going to be leaving Girth anytime soon, that Dante wasn't going to be up and about for a long time, this was the best course of action to take with the horses—put them out to pasture. But that begged the question: Why had he brought me along?

At first I put it out of my mind, dismissing it easily by telling myself that Farol had probably assumed I was bored, that I'd benefit from getting out of the house for a little while, take a little of the open country air. But, after Farol bid the man good-bye, handing him the bridles and lead ropes, I began to doubt that interpretation. My mind shot back to that moment when he'd stroked their noses, his fingers lingering at their flaring nostrils, the light *sniff* Farol himself had made. The more I thought about it, the more I was convinced that it was a goodbye.

We trooped on through the darkness, the steady glow from the carriage lantern, clasped in Farol's fist, guiding our way along the rough pathway. I listened to the faint *squeak* of bats, the *flutter* of their wings, and then, below our feet, the more familiar *scuttle* of mice through the hedgerows. About what I estimated to be halfway back to Girth, I spotted a solid form before us, right on the brink of the lantern's glow. At first I was sure it was a rock, but then, as I took a step closer, I wasn't so sure. It was furry and brown. It had a long, wet snout and beady black eyes that reminded me of Dante's. Before I had the chance to speak, to ask what it was, Farol snorted and said, "Hedgehog."

We halted there and watched it in the light coming off the lantern. It wiggled from side to side as it walked, gradually making its way into the fallow field beside us, its snout pressed to the ground sniffing out grubs. It appeared completely oblivious to us. As I watched it slip from sight, I decided that now was the time to get an explanation from Farol. I craned my neck back to look at him and said, "We *are* going to move on from here, aren't we? You didn't, I don't know, sell the horses, the carriage, to that man, did you?"

I was glad when Farol cracked a smile as he straightened back up. "No," he said, "I didn't sell them. He's just going to look after them for us. That's all."

I allowed the tension to seep from my muscles, allowed myself to draw a few easy breaths and we wandered onward, my mind still flurrying, wanting to know *why* exactly we'd come out here to leave the horses.

"It's for safety purposes," Farol continued. "People'll talk. Someone will recognise the carriage. It's better for it to be out here, where it's hidden for the time being."

"How long do you think it'll be before we can move on, before Dante's well enough for us to move on?"

He shrugged. "Who knows? When we get to talking of Dante I wouldn't be surprised if he just leapt up tomorrow morning, spritely as ever, and was ready to move on." He lowered his tone. "But it's better to be safe than sorry, as my ma used to say."

As we headed back toward the main road, the gas lanterns of Girth now sliding into view, coming brighter with each step forward, I had the urge to tell him about that man I'd seen him strike, the guard stopping us leaving the Forsneers' land. But my nerve faltered. Fear won out.

I listened to the minor *grunts* Farol gave as he plodded up the pathway, like this walk was some great effort for him. I tried to put them out of mind as I placed one foot in front of the other, pressing myself forward, telling myself that tonight I would have a good sleep, that I would replenish my energies.

We arrived at the gate onto the main road. Farol stopped. I stopped beside him. He looked up the road, and then back toward the town of Girth. He scratched the back of his neck with those battered fingernails, and then he turned to look at me.

I felt something hot frazzle through me. I stood where I was, looking up at him, unsure what was going on—and feeling a little strange, that episode with the man guarding the road coming back to me. Might he be capable of striking me too, a child?

"I've decided to go away," he said.

The breath just about stripped my lungs on its way out. "*What?*"

He just nodded glumly.

"But, why? I don't understand. We have to wait for Dante, see if he's going to get better, then we can go on just like always."

This time he shook his head. "Not with me, no. It's just not going to work. We need more time."

"What do you mean?"

"Dante needs time." He surveyed Girth in the middle

distance, its gas lanterns shedding its glow all around, colouring the night sky. "And I can give it to him."

"By going away? I don't understand."

He sighed, his whole bulk rising and falling with the effort of his respiration. "There'll be people coming here soon, people who the Forsneers have sent. You don't really believe they'll let us go after Dante destroyed their home, do you? *Someone* here will read about it in a newspaper, the accusations surrounding Dante, and it won't be long before someone comes to the house, sniffing around, asking questions—"

"But, you put the carriage out of sight—the horses. I'm sure that Finely and his wife will be happy to hide Dante while he recovers. Do you think they'd betray us?"

"I wouldn't want to test their resolve," he said, somewhat enigmatically.

"You think they would?"

"I think it'd be better for everyone if the Forsneers' people, the ones after him, thought that he was somewhere else. A different part of the country."

And then it clicked into place for me. Farol intended to travel somewhere else, another part of England and hand himself in. "But," I said, "what would you do, when they get hold of you?"

"Oh, I don't know," he said, looking down at his shoes. "I'd tell them something—make up some story." He met my eye. "I'd make it convincing, I promise you that."

I thought now of that scene I'd witnessed, and knew that I had to bring it up. It was too big a thing to keep a secret and maybe I thought that it could change whether or not Farol decided to leave. I felt my neck muscles contract as I swallowed, then I said, "That man, you know, the one guarding the

Forsneers' estate . . . I saw you hit him, saw him hit the ground."

Farol's eyes widened in the darkness and I felt the full-force of his stare upon me. "Why didn't you tell me before?"

"I . . . I don't know."

He opened his mouth to speak again and then thought better of it, instead turning introspective, considering his next move. Finally, when he did speak, his voice was grainy, insecure, a little broken, and I knew that he was suffering. A quiet sob entered his voice. "Listen to me, yeah? I've done a lot of bad things in my life, but I never killed a man before, and . . . and, I swear to God, if I that's what happened, if I *killed* that man, then I deserve everything coming to me. I . . ." But the rest of his words were lost to uncontrollable sobs.

My blood froze. I had no idea what to do, how to comfort him. Here he was, a man in his mid-sixties, and he had completely lost it. What was *I*, a fourteen-year-old girl, supposed to do about it?

I didn't dare touch him and I guess that I was so beleaguered by the whole experience that I just kept talking—asking questions. "But surely, you can't change that now. What good would it do for you to turn yourself in?"

He stared at me with tears rolling down his cheeks. "It's the only way, I'm sorry." He glanced back over his shoulder, down the path, back to where we'd left the horses and carriage. "I brought you here—with me—so that you'd see where I'd hidden the horses, and the carriage. Once it's safe to move on, when Dante recovers, I want you to bring them here, and you can go on as it was—escape, find another place." And then he handed me the lantern, began to move forward, to head along the road, in the opposite direction to Girth. "Goodbye, Sara. Take care, won't you? Maybe some day we'll meet again."

I stood there, rooted to the spot, watching him go away into the gloom. Looking back on it that night I wondered whether I should've said something—if there was something I could've said to call him back. But there was nothing at all I thought of in the moment. And before I could tune my logical mind back in he was gone—lost to the night.

CHAPTER SIXTEEN

I JUST KEPT TO MYSELF over the next few days, tried to stay out of Jessica's way as she trotted through the house, bringing things to the recovering Dante. I fobbed them all off with a place-holding excuse about Farol, uttering something vague to our hosts about how he'd gone ahead to negotiate with theatres for Dante's missed dates. They seemed to accept it pretty readily.

Most of the time I spent up in my room. Finely's wife, who asked me to call her Helen, her first name, brought me lots of fat books—apparently worried about my education. I had a flip through some of them but most were so dry, so serious, lacking in colour, that I felt my eyelids drooping as I scanned the words. After a good amount of time skulking away in a corner of the house, I decided that my time might be more politely spent helping *Helen* out with some of the domestic chores. And it was while I was helping her wash the dishes, me drying them up, when the first real crisis occurred.

I listened to the footsteps leading up to the street and then the cry of "Paper! Paper! Get your paper!"

And, before I knew it, Helen wiped her hands on the side of her apron, shot me a smile, saying, "Haven't picked up a paper for days, what with all that's been going on," and shuffled out into the hall.

I had no chance to think up some reason, a distraction, before I heard the door groaning open, and Helen conversing with the boy, handing him over a few pieces of change. I recall that sound, the *rustle* of the newspaper clenched in her hand as she brought it back into the kitchen and then, as if to torment me, set it down on the side.

I stared at it there, that black and white print, rolled up with a piece of twine. I could only read a few letters of the headline, not enough to know whether or not there was anything that could harm us—that might expose everything, have the Finely's turn us over to the police. And in the blaze of my plotting, wanting desperately to get rid of the paper, I thought about how I might feel putting up a group of people responsible for burning someone's house down. Wasn't it just like Farol had declared for himself? Wouldn't we deserve everything we got? I thought about my involvement. Okay, so I hadn't burnt down the house myself, but I *had*, through some means I hardly understood, put paid to our pursuers. My breath chilled in my throat. Perhaps *I* had killed someone. And then my opportunity came. My opportunity to save Dante, Jessica and myself.

Helen strutted over to the stove and whisked off the whistling kettle. She poured out a cup of tea and removed some crumpets from where they were being warmed within the oven. She lifted the newspaper and, along with the tea and crumpets, placed it on a wicker-woven tray. She shot me a smile. "Would you be a dear and take these through to Trevor? I'm sure he's half-starved, hasn't left that room of his all day."

I focussed in on the newspaper, finished drying the plate in my hands and set it into the cabinet with a porcelain *thunk*. I held out my hands and took the tray from her, hardly able to believe my luck.

I walked through the house, headed for Finely's surgery. I stared at that newspaper and thought about what I was going to do. I wondered whether I could risk simply chucking it somewhere and hoping that it wouldn't be found. But what if Helen brought up the matter of the newspaper later on with her husband, made some frivolous comment about it and there was confusion? It would all come down to me and it would draw their attention, do exactly the opposite of what I was hoping to achieve, which was for us to keep a low profile.

And then it struck me, the perfect thing to do. Why didn't I just open up the newspaper and have a look? If I didn't find anything that might put us in danger then it would be okay to take it through to Finely, and if there *was* something to put us in danger I would think of what to do.

I glanced up and down. No one was coming. I set the tray down at my feet, then plucked the newspaper off the top. I untied the string and unfurled it before me. The front page stared back at me. So far so good. No mention of Dante, or the mansion that had burnt down. I kept on flipping through the pages. A lot of it was lost on me, all that talk about economics, politics and crisis—probably much the same today, though, thinking about it, I never can be bothered with all of that stuff. When I reached Page Five, I stopped dead and stared at the paper, not quite able to believe what I was reading:

Farol H Henderson was last night apprehended in the small town of Vickerborough, North Heathwine. He is being held as a known collaborator of magician of nationwide renown, Dante Gobornik, who has been on the run since performing a private function on the Forsneer estate, after being considered the lead suspect in the burning down of the hosts' mansion.

Henderson was apprehended at around six o'clock in the evening by a local police constable, where he reportedly gave himself up. It is understood that the police are following inquiries in the local area, believing Gobornik to be located nearby. They hope that Henderson will assist their inquiries. Police reiterate their request for cooperation from the public in this matter, as they wish to call Gobornik for interview with reference to the incident at the Forsneer estate.

Following the conclusion of the local police's interviewing of Mr Henderson, he shall be transported back to the Forsneer estate and held in the local station there, under the jurisdiction of the region in which the crime was committed, where he shall await trial for his part in the burning of the Forsneers' mansion.

I came up for air and then returned to scan the article again. Short, nothing more than a minor mention. There were a pair of photographs at the head of the article, one of Dante and another of Farol, which had obviously been taken upon his capture. His face looked weather-beaten, skinny compared to how I remembered him.

There was no mention of his being held for murder in the article. Perhaps they were hoping to strike a deal with him, get him to aid them in their search for Dante before pressing charges. Or maybe Farol hadn't killed him at all.

I took in a deep breath and thought about what I was going to do. At least it was a load off my mind that Farol's plan had worked to an extent, that he had apparently succeeded in leading the police astray, managing to get them looking off in—I read again—Vickerborough, North Heathwine. Where was that? It sounded remote at least. I allowed the newspaper to fall in my hands and let out a huge exhale.

"So that's where my paper's got to."

My whole body went stiff. In my panic the newspaper slipped from between my fingers. The sheets caught in the draught on their way down to the floor and the separate pieces all drifted about, scattering.

Finely chuckled and stooped down to help me put the paper back together again. "Never mind," he said.

I forced a smile as I accompanied him, trying to find that page I'd been reading, that article which would bring the reason why we were on the run to the Finelys' attention. I scrabbled through several pages—several tables with figures, percentages, but I just couldn't locate the page with the *damn* article. And then, with a new fear in my heart, I watched Finely straighten up, papers bundled into his arms, the article on Farol's arrest staring right back at me.

"Are you quite all right?" he said.

With deep reluctance, I broke my locked look at the article and met his eye. Still, that article, easily viewable if Finely would only look down, scan the page for some curiosity, remained on my mind. It was torture not being able to look at it—to consider whether or not it really was that bad.

Finely shuffled the pages back into some kind of order, long having lost their numerical sequence. He patted the edges so that they returned to flush and glanced at the portion of his paper that I held in my arms. He reached out. "If you don't mind."

Numb, I handed over my pages. The article was lost now, within that paper, in Finely's hands.

The corners of his mouth tweaked back and he nodded to the tray on the floor. "I have to say that that all looks most appetising but I do wonder whether it might've been a bit tastier warm."

Cheeks flushing, I crouched down and retrieved the tray. "Sorry," I said, in a low voice, that article refusing to leave my conscious thoughts.

He broke into an easier smile, obviously not cross at all with me. "Come on, then, I've got a surprise for you."

"What?" I said, wary that a new threat might be made to our cover.

"Dante. He's woken up."

That mixture of exasperation and delight is difficult to explain. I just recall waddling behind Finely, trying to get another look at the crunched up newspaper in his arms, and, at the same time, anxious to see Dante—to see if he was going to be all right after all. He would have to hear about Farol, among other things.

I picked my way along, following in Finely's footsteps. That familiar metallic stench of rubbing alcohol and bandages hung in the air. I eyed Jessica, standing at the side of the bed, but, as had been the case for a long time now, she didn't so much as sniff in my direction. Then my gaze fell on the bed and, indeed, there was Dante, propped up with a bunch of pillows, looking a touch pale, but without a doubt *awake*.

Forgetting Jessica's cutting stare completely, I burst forward and rushed to him. I threw my arms around his neck, not giving any notice to Finely's warnings, that I had to treat him with care, that he was still recovering. Once I'd got over the initial outpouring of emotion, I felt a touch silly, like I'd made a fool of myself. And then I realised that, really, there was no one to make a fool of myself in front of.

I took up a seat in the hard-backed wooden chair—so different from the cushy armchair in which Jessica had taken up residence—and watched him, feeling my eyeballs twitch about in their sockets, as if he might just fade away if my interest level drooped for even a moment.

When Dante spoke, with the glimmer of a smile, it was with a harsh voice. I could sense the fatigue consuming him, dragging him down, and only then did I realise how badly he was feeling —actually understood Finely's statement that he had been close to death. His voice was, well . . . deathly.

"Where . . . where is Farol?"

Unintentionally, my first reaction was to glance back, at Finely, and the newspaper he held in his hands. I tore myself away, chiding myself for having been so obvious. This had to come out natural, not until we had total privacy could I inform Dante what had really happened. "He went away," I said.

Dante squinted up at me, as if he was having trouble bringing my face into focus. "Went away?"

"Yes."

"Where?"

Again, I found myself faltering for a second, mentally scanning my lie once again, making sure that I got the story straight

—that I wouldn't trip myself up by not staying consistent to what I'd already told the Finelys, and Jessica. "To see to the shows, you know, the ones that you're going to miss."

Dante flexed the fingers of his right hand, slowly forming a fist. He stared at his fingers as if he was stunned as to his own weakness. He turned his attention back to me, a few worry lines forming on his forehead. "I'm going to miss shows?"

I felt Finely's warm breath on the back of my neck, scented a little with the sip of tea he had just taken. He dropped his voice to a whisper. "He's a little mixed up at the moment. His thoughts are all over the place. He's been through quite an ordeal."

Finely had quite a calm capacity for euphemism.

Jessica leant forward over him, smoothing the wrinkles from the covers which were drawn up to his chest. She stroked his cheek and said, "You've just got to concentrate on getting better, okay? Then we'll think about what we're going to do." On her way back down into her chair she shot me a scowl.

Finely looked about our faces, squeezed his lips together and smiled vaguely. "I'll leave you all alone for a while, shall I?"

Although none of us responded, I could feel the silent pleading for him to do just that. We had to speak frankly.

Without another word, and taking that *damn* newspaper with him, he shuttled out of the room.

I felt the wooden ribs of the chair digging into my back and I looked over Dante once again, listening to Finely's retreating footsteps, and then the muffled conversation he was having with his wife in the kitchen. I snapped to attention, knowing that now was my opportunity. Seeing that Dante was in no condition to absorb the gravity of what I had to say I, reluctantly, turned my attention to Jessica. "Listen," I said, "Farol's sacrificed himself—he's gone off to some godforsaken part of the country and handed himself into the authorities. He thinks that he's helping us by misleading the police, informing them that Dante's up there—near where he's handed himself in, and—"

"Where exactly?" Jessica said, announcing the syllables in a cool and sharp manner.

I recalled the newspaper article. "Vickerborough . . . North Heathwine."

She nodded to herself, apparently knowing of this place.

My curiosity got the better of me. "Do you know where that is?"

She curled back her lips in a smug smile. "That's where Dante performed his first show."

"Oh."

Jessica returned to her fawning over Dante, her light fingers lightly stroking his dark hair, winding in the downy fluff of his days-old stubble.

I decided that I should get everything out at once. "The carriage," I said, "Farol took me out in it, to the fringes of town, and we went through a field, then saw a man. He left the carriage there, the horses too, so that they'd be hidden. I . . ." I fumbled over the words, and then, finally they came to me. "The newspaper. The *Finelys*," I said it in a hushed tone. "They took a newspaper today and there's an article inside about Farol's capture."

At this, Jessica arched an eyebrow.

"What should we do?"

She resumed her fondling of Dante, then said, with no emotion, "I'll take care of it. Don't you worry."

I supposed she was enjoying this, what with being the *de facto* leader of our group while Dante was incapacitated. I hoped, for my sanity, that Dante would get better soon and things would go on being as they had been before. My mind stumbled back again, and I knew that I had to keep speaking, even if Jessica just wanted me to button my lip. "I'm worried about him."

"Who?"

"Farol. I mean, what's going to happen to him?"

She shrugged. "Oh they'll keep him in custody for just being associated with Dante, but there's nothing they can charge him with."

I thought of that man, the man that Farol himself was sure that he had killed. And I knew, full well, that the police might very soon have a good reason to keep him. But I decided to keep the information to myself, for the time being. Despite everything, I felt a little outraged that this man—the closest thing to a *family* member of both Dante and Jessica—who had cooked for them, driven the carriage unknown thousands of miles, and now he was just to be cast aside as useless. No, that wasn't the right thing to do, and I was determined to make my voice heard, even if it served to rile Jessica.

"Aren't we going to go after him?" I said.

A dour expression descended over Jessica's face. "Look," she said, "what he's done for us—this giving himself up for us—whatever the ins and outs of it may be, whether or not it was a reckless thing to do, or not, it's simply the way things are. We're on the run, Sara—Dante's on the run. We're all implicated"—she paused a moment—"you and Dante more than most, but they'll take me too, just for being associated with you. And if that's not enough I'm sure that Gerald and his friends would be all too pleased to speak out against me in court, to expose me as the thief I truly am." When she looked at me I saw that there was a nascent tear in her eye, and I knew that I had underestimated her in thinking that she was heartless—that Farol was just a convenient imbecile. "We have to run, Sara, can't you see that? If we go looking for him they'll take us too."

I did understand it, everything she said. Despite the subject of the conversation, the depressing tone it had taken on, I was glad that the air had thawed somewhat between myself and Jessica. The way she'd spoken to me, the tears in her eyes, showed me that there was more to her, more below the surface. And I wondered whether her frostiness toward me, especially in the wake of our escape from the Forsneers, was just a natural defence mechanism, something she'd developed to keep what she loved most safe. To see off any threat she saw to Dante.

From the bed, Dante stirred, tilting his head upward, as if he had caught a scent. "What's that about Farol? He's a good man, Farol. Trusted. A loyal sidekick."

I caught Jessica's eye and found myself with a light smile coming across my lips, and then I knocked my head back against the rigid chair and stared up at the eggshell-white ceiling.

CHAPTER SEVENTEEN

A S THE DAYS passed by I read through more and more of Helen's books, with nothing else to do. I kept half an ear out for any more newspaper boys in the street, but it appeared that they only turned up in Girth once in a while—certainly no more than once a week. Jessica informed me, the same day I'd taken the tray through to Finely, that she'd managed to get hold of the newspaper and dispose of the offending page appropriately. And so that put my mind at rest for the time being.

Among all those black letters, those white spaces, I turned my mind to the Forsneers' investigation, and whereabouts they were up to with it. Had they worked out that Farol's admission had merely been a diversion? Maybe they'd given up on their search of North Heathwine. There was no way of knowing so it was better to just lose myself in the books—in those stately gentlemen's words, attempting to work out what made them so widely respected, their opinions so widely sought. After hour upon hour I was still at a loss. The only power they held over me was their ability to send me off to sleep.

There was the *shuffle* of footsteps outside the door and I anticipated a visit from Helen. I worked out that this might well be her next attempt at having me live on with them. I estimated that she'd left enough time between the last time she'd offered and this. She'd be entitled to ask me whether I'd thought the matter over at least. When she did come I knew exactly what my answer would be.

A stiff *knock*, and I asked her in. Only it wasn't Helen at all. To my utmost surprise it was Dante. He appeared a little confused still, his wits still not quite about him, and he walked with a limp as he rounded the door into my room. I noticed him drag a cane after him, black with a silver handle in the shape of an snarling cat's head. He closed the door behind me and looked me up and down. "Are you ready?" he said.

"Ready for what?"

"Your lesson."

In a way I liked that he was still a bit dopey from the episode he'd had, in that there was no attempt on his part to cover up his natural accented English. I knew that it was the real him—not some sort of imitation. Still unsure what it was Dante was doing in my room, let alone with all this talk about a 'lesson,' I gave him a blank look.

"Surely you've wondered about the souls I stir up."

A twinge ran through me. "You're . . . you're finally going to tell me what's going on?"

He gave me a sure smile, more the Dante that I knew. "I think I owe it to you. You must have a lot of questions."

Again, it was like he'd read my mind—even if it had taken him a while. He had a good excuse, I suppose, but still . . .

He rested his cane up against the wall and then sank to the floor, crossing his legs as he did so, and looking at me through narrowed eyes.

Feeling a tremor of apprehension pass through me, I said, "Does Doctor Finely know you're up and out of bed, Jessica . . ." But my words just disintegrated in the air, with that look in his eye, that pure darkness, stirred pools of oil, both his irises.

He held his palms flat, indicating the space on the carpet, suggesting that I sit opposite him. So I did. We sank into silence for a long while, each of us lost to our own thoughts, and then, out of nowhere, Dante tilted his chin up and looked at me, as if some desperately important item had just struck him. "What have the others said about me?"

"What others?" I said.

"Jessica, Farol."

I hunched my shoulders and crossed my arms over my chest, feeling that familiar biting chill—afraid of it, that at any moment those shadows would be back, that I might see my mother again. "They said that a 'darkness' surrounds you, that you can't escape."

He gave me a firm nod, lips pressed tightly together.

I waited and waited, hoping that he might fill in this titbit, give me some sort of meaning to all these muttered words, the conjecture that seemed to hover all around Dante Gobornik.

"So now you know why I cannot stay in one place for too long."

"No," I said. "Not really."

He rubbed his thumb against the side of his index finger, thoughtful. I wondered if he was disappointed that I hadn't grasped what was going on already. Disappointed he might've been, but there was little I could do aside from be honest with him.

"My life," he began, not meeting my eye, "is quite similar to your own. In fact, although I hesitate to say it in such concrete terms, it appears that we are linked—that we share . . . whatever it is that follows me. My parents died mysteriously, when I was a little younger than you are now. I had to take to the streets—beg. I made ends meet for a year, maybe a little more. It seemed that someone, or something, was looking out for me. For some reason I never felt alone. As fate would have it, I had the good fortune of being taken in by a gentleman—an English gentleman —who happened to be passing through my town and saw me in the street one day, begging for bread at a baker's window."

"Where . . . where are you from?"

Dante shook his head. "I do not remember the name, unfortunately." He snorted. "Not even the country of my birth." He glanced up at me. "Can you believe that? If anyone asks me where I am from originally I cannot truthfully answer. The best I can say is that I am from *Europe*, that seems to satisfy most, confirm to them that I am a foreigner. After that the questions normally stop."

I thought about where I'd come from myself—where my family had originally come from. No one really knew for sure. I mean, I had ideas, but they were little more than that. I supposed I was lucky to be able to call England my home, I *was* English after all.

"This *gentleman*," he said, flexing his tongue as he uttered the word, "I could hardly believe my fortune in his taking me into his care. I soon learnt why he was so eager to take me on, why he wanted so badly to *adopt* a child—a son. I recall one night, while I was down in the pantry, of the house the gentleman kept in the countryside far away, the butler, the man he had brought with him from England—his most trusted employee—informed me that the gentleman's wife and son had passed away the previous summer." His cheeks drew taut, his Adam's apple bobbed in his throat. "That he did not intend to remarry, but he wanted an heir, someone to take on his mantle, someone . . . no, that's not the word at all . . . what he wanted was a *replica* of himself. And so he would give me books, he had the butler tutor me in etiquette, he worked on my accent, my *Eng-lish* accent," he said it with near perfect delivery, just the merest lingering suggestion that English was not really his native tongue, but so subtle as to be almost disregarded.

He screwed his mouth into a scowl. "And it took me so long to notice, to realise exactly what it was that he was doing. I cursed myself for being so stupid, so blind. Believing that this man merely wanted to feed and clothe me, that it was out of the goodness of his heart that he wanted to see to my needs."

"When did you find out that he intended to turn you into a replica of himself?"

"The day that a strange man came to the house—a foreigner, although I have the impression that he had a French accent from my grasp of English at the time." He waved his hand above his head. "But that's no more than speculation, and it is unimportant where he came from. He was nothing less than a, uh, magician."

"A magician?" I said. "Like you?"

"Yes, like me, except while I am what some might deem to be a master at what they choose to call 'conjurings,' this man, this *magician*, was what you might name a master of mind tricks, those feats of mentalism that I try so hard to work into my own acts, which I mimic in my own particular way."

"But you use a stooge, you use Jessica in your acts."

"That's correct," he said, with a sigh. "And it is because I've never understood, let alone been able to master, those feats. Those little sideshows, that beginning and end to the act, they serve as a reminder, if nothing else, of this magician, this man who came to the house."

"And what did he come to the house to do?"

"To wipe my mind."

My heart skipped a beat and I glared out into the air before me. "Is that even possible?"

Dante allowed an easy smile to form on his lips. "Oh yes, to a skilled practitioner it is quite a powerful ability too—much in demand also."

I wrinkled my forehead. "But why would he want to wipe your mind?" And then it struck me, and I admonished myself for my thick thinking—for not thinking before speaking. All the pieces of the puzzle were there and I'd been too dense to fit them together and form the bigger picture. "Because the gentleman wanted to make you *just* like him?"

Dante inclined his head in a slight nod. "But the gentleman, he had bargained on my passivity, my *innocence*, up until that point. Even then, when he sat me down in that room, with the blazing fire, had the butler bring me a blanket to keep myself warm, and left that magician with me, I have to admit that I had no idea that anything might be the matter. I remember his voice, deep and smooth, like treacle, and twice as sticky. I felt my head nod forward onto my chest, like his," he said, demonstrating. "It's hard to describe but, ah, it was like my whole mind was a spinning mass of curds, and this man, this *magician*, was forming it into a cheese of his choosing. And I felt myself losing my mind, my identity. And then, something inside of me . . . no, it was something *outside* of me—I remember—this something woke me, and I recall looking up, my mind feeling like mulch and seeing an outline, nothing more than a shadow in the corner of the room, watching over me. And . . . and I was certain, completely certain, that it had the face of my father."

My heart tingled and I yearned to add my own tale to his, so that I might feel better—cleansed in company—but I knew that I had to wait my turn, because Dante hadn't yet finished.

"I screamed out, into that magician's face, right into him. I read the fear in his eyes. It blew away all the cobwebs, the mist that had descended over my mind. The magician, he stumbled back, fell over onto the floor, if I remember correctly. I just remember sitting in that chair, trying to remember who I was, what my name was, and the expression on the magician's face— wide-eyed shock, his mouth like a puckered arse, if you'll excuse my lewd choice of language, but that was how it looked to me. And his words, they began with a mere whisper, so quiet that I had to lean forward to hear him, and he said to me, 'You, my dear boy, tell me, you saw them, didn't you? Yes, yes,' he said, looking about him, 'I can feel them, the cold, I've had that sensation before,' and from that moment on I knew exactly what he meant, and they were with me forever after, if they hadn't been so before."

I opened my mouth to speak, but Dante waved me away with the waggle of his finger. "There was one thing from that meeting, as I sat there in that high-backed armchair, desperately trying to cling onto the memories the magician hadn't banished forever from my mind, like a boy scrabbles for his marbles as they roll off down a hillside, the magician, he crawled toward me, fear in his eyes. I knew that he was terrified, that his natural, animal instinct would've been to run from the room and never return. But he had to know, to be sure of one thing, and I recall him gripping onto my knee, holding on tight, and in hurried English I barely understood, said, 'My child, please, I beg of you to teach me how you see them. Please, won't you teach me?' And with all that pleading in his eyes, that desperation, and the combination of my muddled thoughts—I really wished to placate him, to pass on whatever it was that I possessed that he wanted. But, I knew even then, that I just couldn't, that whatever force it was that had claimed me, that would lag at my heels forever more, it wasn't something that could ever be taught. It was a *gift*."

After he'd uttered the final word, he rocked back on his haunches, apparently exhausted just from the telling of the tale, and he scanned the window behind my head, looking out at the blazing blue sky overhead, and I saw his sooty eyes reflect the sun, twinkle there. I thought, just for a moment, I saw that boy trapped inside, desperate to escape from his prison inside Dante's skull—to escape from whatever held him there.

Right then I knew that was the perfect moment, so I just spoke up, trembling as I was, I said, "I've seen my mother too. In those shadows, those *things* that you conjure up."

Dante cocked his head, still staring over me, at the sky beyond. I wondered if he'd truly got over the effects of his own reanimation.

"Is . . . are you saying that *I* have this gift too?"

For a long while I was sure that Dante had slipped away again, in fact I was terrified that he might be about to have another episode. A shrill cry for Doctor Finely was on the tip of my tongue, and I would've called out if Dante hadn't, so calmly and gradually, turned back to me and said, "Yes, Sara, that's exactly what I'm saying. How else do you think you saw off those pursuers, when we were in the carriage? If it hadn't been for you we would all have been caught—and goodness knows where we might be." He snickered to himself, and it seemed so out of place, tinny in the tiny cramped room, what with the oppressive atmosphere drooping over us like a damp bed sheet. "You don't know the things that go through my mind sometimes, it's just, if anyone ever found out that the show—*my* show—was all real, that there was no smoke and mirrors about it, then I'm certain they'd hunt me out, like a modern witch hunt, would they burn me at the stake?" He chuckled to himself again, this time louder, a little manic in tone. "Duck me in a lake to see if I'd float?" He burst out into a haughty laugh.

The only effect it had on me was to make my body feel like an empty, freezing cold metal chamber. Dante was scaring me. I wasn't ready to hear all this. Just because he'd found someone like him didn't mean that I should automatically become his *confidante*. I wasn't . . . old enough yet for that.

Dante seized control of himself, bringing his hand up to his mouth, actually having to pinch his lips together to prevent himself breaking out in a fresh batch of giggles.

As for me, I'd never felt so serious in all my life. I was ready to ask the question that had been haunting me all along, that had stung my throat on more than one occasion. "Did you . . . Did you murder my parents?"

If any grin had remained on Dante's face, it was now well and truly gone. He stared at me, his eyes glassy and empty all of a sudden. I had the horrible premonition that he himself was one of them—a shadow—but then his focus shifted, life seemed to return to him and he said, "Sara, I honestly don't know how to answer that question."

"It's easy," I said, feeling a lot more assured, my guts much steelier than I'd expected. "You say either 'Yes' or 'No,' which is it?"

"I don't know . . . what to say."

"You can't give me an answer? You either know or you don't, Dante." My voice grew sterner and I locked eyes with him. "*What* did you do to them?"

"Listen, Sara, I know what you're thinking, you're going out of your mind. You're confused—believe me, I felt the same when I lost my parents, what I can remember of it. Please, just let me finish the story, my life story—as much as I can recall—and then, if you still wish, I shall answer your question." He gave me that slanted look of his, that slightly lopsided grin. "What do you say?"

Now I was more than a little anxious. For the first time in my inquisition, my voice trembled in my throat, making me feel probably just how I looked—a silly, frightened little girl. "Okay," I said.

Dante opened his hand wide and stared at the back of it, the skin stretched out there—blue and purple veins, all filled to bursting with that thick blood of his. "There's really not a lot more to tell. After the meeting with the magician, I never saw him again, that was the end of our relationship. The gentleman, while he never admitted what it was he did—or tried to do—he continued to attempt to mould me in his image through more . . . organic means. He still gave me the books, of course, and the tutors, they arrived by the truckload, right to the house. I took my classes in the front room, the biggest room, my favourite. That same room the magician had tried to convince me to forget everything I'd ever known, and where I was still conscious of having beaten him. Of course, it was also where I'd seen my father's face, so that was another reason I felt tied to it.

"When I came of age, the gentleman sent me off to England, sent me here, to study at university. Oh, he had me put down for medicine, and I tried my best, but really, from that point on my heart had slipped from the matter. My friend, Trevor Finely"— now I understood how the doctor fit in, an old university friend of Dante's, perhaps he could be trusted after all—"he did his best to get me up to speed on my studies, and to his credit—his brains and hard graft—he did get me through that first year. But I knew that medicine was never going to be my vocation. My head had been turned, you see. There was only one field for me, and that was magic.

"At university, I recall lying in bed, staring up at the ceiling and thinking over my encounter with that magician, analysing it from every angle. What struck me was not that I had this power, that I somehow had this connection to another world." He paused, his voice taking on a firmness that it hadn't before. "This . . . this *darker* world, although it is true that it would serve me well. No, what really caught my attention was my potential, what that magician had seen in me, valued in me. Something my own, something which I owed to not one person on Earth. Not a living person, in any case. And so I advised the university of my decision and never returned."

I felt my breaths wheeze through my nose, that acute sound nagging away at my hearing.

Dante continued, "I never went back to the gentleman, there was no need. He had led me as far as he could. I . . . once I did return to the mansion, while I was learning of my abilities, prac-tising, shall we say, and I took a trip out of my way to visit." He pouted. "There was nothing left."

"What do you mean nothing left?"

"The whole place had burnt to the ground."

Of course my thoughts flickered straight to the Forsneers' mansion, and what had happened there. I wondered if Dante had had a hand in both. It seemed like too much of a coincidence not to be the case. But could I really presume?

Dante shook his head, and genuinely looked a touch upset about the recollection, and then a moment later it passed completely and he took on the most neutral of expressions. "It was nothing but a burnt out structure—a few scraps remained, the pages of singed books scattered about, but there was nothing worth saving, at least not in my opinion." He let loose a sigh. "And then I just turned away and left."

I allowed the silence to billow up around us before picking my moment. "So, my parents?"

He gave me a light-hearted shrug, smiling nonchalantly. "As they say about me. Darkness lurks nearby. Sometimes I don't choose, things just happen. Why do you think I like to dress up?" He snorted a laugh. "The Man in Black, the Beggar? Those are disguises, and I'm sure that sometimes it fools them, but not always. They're not always fooled."

I gritted my teeth. "Like the night with my parents?"

Dante slipped into a straight face once again. The room chilled a couple of degrees and I was sure that the light dimmed. "I saw what you had—the gift. In the same way that the magician who came to wipe my memory sensed it on me, had read about it, I've read long and hard about it too." He glanced back, at my pile of books, leafed through a few of them, and smiled to himself. "I see that Helen has been trying to get you to read something."

I looked to the books, annoyed that he was getting sidetracked, still evading my simplest of questions, the question which I had a right to know the answer to, whatever it was. Was he afraid that I might get angry, that I might attack him? What damage could a fourteen-year-old girl do a full-grown man? Or was it something else. Now, now that he'd found me was he afraid that I might leave him? I considered it from his point of view, his endless searching, wanting to understand his condition —and now he'd found another. Maybe that was it.

Dante dabbed his tongue on his bottom lip, now three or four books down. As he read the title of the next book, he knocked the books resting on top of it over. They dropped to the ground, pages fluttering, a couple of them landing down on their fronts, inelegantly sprawled.

I wanted to reprimand him, tell him to respect the property of others—if that story he'd just told of his childhood was true then he had probably developed spoilt-brat tendencies, thought the whole bloody world revolved around him.

Dante slipped his chosen book out and glanced to me. "Didn't get to this one yet?"

"No," I said. "To be honest, I'm not much of a reader. I've only skimmed through those ones you just *chucked* on the floor."

He broke into a grin. "Oh, those are a load of rubbish, I wouldn't bother with those. Helen, she's just trying to build up your knowledge, give you a grounding in other . . . some would say, frivolous matters, *this* though"—he tapped the cover of the book—"*this* book is most important." He inspected the dark green cover, the faded gold lettering, its hardback cover battered around the edges. "Why, this was the very book Trevor showed me the first time I came to visit, after he and Helen got married. God bless him, he's always been at the forefront, most interested in understanding my condition—although I do imagine that he's got something at stake, that he'd like to be the first to medically document the phenomenon. The book's really quite enlightening, knows his stuff the author—one of the reasons I recognised you for who you were. I think you'd enjoy it." He tossed it to me without warning.

I caught it between my hands before it could spin into my chest. I read the cover. "*Newbert's Study of the Hyperactive Connection to the Spirit World.*" I looked back at him. "What *is* this?"

"Nothing less than you need to know," he said, wrenching himself up from the floor and hopping over to the door, plucking his cane from the wall on his way.

Caught off guard by the book he'd so unceremoniously thrust into my hands, I snapped back to reality and said, "My parents. You still haven't said what happened to them."

He lingered in the doorway. "Sara, I wish that I could give you an answer, but I straight don't know. All I can say is that I saw you and knew that I wanted you to come with me—you were the one I'd been looking for, you saw the poster. It could have been a gas leak which killed your parents, perhaps it was *something* of what plagues me that decided to interfere in our fates, or maybe"—he paused, his eyes lolling about the room, once more passing over the book I held in my hands—"or maybe, it was your own power that caused it. How can we ever be sure?" And then, with a swift, out-of-place smile, he slipped from the room, and I listened to the juddering rhythm of his uneven step pass along the landing, then back downstairs—maybe Finely was going to give him a check up.

I clutched the book in my hands. *Newbert's Study of the Hyperactive Connection to the Spirit World.* Was that what it was, then? The 'spirit world?' I felt myself falling back, landing on the edge of the bed, my body feeling half torn apart, my mind more than ever swirling with confusion. I processed what he'd said. Could it be that I was really responsible for my family's death? Dad, the babbie, Mum, all three of them? It just seemed too horrible to even contemplate, too confusing. In fact, the more I thought about it, the more it seemed that Dante had pulled a fast one on me, somehow got me going off along some other path of under-standing. Was he just covering for himself, his own culpability?

I rested the book down on its spine and lay on my front, on the bed, turning to the first page. I hoped all the answers I needed, I craved, would be contained within the covers of *Newbert's*.

CHAPTER EIGHTEEN

T HE SOUNDS of hurried voices brought me around in the morning. I looked about myself and realised that I'd fallen asleep on the floor, clutching the copy of *Newbert's* to my chest. I laid the book down and hauled myself up with the aid of the sturdy bedpost. I blinked in the fresh morning light seeping in through the curtains and tried to make sense of the commotion taking place in the house.

I could hear a gruff voice, Finely I was sure, and a higher-pitched more measured one, that I pinned as being Helen. I hesitated a few moments, still caught in the daze between sleep and waking, before deciding to slip from my bedroom, along the landing and to the top of the stairs, where I could just make out the two figures conversing down below. I kept myself hidden behind the banister and listened in.

". . . I don't care what *he* thinks, dear," Helen said, and although her words carried a fierce weight, they were controlled —never close to losing perspective or raising in tone, "there's one thing that's most important and that's her safety. She deserves a normal upbringing, and we can offer her that. Remember how down we were last year about the . . . the . . ."

But even the measured, emotionally-in-check, Helen couldn't bring herself to finish her sentence. I realised, right away, that they were talking about me. My body shuddered a little at the prospect, and I wondered whether that might be something like the sensation a 'spirit' feels when someone walks over the grave of its physical body.

This time Finely spoke. "But *us*, really, you think that it'd be appropriate?"

"Why not us? We're stable and we're one of those few people in this country that understand her condition—or at least know *of* it. If she was to go with Dante then she would be putting herself in great danger. We could offer her something of a normal life, a normal upbringing."

Finely broke in. "And I could study her, learn more about what it is that plagues them."

For the first time in the conversation, the first time in all of my acquaintance with Helen, I noticed an iciness enter her tone. "You're *not* going to turn her into an experiment. That's out of the question. If she does come to live with us then it's as our daughter—and, don't tell me that you would even hint at the idea of experimenting on your own daughter."

Finely's silence spoke mountains.

"I wouldn't allow you," she said.

I felt for my grip on the banister of the stairs, slowly helping myself up, into an upright position. I listened in intently, hoping that they hadn't heard me—that I wasn't the reason they'd decided to curtail their conversation. I realised that quite simply they'd reached a natural end, they had nothing else to say to one another. Both sides had drawn their arguments, stated their position, and all that was left was to wait and see how it all turned out. Well, as for me, I knew just how it would turn out. I had already made *my* choice.

Just as I had expected, later in the morning—after we'd taken breakfast—Dante came to me and told me that we were taking our leave. Although I'd enjoyed my stay with the Finelys, been so glad for their kindness in taking us in, and above everything else ecstatic that Finely had managed to heal Dante, to bring him back from the cusp of death—whether or not this spirit world had had a hand in his 'resurrection' or not—I was also happy to be moving on. I knew that there was danger out there, that Dante was subject to a national manhunt, but I also knew that this was my life, *our* life now. We would forever be moving on, going onto the next place. It was the new normal for me, and I relished it—wanted to dive head first into my new life.

So, with *Newbert's* tucked beneath my arm, the other books left in a scattered pile in my room, I wished Helen and Trevor Finely goodbye at the door. Helen examined me with moist eyes, her bottom lip jutting out. She rested her gentle touch on my shoulder and stared into my eyes, not even needing to ask, already knowing the choice that I had made. "Here," she said, "there'll always be a life for you, never forget that. Whatever happens, wherever you end up, just remember that you can come back here."

I swallowed, feeling myself welling up.

"Think of us as your backup plan, if you like," she said.

Feeling my voice waiver, my heart pound, I just about got out, "Thank you. Thank you for everything."

And, all of a sudden, she lurched forward and seized me in a strong hug—a so strong hug that it betrayed her frail frame. Her fingers dug into my back, drawing me closer and closer to her chest, and it was only when Finely's sure touch intervened, to pry us apart, that we finally stood back from one another, each of us taking in the other for the final time. Without another word, Helen turned away from me, her sobs chattering out of her, and she disappeared into the house.

Now it was Finely who was bearing down on me, his large frame towering above. I expected a firm handshake, some off-handed show of affection. What I got instead was a rough kiss on the forehead and a gentle squeeze of a hug. He stepped back from me, looked over Dante and Jessica, standing about ten paces away from us, and then forcing on a smile, turned and followed his wife back inside.

The walk to the carriage seemed to take forever. I guess that I hadn't taken into account the horses that had towed us there the first time I had visited—or the emotions jiggling about inside of me as I'd accompanied Farol back to the road on the way back. Dante had cast aside his cane soon after leaving the Finelys' house, and he walked with it tucked beneath his arm, a slight limp still bothering him, but otherwise mobile.

My heart ached at having to leave the Finelys—those two marvellous people—behind. And it was made all the worse for knowing that it was my fault, I was the one who had made them sad, left them feeling empty in their own home. If only I'd stayed, been their daughter, then I could've brought them untold happiness. And yet, I knew that my destiny lay with Dante. I had to honour that. Perhaps fate would decide for me—and I would end up back with the Finelys after all. There was no way of telling.

The hermit guarding the carriage regarded me with a wistful eye as he sat back on a wooden rocking chair on his porch, feet resting up on the fence surrounding his house. He watched us approaching, his eyes never leaving us even for a moment. When we arrived beside him we didn't greet him, there was something in the air that suggested that wasn't necessary, and he simply swung himself gingerly up to his feet and stomped off in the direction of the cave which concealed the carriage.

In the course of the few days—or had it been as much as a week, a couple of weeks?—the carriage had become ravaged by a dusting of cobwebs. Incredible how such a short period of neglect could affect the carriage so dramatically. Together, all three of us wheeled it out from its hiding place. When we emerged from the darkness, blinking back the daylight like a trio of freshly emerged moles, the man stood there with Old Billy and Silver, holding onto each of them—both horses silent and still, like a pair of well-trained dogs. Without speaking, he handed one lead rope to Dante and the other to Jessica, before turning on his heel and heading back to his shack.

It was Jessica who broke the silence. "It's better if I drive the carriage—they'll recognise your face anywhere," she said, to Dante.

Dante shook his head, long and dolefully. Then he leapt up onto the carriage, unbuckled the tarpaulin, and fished around inside. He brought out those rags that I recognised from his disguise, the one he'd greeted me in, when he'd played the beggar. I don't know how he did it but with that same . . . sleight of hand . . . he threw them on over his current clothes, his smart suit. He took on a crooked posture, half-bent over, almost the same height as Jessica now, and he busied himself tying Old Billy and Silver to the carriage, snaking their bridles over their elongated faces, before hoisting himself up into the driver's seat.

Jessica and I exchanged glances and the both of us got into the carriage through the bullet-marked door. As she brought the door shut with a solid *snap*, the earthy odour of dried blood seeped through the stale air. I brought the neck of my tunic up over my mouth and nostrils to guard against the stench and felt the carriage moving beneath me, that mechanical jerk of the wheels, the *creaks* and *groans* as it shuddered into action—like the waking of an elephant following a coma. And that gentle *clopping* of the horses' hooves lulled me into a hypnotised gaze, and my concentration drifted onto the passing countryside, those thickets, spindly trees and bushes, the sludge browns and emerald greens, and all those ruby reds and burnished yellows in between.

Soon enough, we arrived back at the main road, and I was taken a little by surprise when Dante steered the carriage back toward Girth, in the opposite direction of where we should've been headed. I looked to Jessica for explanation.

She gave me a gentle smile. "We need to pick up the trunks," she said.

Sure enough, we arrived back outside the Finelys' house. Looking at it from under glass it seemed cold, unfamiliar now, just another *lovely* house on a street filled with lovely houses—its steel-blue front door and sign jutting out from its façade, the only aspects which marked it apart from its neighbours, that and the knowledge that the Finelys lived there. And it shocked me, how they lived such a normal life amid all the other chaos. I reflected on how far apart their lives were from those of the capital. I pondered whether or not it was a good or bad thing to detach one's self. And then, a pair of hard *thuds* announced the fall of the trunks on the roof rack. I heard Dante draw the tarpaulin back over it all, fasten the canvas back down before reassuming his position back in the driver's seat, striking the backs of the horses. Apparently he had his strength back too. The carriage lurched on, leaving the Finelys behind.

I glanced back over my shoulder to the house, and saw, up in the first floor window, staring out from the bedroom which had been my own, Helen there. Her palm was pressed up against the glass, her features flattened against the surface. She was waving me off.

I raised my hand in response, a static wave, and then we turned the corner, and we were gone for good, heading back along the road, on our way to more adventures.

We were a good hour or so out of Girth before I plucked up the courage to ask Jessica the question that had pecked away at me —forever, it seemed. And now seemed as good a moment as any. "What happened?" I said. "Back at the Forsneers' mansion?"

Without turning her head away from the window, she focussed upon me, fixing me in periphery of her glance. I wondered whether she was going to tell me, or if she'd continue to keep that episode to herself as some sort of display of the power she had over me in terms of our respective relationships with Dante. And then, just when I'd resigned myself to playing more power games with her, she opened up to me.

She turned in her seat so that she faced me straight on. She flicked a curl out of her eye and began. "It's not like it hasn't happened before," she said. "I mean, never on that sort of a scale before, but Dante, he's jealous, always has been."

I risked putting our freshly thawed relationship under a little tension and said, "So why did you allow yourself to get into that situation?"

She scowled a touch and then, appearing to realise that we were supposed to be being nice to one another, returned to a neutral expression, looking wistfully out the window. "There wasn't much choice, was there? I mean, what would you have done in my place?"

I had no answer to that.

"Exactly," she said, flashing her eyes. "Sometimes the benefit of hindsight can distort—and maybe there was something that I might've been able to do, but you could equally ask why Dante got himself all stirred up, and allowed his power to overwhelm him like that."

"What actually happened, though?"

"Well, I was off down the garden with Romeo, just like you saw, and next thing I knew Dante's Man in Black was striding his way through the crowd, shouldering people out of the way. It was funny because just at that moment Gerald was prompting away for more answers to Dante's act—wanting to know the ins and outs of it, and getting progressively exasperated about it." She inspected her hands, which—the way she was looking at them—one might've assumed, had begun writhing of their own will. "I remember looking over Gerald's shoulder, seeing Dante approaching. Gerald got irritated, wanted to know what it was that was distracting him from his *marvellous* good looks, but when he turned to look he didn't recognise Dante—of course, no one ever does the first time."

My breath hitched in my throat.

"On seeing this stranger approaching, Gerald decided that he was going to take a stand, that this upstart was trying it on with *his* girl. I remember Gerald puffing himself up, looking down his chin at Dante, waiting for him to draw closer. Dante arrived beside us and just stood there, watching, head slightly cocked to one side. He produced a flute of champagne that he'd kept down by his side and passed it to Gerald, that diffused him somewhat, prompting him to set his empty glass down at his feet. Dante then proceeded, still unrecognised by Gerald, to ask us how we'd found the evening, and invited our comments on the magician, and how he'd managed to do what he did. At that point, Gerald declared himself totally befuddled, not having the faintest clue how it was done. And then . . . and then, Dante said that he'd be willing to reveal all his secrets on the basis that Gerald would allow him to speak with me for a few minutes. Well, Gerald spent about a second weighing up that offer being throwing it back in Dante's face, telling him to get shot of us to boot. And that was when I noticed Dante getting cross, those lines appearing on his face. A few moments later and Gerald twigged exactly who he was speaking to.

"A sliver of a smile appeared on his lips and he stepped forward, prodding Dante in the chest, demanding to know exactly how he did his tricks—what he did to bring up those conjurings that had had the whole audience so enraptured. And, for the first time since I've known him, Dante told the truth. He said that, quite simply, he did nothing. There *was* no trick. What he was doing—raising the dead, their spirits, bringing them back to walk upon the Earth—wasn't false, it wasn't a fakery at all.

That was the one answer which Gerald didn't want to hear, he wanted to know the secret behind it all and he believed it to be just one of Dante's stock answers, one of those responses which he gave with a wry smile and a wink. Gerald got crosser and crosser, demanding to know the real reason, and then, after he'd swigged the rest of the champagne in his glass and tossed the flute off into a bush to the side of him, he shoved Dante in the chest. Well, that was just when everything went a bit crazy— when the confrontation got out of hand.

"Maybe it was because of the especially charged show which Dante had put on, something of his power still lingering near the surface, always threatening to break through, or perhaps it was a willingness to show Gerald that he wasn't lying, on the contrary, that he was simply telling the plain truth. Whatever happened, I felt that chill descend over whole garden, I remember the remarks of the ladies to their husbands, proposing to go inside, while the gentlemen claimed that it was preposterous, that they must've just been feeling the weather *wrong*, while they shuddered in their jackets and knocked back their whisky, or whatever it was they were drinking. Before I knew it, all around me the whole garden was stuffed full of those shadows, all around, their blank faces, expressionless, subhuman things. Then Dante grasped hold of my hand, his fingernails broke my skin, I noticed later—just like you did in the theatre—and he dragged me through the crowd, Gerald's protestations thick in our ears. When we got back into the house, headed for the front door, Gerald seized hold of my trailing arm, twisted it behind my back. I felt like a ragdoll there—Dante jerking me forward, Gerald with all his drunken strength pulling me back, both keeping me rooted to the spot. Something had to break the deadlock, and I admit that my money was always on Dante—it always is. All of a sudden flames shot up all around, fire every-where, smoke pluming about. Dante didn't wait, the spectacle had taken Gerald off guard, and he managed to get me out into the hall, but not before, glancing back over my shoulder, I saw Gerald pointing a rifle at us. Dante dragged me out through the front door and I recall that rifle *crack* in my ear, the puff of paint and stone flying up, and then I was outside, we were rushing for the carriage." She smiled lightly. "I saw your face peering out at us, and I knew that we'd almost done it—almost escaped." Her smile faltered. "Then that horrible deadweight, that tug of Dante on my arm after Gerald shot him. But we got him inside, got him better, didn't we?"

I snapped back to the present, having lost myself in that evening once again. "Yes, yes we did, and now everything's going to be fine." My mind wheeled around and I found myself saying, "Only, I wish that we had Farol with us, it's terrible to think that he might be in the Forsneers' hands, even now. I wonder what they might do to him."

Jessica gave a wry grin, her eyes gleaning a little from the emotions stirred up by remembrance. "Oh, don't even *wonder*," she said. "They'll have him—I can bank on it. The Forsneers, they have everything they want, they pay all the right people, how else do you think they've got along for such a while?"

"So, what you're saying that they'll have hold of him?"

She nodded solemnly. "You read the newspaper. Yes, there's no other possibility I'm afraid. But," she said, drawing a sigh, "we have to look forward now, look to our future. Farol, he was a terrific companion, loyal and kind"—that remark made me think of that show of brute strength, the act which had sent him away from us—"but he's gone now, he sacrificed himself so that we might have a chance at continuing—going on." She shook her head, looking out the window. "If there's any karma at all, he'll find his way back to us. That's our hope now."

I wondered whether I should tell Jessica about Farol—about what I had seen. But what would it achieve? As far as Jessica was concerned it was enough that Farol had simply wandered off in the middle of the night and turned himself in. If I spilled the story about him hitting that warden, the man guarding the exit to the Forsneers' estate it would only give her another reason to believe that we were doing the right thing in leaving him behind.

I peered out the window, losing myself in my thoughts once again, resigning myself. What *was* there that I, a fourteen-year-old girl, could do to help him now?

The carriage slowed on its way, approaching a junction I saw out the window. There was a post which marked the directions of the compass. I picked out just two of them: north, where we had come from, the direction of my home, and then south, where we were going to—our future. I felt a tingle pass through my stomach at the thought of France, of *going abroad*, as the posh folk in the capital would've said. Now I was going to see something of the world myself, and the heat of the chase, the fact that we were fleeing, only added to my anticipation and excitement. Then, without warning, the carriage careened to the left, taking a sharp turn back to the North.

For a moment or two I was confused, thought that Dante might've got himself muddled—he still wasn't quite himself after all. Only when I glanced across as Jessica did I realise that this was no mistake at all.

Jessica leapt out of her seat and, with the carriage wheels still revolving, the carriage jerking about all of the road at a steady pace, she threw open the door, and jumped out.

CHAPTER NINETEEN

FOR SEVERAL HEARTBEATS I was resigned to staying in my seat, staring into space, trying to absorb what was happening, what it was that sharp turn to the left had signified. And then I heard the raised voices outside the carriage, Jessica's *screeches*, Dante's calm, gathered responses. I could feel the horses stirring up the dust with their hooves, snorting to themselves as they witnessed the spectacle. More out of concern for my own safety than curiosity, I dived out of the carriage, just as Jessica had done.

It wasn't before time either, because, as I landed facedown in the dirt, feeling the gritty ground scrape away the skin from my knees and the palms of my hands, I looked back to see the carriage toppling along precariously at full tilt, Silver having been thoroughly spooked by the argument erupting between Dante and Jessica. Poor Old Billy, he just lagged along, like a madman's conjoined twin, with no sense of control whatsoever.

I watched Dante and Jessica stop arguing and turn their

attention to the out-of-control carriage quickly bombing away from them. Dante made a feeble attempt to dash after it—for a few paces breaking out of his beggar persona and going after it at a strapping young man's pace—a strapping young man with a gammy leg—before giving up and simply pattering to a vain halt.

All three of us remained engrossed on the passage of the carriage, still going at full-tilt, because of Silver's effort, and Old Billy's reluctance to contribute, veering sharply to the right of the road. A few seconds later and a devastating *crunch* chopped through the air as the carriage overturned in a ditch, both horses going head over heels, neighing wildly. I saw them come down and knew immediately that something was wrong with Old Billy.

Following the crash, while Silver righted himself almost straightaway and, now freed of his harness, cantered into the field which ran alongside the road, Old Billy just stayed on the ground, lying on his side.

I looked over to Dante and Jessica, both of whom remained steeped in silence. So I saw that it would be up to me to be the first to run over and take stock of the damage. As I drew closer, I could make out that strained breathing, that horrific sound of Old Billy's lungs pumping like a bellows, desperately trying to keep his heart beating. Once I stood on the precipice of the ditch, I saw the problem right away. Old Billy's neck rested at an impossible angle, almost at thirty degrees from a straight position. In the tumble, coupled with the speed of the crash, he had broken his neck.

I lingered there, afraid to go forward, hearing those frivolous *snorting* and *geeing* sounds which Silver gave off as he danced free through the field on the edge of my vision. Did he realise what he'd done? What his foolish action had resulted in? I just told myself, over and over again, that he was just a horse. And then, on that same tact, I thought about Dante—about whether this would've happened if Farol had been here, driving the carriage. If Farol had been there with us there would've been no need for us to steer up toward the north at all, right at this moment we would've been heading straight for France. I stared down at the doomed animal, at the fear flaring up in Old Billy's eyes and there I saw death—*real* death—glaring back at me, taunting me, measuring my strength and scoping out my weaknesses—plotting its advantage. All in that moment, in that beady, marble-like eye.

Dante and Jessica shuffled closer, I felt them come to a stop at my shoulder, could feel their wandering eyes, taking in the image before me—that poor, dying horse.

Old Billy's breaths came harder and faster as panic, and pain, set in. His eyes lolled back in their sockets and his tongue prodded out between his hairy lips. He got caught in a spasm, shutting his eyes completely now, his breathing irregular and fainter with each inhalation. And then he was gone.

All of us stood around staring at the dead horse, the carcass before us. Obviously no one wanted to be the first to say something, so I decided to speak up. When I spoke I surprised myself with the fortitude in my voice, how I managed not to well up. I guess I was thinking more of Farol and how he should've been there with us, there to comfort Old Billy in his last moments. But all Old Billy had was us three. I pointed over into the field, into the foreground, Silver still strutting and snorting in the background. "Just here," I said. "Let's dig a big hole and bury him just here."

Neither Dante or Jessica said anything.

I turned back, thinking that they hadn't heard me. However, the two of them continued to stare glumly at the dead horse, clearly unable to believe what they'd just witnessed—such a pointless death when there'd been so much hope, what with Dante getting better and us moving on to our next adventure. And now they'd lost an old friend.

Dante was the first to snap out of his stupor. He gazed at me, eyes devoid of emotion, lips thin and expressionless. "What'd we dig the hole with?"

It was a good question, and one which, if Dante didn't have the answer, I wondered how he could expect me to have it. I didn't know everything he kept up in that trunk loaded beneath the tarpaulin on the roof of the carriage. Surely he had something appropriate?

Jessica spoke with a weak, floaty voice, as she trod down into the ditch. "I'll find something," she said.

The carriage itself lay on its side, the tarpaulin still firmly fixed in its place. Slowly, with me and Dante watching on, she peeled it back and peered inside. I caught sight of those trunks nestled there. She fished inside and, with a great big *groan* tugged one of the trunks free from its place. Dante had to help her carry it right away from the carriage, where they set it down on the roadside and popped it open. She rummaged about inside for a few moments before straightening up, holding up the item which she'd searched for. I made out the object in the midday sun. A trowel. A bit battered and rusted in places, but a trowel nonetheless.

Dante flashed his eyebrows. "And you expect to dig a hole for this guy"—he inclined his head in the direction of Old Billy's body—"with that little thing."

Jessica tossed the trowel at Dante, who caught it, then she said, "No, I expect *you* to dig it. *This* is all your fault."

I saw Dante's features darken, his mouth become a narrow

slit. But he said nothing to her. He merely took that trowel, leapt across the ditch and stumbled into the field, where he started digging.

At that point I thought of raising the issue about the owner of the land, whether we should go and seek him out to ask permission, but it was too late. Jessica had stormed off to the other side of the road, where she'd picked out a tuft of grass and sat herself down, while Dante was already on his knees, trowel in hand, digging a hole big enough for a horse.

I spotted a nice looking shady spot a few paces away, equal distance from Jessica and Dante—just to emphasise that I wasn't taking sides—and I made for it. On my way around the lip of the ditch I couldn't help but look down once more, to that husk which had once contained life. Was there any way for me to see animal spirits? I waited, staring at it intently as if Old Billy's spirit might leap up and lick my hand, searching for a carrot or, if he was lucky, an apple. But nothing at all happened. Maybe *Newbert's* had some sort of clue concealed inside it, but there was more than a thousand pages to be read, and I had no interest in scouring through it right at that moment—nor floating the prospect with Dante. So, in the end, I just decided to take up that spot in the shade and wait for Dante to finish the hole.

It was about mid-afternoon by the time Dante had finished with the hole. He looked to us and that was enough of a gesture for us to go over to him and stare back down into that ditch, that same question on all our lips of how *on Earth* we were going to lift Old Billy's body and get it over to the hole. I guess we should really have thought about that before Dante had dug the hole—but, what with emotions running high at the time of decision-making, there wasn't a lot of logic floating around.

All together we shovelled our hands beneath the still-warm body. I felt the fur rough on my fingertips, and that healthy stench of horseshit and grass still clinging to him. Until I'd headed out into the country I'd never thought of horseshit as being an attractive smell, but now I felt that way. It was earthy, natural, organic. Farmers used it on their crops as fertiliser. I had indirectly ingested huge quantities of it. More than anything in that moment I think I twigged that it represented life—it was some substance strong in life, and with all the death around me, God help me, I needed something to remind me that I was truly living.

In the end we could only drag the carcass up the other side of the ditch, and then across the small patch of field to Dante's hole. It wasn't ceremonious. We merely let him go from our clutches and his dead body thudded as it landed at the bottom.

As it turned out, Dante had hardly dug the hole deep enough. Even standing at the side of the hole it was easy to make out the horse's flank rising above the ridges. Still, there wasn't time, we were losing light and we had a long way to go—in which direction was another question entirely.

Together we buried our hands in the mud and tossed it on top of Old Billy's body. I had a strange prickly sensation as I participated, watching the mud slowly accumulate upon him. I got a very real sense that we were giving Old Billy back to the earth, that soon he would simply be dirt, powder.

We finished the grave about an hour later—more of a funereal mound from the way the dirt all piled up upon Old Billy's body. I had no doubt that the farmer—or any passing traveller for that matter—would notice something a cropper about the earth here. Did it really matter? If anyone did come looking, found the horse, we'd be long gone. I was sure that we wouldn't be the first to bury a dead horse in the countryside.

Before going to fetch Silver, we decided to get the carriage out of the ditch first. This was a much easier task because, apart from a broken strut here and there, nothing essential to the movement of the carriage was beyond repair. We could at least limp our way to the next town where we could get some professional help.

Once the carriage stood back on the roadside, now looking more battered—and untrustworthy—than ever, what with its scratched-up paintwork and the chunks of wood sticking out at odd angles. I just hoped that we didn't come across a policeman, or another of those road wardens, because we would be prime candidates to be stopped and our identities well and truly scrutinised.

It fell to Dante to go off and fetch Silver from where he bucked and whinnied on the other side of the field. I thought it would be a thankless task, that he would end up on his backside with the horse a dozen acres away before he got up. But it turned out quite different.

Leaning up against the carriage, I watched Dante—still dressed in his beggar's clothing—sneak up on Silver, slowly, creeping his way along. There was no doubt that Silver could see him, even if it was just out of the corner of his eye. And yet he didn't stir from his place, made no effort to run. Soon Dante didn't even have to creep, he merely picked his way through the field, up to Silver's side and then lassoed him with the lead rope. Silver didn't protest that time either. It was like they shared a connection, an understanding. I watched the two of them gradually make their way back toward me and Jessica, standing at the roadside, side-by-side, like a horse and rider who had spent their whole life together.

Dante helped Silver back into his harness and then took up the driver's seat once again. He looked down to me and Jessica, seeing us gawping at him, then said, "What're you too so fussed about? Come on, we've got to get a move on."

I turned around right away, but Jessica stood her ground—just a few moments more—before giving in and joining me in the carriage. With that gentle, solitary, *clip-clop* resounding in my head, and the dusk drawing in on our heels, I found my head lolling to one side, my eyelids drooping, I got one last look out the window and thought to myself, *We're going back north. To save Farol.*

CHAPTER TWENTY

E ARLY NEXT MORNING I woke when the hooves stopped sounding on the road, when the carriage ground to a halt. I rubbed my eyes and yawned long and wide, looking about me, trying to ascertain where exactly we were.

The house alongside us was grey—covered in pebbles. Quite pretty in a way. I craned my neck to see as far as I could, along the road, and back where we'd come. This seemed like a tiny hamlet. Only a few houses scattered along the roadside, living off passing trade.

A man dressed in a black-stained apron emerged from the house, wiping his hands on a torn-off piece of cloth. He approached Dante, who was out of sight, and conversed with him.

I turned my head to look over at Jessica. She slept on, using her clasped hands as a pillow. Only the occasional flicker of her eyeballs beneath her eyelids suggested she was alive. My limbs felt stiff and my muscles ached so I clicked open the latch and dropped down onto the dirt road, landing beside the carriage. I rounded it and came face to face with Dante.

Dante remained focussed, his gaze watchful as he examined the craftsman examining the carriage for the damage. He shot me a swift wink then turned his attention back to the man. "You don't happen to know where I might acquire a horse around here, do you?"

Hands on knees, head almost beneath the carriage, the man replied, "Not around here, nope, afraid not, pal. You might have more luck in Donneston."

"And how far away is that?"

He pulled his head out from beneath the carriage, straightened up and then fixed me with a long, pondering gaze. I thought he was going to address me directly and then, at the very last moment, instead he addressed Dante. "Due west from here. Twenty miles. That any good?"

Dante shook his head, then said, "No, that's too far out of our way."

Again, the craftsman shot a glance at me. He wiped his hands on the dirty cloth. "Where're you headed if you don't mind me asking?"

"North."

"North?"

"That's right."

The craftsman scratched his neck. He squinted up the road, in the direction we were headed before turning his attention back to us. His swift eyes moved between me and Dante, then finally they rested on me. "Listen," he said, "I'll level with you, okay? I know just who you are"—he nodded in my direction—"I seen that girl on the posters they've been handing out."

Dante blinked rapidly. "What posters? Who's been handing out posters?"

"Why," the craftsman said, "posters of you, Dante Gobornik —who'd you think? I didn't recognise you right away, but when I saw her here it rung a bell, then I took a closer look at you, and I've never been more certain of anything in my life. Oh, you're him all right, ain't you?"

Dante was struck dumb for several moments. "Who was here handing out the posters?"

The craftsman shrugged. "Some messenger boy for some nobleman." He made a hollow sucking noise and then spat a great wad of chewing tobacco down at his feet. Slowly he raised his head back up. "But I ain't got much time for noblemen if I'm honest about it—in fact you catch me on a bad day and I might just tell you that they're the scum of the Earth."

"Why's that, if you don't mind me asking?"

"Oh," the craftsman said, in a tone that suggested he was about to impart something casual, something for our convenience, when really he was just about bursting at the seams to tell everyone he met, "they took away my family's land—a while back now. The *bastards*." He pointed off in the direction we'd come. "Back there, Hallough Fields, those were our lands for the longest time—six generations, at least. Then, one day, someone came along—on appointment of the king"—this warranted another spit, and what I supposed to be the remainder of the chewing tobacco splattered into the dust—"and they had this long old piece of paper and read to us about how it was the king's *right* to take whatever was of his choosing, whatever was to his liking, and he'd up and decided one day that our land was precisely the thing he was looking for. And that's how we lost Hallough Fields."

"I'm very sorry to hear it," Dante said, actually sounding genuinely sorry.

The craftsman pressed his lips together and nodded. "Yup, that's the way of the world, I guess. King got his big old estate built, oh they put up a whole mansion house, and converted the whole lot into hectares of hunting ground." He shrugged. "If my great granddad had been around to see it, it would've killed him —if he weren't already dead. I would say that he'd be turning over in his grave but those men, those *noblemen*, they turfed us off the land before we could go by our graveyard and retrieve our dead relatives. So he don't have no grave no more."

Dante nodded to himself and then, having waited what he'd obviously thought to be a polite amount of time, leaving enough of a reverent pause for the craftsman's dead great granddad to be honoured, he said, "So, how long do you think these repairs are going to take?"

The craftsman wiped his forehead with the rag. "Oh, I'll get going on them right now, I will. Won't take me too long, should have them done by noon." He broke into a conspiratorial grin. "Say, what you said about that horse, if that's what you're interested in, I might have the very thing."

This caught Dante's attention. His eyes sparkled. "Really? Honestly?"

The craftsman nodded then inclined his head in the direction of his workshop. "Out back we've got a field, couple of fillies in it. Young ones, but they'll learn. Broken and everything. I've taken them in carts a couple of times myself. Docile as anything." He arched an eyebrow. "Take a look?"

"Okay," Dante said, following him, gesturing for me to follow.

We passed through the workshop and I took in the various

tools which beyond: hammer, tongs and axe, I couldn't even name. The air smelt lightly of sawdust and grease. There was a touch of paint in the air too—I soon saw its origin, the tin of white paint in the corner, at least a gallon's worth.

Despite the stature of this tiny village, and the filthy appearance of the craftsman, the workshop itself was kept reasonably clean—the floor was swept, the tools all in their places, the offcuts of wood stacked neatly over in a corner. I could tell that this craftsman took pride in his work.

As I followed on Dante's heels, I caught the light beaming in from outside, setting the dust tumbling through the air. I gawked at that ray of light all the way through, until I emerged on the other side, through a back door.

There was a field standing there. It wouldn't have been more than the plot of land required for a house, left fallow. There was a well-built, sturdy gate around the perimeter that looked as if it had been erected fairly recently—the wood hadn't yet been given any sort of protective coating. I liked that. It made it seem more . . . natural.

As we rounded the fence, wading through knee-high grass, I listened in on the craftsman informing Dante that they'd bought these two lots—the one with the workshop and the field we were standing in—with the compensation from the hijacking of Hallough Fields—this warranted another spit, and I wondered whether he had a whole tin of chewing tobacco concealed in his cheek. He explained that they also had another property in the village where his family: just him and his father—his mother having passed away a few years earlier—resided. He informed us that his father had grown quite fond of drink over the past few years, though his determination was just as dogged as ever. This workshop had once been run by his father, but the craftsman had had to take over the running when it became clear that his father couldn't handle it any longer. Apparently he had found his father one day lying pinned beneath a pile of sledgehammers, all criss-crossed, and the doctor had informed them that he'd broken three ribs and his coccyx. His father, of course, was slouched up against the workshop wall, blasted-drunk, laughing away till he was red in the face, apparently unaware of the pain.

The two horses—as promised—stood before us in the field. One was a creamy white colour, a little like Silver, while the other was a light honey colour with a few white splodges on her nose. They were around about the same size, so I guessed they were about the same age.

The craftsman leant over the fence, propping his elbows on the top rail. With his elbow still resting against the wood he pointed to the creamy horse. "She's a fiery old thing, she is." He chuckled to himself. "Why, I remember once when I had her harnessed up to a cart and we were heading through the hills around here. Everything was going just fine till this squirrel popped out of the hedgerow and dashed right across her path. Well, I didn't think anything of it till she decided—out of the blue—to up and chase after it." He shook his head, his eyes a little wet with tears of joy. "I just about got myself clear of that cart before she jumped that fence. Of course she got herself stuck on the other side, cart held her back. She couldn't get the cart to make the jump with her."

The craftsman's anecdote was a little close to the bone, what with that image of the carriage toppling over into the ditch, sending both horses tumbling—breaking Old Billy's neck—still fresh in my mind. I swallowed back the lump in my throat and concentrated on the horses, trying to put the man's story out of earshot. But, to my relief he seemed to have wrapped it up.

The craftsman got a hold of himself and then pointed out the other horse. "Now *she*, well, she's a completely different prospect indeed. While that one's a firework and a half, that other one's a real worker, solid, hard to scare. Never does anything that you don't expect. A dream horse, in short." He winced a touch, as if he was regretting having sold her so hard, and then said, "Not all that quick, though, and . . . well, she does like the taste of grass. Why, you leave her in a field and it'll be just about gone by morning, and that gut"—he pointed to her, rather round, stomach—"filled with the whole damn thing." He looked back to Dante. "So, sir, which would you like to take along with you?"

Dante looked pensive for a moment, he parted his lips then thought better of it, instead turning to me. "Which do you think, Sara?"

There was no decision to be made. So I just got it out straightaway. "Let's take the honey-coloured one."

The craftsman sucked his teeth and chewed rapidly—as it turned out, he had a great deal more chewing tobacco still left to get through.

Either not noticing the craftsman's reaction, or sidestepping it, Dante said, "How much for her?"

The craftsman looked between the two of us. "You're sure about her? I mean, the other one, she's not so bad—in fact I'd quite happily declare her to be the fastest horse this side of the Twin Valleys." I don't think either me or Dante had much idea what that qualification meant, so it was pretty much lost on us. "Tell the truth, I'm thinking of getting her out into the racing circuit, see if she might be able to channel her energy in that way. But," he said, pausing again, obviously realising that he was cutting holes in his pitch all over the place, "she'd be great for tight spots, get you out of anything real quick."

Dante, however, remained unmoved by this argument. "We'd like to know the price for the honey-coloured horse."

The craftsman seemed to give up, nodding his head lightly, as if—deep down—he would've said just the same thing in our position, and it was only in his role as salesman that he regretted our choice.

"So, how much?" Dante repeated.

The craftsman met Dante's eye slowly. His munching ceased and his face took on a childlike quality, as if all the wrinkles embedded there smoothed out—unwebbed themselves. "Why don't you tell me where you're going first?"

Dante shrugged. "Up north, like I said."

"No, where're you going specifically?"

Dante settled into silence.

The craftsman turned his attention back to the field—I saw him return his gaze to the honey-coloured horse with a wistful longing that only someone who's come to terms with losing something they hold dear can look. He began to chew again. "Because if you said to me that you were going up to see to the Forsneers." He turned straight-on to Dante, an intensity entering his eyes. "If you said you were going up there, I don't know, to settle some kind of score, to give them a bit of a kicking, I'd give you this here horse for free."

Silence billowed all around.

"Well?" the man said.

Dante looked over to me, and I gave him a nod, as if to agree that this was the moment to tell the truth. "Yes," Dante said. "We're going up to see the Forsneers. It's one of my companions

—you see, they're looking for me, as I'm sure you've read, and I intend to go up there to free him."

The man twitched his mouth. "And how'd you intend on doing that?"

"By giving him what he wants."

The man arched his eyebrow, then he stepped back from the fence, crossing his arms. "You've got some balls, Dante, I'll give you that. And I appreciate you being honest with me, I knew you would be eventually, once I pressed you." His gaze returned to the field. "I know you're a common man, just like us—like *me* —and I hope you understand that when it comes down to it, when it's *us* again them, you know which side you're on."

Dante inclined his head, smiling lightly. "I think I understand," he said.

"Good," the man replied. "Then there's just one thing I want from you—before I gift you this here horse and the repairs to your carriage."

"And what's that?"

"My mum, I'd like you to bring her back."

Often I wondered about the status of Dante's finances, how much he actually had to keep going, but—at that moment—I was more or less certain that he had at least enough to last us for several months, once I'd factored in the cost of crossing the Channel. But it wasn't about the money, I learnt that on that day. What this man—who's name it turned out was Oliver—wanted from us was something he valued much higher. He wanted a mutual respect to flow between us, to know that we were of one body: the same flesh and blood. Family. And family doesn't hold debts over the other, everything flows inside of it, because it's a part of it.

True to his word, Oliver fixed up the carriage, just like he'd said, and he brought the horse around to the carriage, to be introduced to Silver. They seemed to get on fine, which was to say that Silver nosed her flanks and gave her a squint-eyed glare before turning and facing in the opposite direction. Everything was set for us to go. Despite this being a quiet village, according to Oliver's testimony, he advised us to lock the carriage and horses up in the workshop while we went to visit his house, just in case some, less-well-intentioned, travellers passing through, happened upon it, recognised and reported it.

Now with Jessica along with us—me having woken her on our way out of the workshop—I jogged to keep pace with Dante and Oliver, who had descended into total silence ever since he'd given out his offer. Dante glanced back over his shoulder and, saying in a whisper which befitted the stern quiet enshrouding us, "Why'd you pick the honey-coloured horse?"

A smile quivered on my lips then drooped. "What he said, her character, she reminds me of Old Billy."

Dante grinned. "Me too."

We marched on along the village road until we got pretty much to the outskirts of the houses. Oliver led us down a winding, decrepit old mud track, with a tuft of unruly grass sprouting out the centre, and then right up to his house—where he and his father lived.

The house was painted a light pink colour and it was kept in the same order as the workshop, which was to say that although it looked quite old, windswept and battered, the grass was cut, there were no broken windowpanes and a healthy coil of white smoke curled out of its chimney. Oliver invited us inside.

As I crossed the threshold, the stench of liquor was overpowering. I got a whiff of everything: wine, beer and whisky, one great big mix. I held my nose, recalling the time I'd met Dante, down that side alley at *The Tom Cat*. I gave Oliver a fresh lookover and decided that he wasn't the drunk of the house, which only left—

"Son? That you?" came a croaky, quivering voice from inside the house.

Despite the fire I'd seen from outside, the actual interior of the place was gloomy and smelled of damp. I wondered if Oliver's father literally threw his alcohol at the walls—if the house itself was drunk.

"Son?"

"Yes, Dad," Oliver replied. "It's me." He shrugged off his coat and hung it up on a hook at the door. "I brought some friends, hope you don't mind."

His father made an impotent sound, something approaching a "*Gahh.*"

Oliver led us into the kitchen and prised the lid off a large saucepan sitting on the stove. "Have to get myself up at the crack of dawn to cook for him, otherwise the old fool don't eat, if there's nothing prepared." He looked us over. "Any of you fancy some stew?"

None of us responded.

Oliver smiled a touch. "Go on, you've been on the road, I'm sure you've all got appetites."

Oliver wasn't wrong and, just like he suggested, we all crowded around the table, sitting ourselves on jaggedly put together stools, which I guessed were rejects from the workshop, pieces that he had either used as practice or deemed of inferior quality for sale. It was interesting to think that he hadn't always been the competent craftsman that he clearly was now—what with his handling of the carriage. In a way I was glad—it made me think about my power, and how I had the capacity to yield something truly unknown, that, little by little, I would have to learn its intricacies, study under Dante, to truly realise my potential.

We polished off our stew in no time and every single one of us—even Jessica who protested that she was trying to watch her figure—had a second helping. There were a few jokes thrown around the table, mostly at the expense of the *noble* classes, and some jokey threats from Oliver of what he would do if he ever found himself in a dark alley with Gerald Forsneer, before the mood changed. It changed because Oliver brought up his mother again.

He told us about his father, how he'd just fallen apart since his wife—Oliver's mother—had died. That was when the drinking had started, so unlike him. All he wanted from Dante was for him to bring her back, to have her talk some sense into his father. For the first time I noticed Dante growing twitchy—nervy—about agreeing to anything, to actually being able to bring Oliver's mother back for such a chat.

"Really," Oliver said, "all you've gotta do is try. Who's to say if it works or not, but at least you'll have tried—and that'd be enough for me. You're Dante Gobornik, I know what you stand for, and you've more than earned those repairs and that horse I gave you."

This appeared to soothe Dante's nerve somewhat.

As we were on the point of leaving the kitchen, Oliver rested his hand on Dante's shoulder and said to him, in a voice that clearly was only meant for Dante, "And I don't care if it's all a trick—just some illusion. All I need's for you to scare the old man back onto the straight and narrow, got it?"

Dante stared back in Oliver's eyes—like a terminally sick patient being asked by a doctor to just show his symptoms a little more.

The sitting room, where Oliver's father passed the majority of his day—judging by the several emptied flagons of ale, the rampant stench of whisky and the rows of emptied wine bottles all lined up in a crooked row on the window sill. Oliver father, himself, shifted in his armchair, his eyes large and bulbous as he took us in—like an owl spooked into a corner of a barn by a group of cats, a broken wing preventing it from flying away. "Who . . . who *are* you?" Oliver's father said.

Dante rolled up his shirt sleeves, like a doctor making a house call. "My name," he said, "is Dante Gobornik. I am a Great Purveyor of Mind Tricks and Conjurings of Nationwide Renown."

This just begat a blank stare from Oliver's father.

"We're here to see if we might be able to bring back your wife, for a little chat."

Oliver's father's eyes just about popped from their sockets. "What did you say?" And then darkening a little in anger—his vein-stained face, the blotchy purple skin making him look a lot like a beetroot. "Who're you to talk about my Susan?" Then he wobbled up out of the armchair, hands waving, swaying from side to side. "Get out of my house! All of you!"

At this juncture, Oliver rounded us and calmed his father, quite miraculously. I got the impression that his father often flew into rages such as these, and so Oliver was well practised in bringing him back down from the towering spiral of fury. He got him sitting back in the armchair, while he surreptitiously removed the cask of wine which his father had tipped over during his rant, and which was bleeding red wine onto the tanned oak floorboards.

Oliver's father just resigned himself to sinking back in his armchair, eyes forever watchful, ready for whatever our next move might be.

Entering performer mode now, Dante shifted before Oliver's father, staring right into his eyes. "Mr Hallough, I must first inform you that the extent of my gift is such that, while I shall try my best to bring back your wife, it might be that I cannot do so. There are various reasons for this which I shan't bore you with for the time being, however once we've concluded our contact with the other side if you're interested in asking any questions I shall invite them then." He cocked his head to one side. "Is that clear?"

Struck dumb, Oliver's father waggled his head up and down, eyes fixed on Dante. Then his lips moved up and down, only joined a few seconds later by the light whisper of words. "You . . . you can really bring my Susan back—back to me?"

"I'm going to do my best, Mr Hallough, okay?"

Oliver's father—Mr Hallough—remained where he was, apparently too terrified to respond on any level at all.

"Now we shall begin," Dante said, closing his eyes and stooping forward, resting on his knees. Almost at once I felt the light *hum* in the room, that giveaway sign that, soon—in a matter of moments—a connection with the other side would be opened. And there would be no turning back.

A tremble ran up my spine and then, all at once, I felt the

touch of Jessica's hand—warm, much warmer than my own. She intertwined my fingers with hers and squeezed. With the atmosphere in the room reaching oppressive levels—like the pressure bearing down on a cloudy, hot summer's day that never seems to break. Only there was no heat in the room. None except for Jessica's touch.

Outside, the gentle breeze that had blown seemed to still. I thought I could hear the *crackle* of the stove cease. And then, I knew, in that moment of stillness—like the eye of a storm—that they were here. That their presence was within us, and among us, walking about just like shadows.

I kept my eyes clenched tight only to be blinded by white light. Equally, almost in pain from the brightness of the sensation, I attempted to open my eyes again, only to find that I could not. Something was preventing me. After fleeting moments of panic I told myself to calm down, reciting some titbit or other that I'd read in *Newbert's*, that line about the land of the dead being one that was fraught with worry and dystopia, and that any worthy voyager—someone who had the gift—had to learn to breathe there, to allow themselves to relax into it. Because, only then, would they truly be able to turn the tables, to control the dead, rather having the dead control them.

And as I forced myself to relax, demanded that my muscles release all their pent-up tension, I began to slip into the world, to see around me. The light wasn't blinding any longer. In fact, I could see quite clearly. It was like a bright morning blighted by fog. Slowly, gradually, the sun burnt it off, brought back first the familiar shapes, those dark outlines, and then shirked a little detail—the arms, the legs, the torsos, the heads. And then, before I had really got used to the sensation, I knew that I was feeling all those beings—their unquiet souls—sailing around me as if caught in an almighty storm, and then, feeling what I could only identify as Dante's influence, something like a calm, light blue light, their forms drew clearer, the hurricane in which they sailed—spiralling up before being hurled mercilessly downward again—slowly blew itself out. And all those souls. They dropped to the ground. I felt them. Their ticklish touch, their ghostly flesh, their waiflike hair, brush against me—send sparks through me. Again and again I told myself to relax. I concentrated on every one of my breaths, and focussed on Dante, in the middle distance and yet hundreds and hundreds of yards away from where I knew he crouched—in the real world. Here he was a mercurial figure. Nothing less, I saw, than a channeler, a magnet drawing all these spirits into him.

That was when I felt her touch, my mother's touch, her gentle fingers stroking the downy hair on the back of my neck. I had no need to turn to see her, I knew it was her there. And she was watching over me, staring over my head, watching what Dante was doing just like I was. Voiceless and yet . . . *there*.

It was eerie watching those souls all descend on Dante, surround him in a circle. And I watched on as he tilted his head upward—something approaching a half-smile on his lips—and appeared to converse with them. I strained my hearing, wanting to listen in to the conversations, but I had no luck. All seemed intent on listening to what it was he had to say and I observed as, following the conclusion of their mute conversation, several of the spirits floated off, on their way bumping into others, their shadowy auras colliding with one another. They reminded me of ants on their way to or from an ant hill—nuzzling the next in line, passing its orders on from the queen. Was that all these spirits were reduced to now? Nothing more than simply insects? Half beings? I considered my mothers touch on my shoulder and knew that she was more than that, she recognised exactly who I was. There was no way that she was *just* an ant.

It felt like hours passed by. Whenever I attempted to move my limbs, waving my hand before my eyes, it would take an awfully long time—and only then being a series of waves, blurred motion before me. It reminded me of waving my hands before me under streetlights, at night, that ever-so unreal representation of my skin—nothing more than a blur of pink.

When I looked back to Dante, feeling as though I'd already passed a whole day in this realm, from the way that my legs felt like they carried lead weights and how my brain felt like molten sludge, I saw that the other spirits all parted for another. A new shadow. The one that I supposed he'd summoned—what all those Chinese whispers had been about. It turned up before him, gliding gently and then stopped, like a phantasmal soldier awaiting their orders.

My mother clasped my shoulder tighter and I knew that Dante had found what . . . who, he was looking for. Mrs Hallough. And what happened now? I was witnessing it unfold. How he reached out for her hands, his upturned and facing hers, like a prince offering a dance to an embarrassed young princess. She accepted him and together they gently floated upward, resting in mid-air, above our heads. All the other spirits watched with their necks—whatever they had in place of necks—craned upwards to observe the two of them.

I thought I could hear the stirring of wind on the horizon, like another one of those storms brewing—like the one I'd found myself in upon arrival in this place. I kept my eyes fixed on Dante and Mrs Hallough, spiralling slowly about one another. The storm grew in strength. The gusts became howls. The light was returning. With all my strength, I clung on to the vision inside my brain, but I knew I was slipping, slowly. It was like I held by the tips of my fingers at a cliff edge but, no matter what I did now, it was inevitable that I was going to drop, fall into the unplumbable depths below. Just as I felt myself slipping, my grip giving out as the last ounce of strength departed me, I heard clear words, right up close, almost directly spoken into my eardrum, "Sara, I love you."

And then I did drop.

CHAPTER TWENTY-ONE

M
Y BREATH HITCHED in my lungs. I felt it ragged in my chest. My eyes snapped open and I took in the room. There, over at Mr Hallough's chair, was a shadow, standing over him, staring down. I saw that their hands touched. Only a few seconds later did I realise that Dante was there too, only a matter of inches away. His mouth moved slowly, and his voice had taken on a floaty, otherworldly quality. He was speaking for Mrs Hallough, I knew that. But their words, I couldn't hear them. I knew they weren't for me in any case. These were private things—thoughts shared between a husband and wife. I had no right to hear them. And yet, I was curious. That was my mother's voice I had heard in my head, she had told me that she loved me. But just as soon as I'd heard her she'd slipped away from me. Again.

I dared not steal any closer, both since Jessica continued to clutch my hand, and that the scene between Mr and Mrs Hallough was just impossibly still—their fingertips touching,

Mrs Hallough's mouth moving silently, Dante's voice just below a whisper. I glanced around to see Oliver standing over at the stove, his complexion totally pale, mouth slightly ajar and tears snaking down his cheeks. This was a time to stand back and watch. Not to interfere.

Slowly, and with great delicacy, Mrs Hallough withdrew her hand from Mr Hallough's. I thought I caught whispers in the air, gentle words that I could just about make out. Those quiet voices I'd often thought, lying on my side at home, to be the neighbours speaking to one another—made just inaudible by the insulation of the walls. Now I knew better than that.

Mrs Hallough retreated all the way, her shadowy form moving away, past Dante, and into the corner of the room. She seemed to be taking it all in. The mess which Mr Hallough kept around himself. I concentrated hard, trying to strip back that ever-changing face, to bring it into some sort of focus and, *finally*, I made out something of her features. The knitted eyebrows. The slender lips. The delicate, pointed nose. From this composite I established that Mrs Hallough, when she'd been alive, and in her time, had been quite a beauty. Now, traumatised by death, dragged through the ditches she still held onto its essence, if only it was slipping away from her moment by moment, like a gradual tide.

And then, all of a sudden, she just faded. Her whole spirit disintegrated into thin air.

Dante stumbled forward and then collapsed, flat on his front.

For a brief moment everyone in the room was totally still, completely absorbed in what they'd just witnessed—unable to process the swiftness of what had just occurred. And then, all at once, the room was abuzz. Mr Hallough, now apparently sober, leapt up from his armchair and flipped Dante over onto his back, with the vitality of a man twenty years younger, while he barked orders at his son, to fetch water, to bring a cloth. As for me and Jessica, we just held back, afraid—I suppose—to infringe on that territory in which Mr Hallough's wife had until moments ago drifted.

Oliver brought the damp cloth and a jug of water, which he immediately poured out into a tumbler. Between father and son, they raised Dante up, taking his weight upon them. Mr Hallough brought the glass to Dante's lips, wetted them, forcing him to take the liquid down.

Dante spluttered the water out almost as soon as he had taken it in his mouth. His eyelids flipped open and his eyes wildly danced about in their sockets, looking blindly about him. Now, having been in the realm, having shared something of the experience, I knew the confusion of jumping from the spirit world, coming back into the real one. He took several seconds to get a hold of himself, and with father and son's help, to get back onto his feet. He stumbled a couple of times before finding his balance, using the cornice to stop himself from toppling over. Oliver and Mr Hallough dared not stray too far from his side, not willing to trust his legs as much as Dante did himself.

And then, after the air in the room settled, once Dante allowed Oliver and Mr Hallough to seat him on a settee, to bring him a fresh mug of tea, steaming with hot milk still swirling about in a creamy spiral, the sobbing began.

First I didn't really know what it was. I thought that it was a squeaking somewhere distant and out of sight in the house, but then, looking to my side, I saw that it was Mr Hallough who was crying—bawling his eyes out, like a toddler. He clenched his fists and brought them down with hammer-like strokes on the arms of his chair. The tears dripped off his chin and landed on his shirt, dampening it, becoming undistinguishable from the long-left, well-set stains. Oliver, too, I saw was weeping, albeit more quietly than his father, and with his face half turned away, so that from a fleeting glance it appeared that he was simply looking out the window wistfully. Myself, I felt like crying too. Those words of my mother's slowly penetrating me, seeping into my skull and taking on meaning. But I held off. I've always done my crying in private, and I decided that, although it was an emotionally volatile situation, there was no need for me to alter my habits.

I kept expecting Dante to rest an easy hand on my shoulder —perhaps shaking a touch from the trauma of the occasion, of *crossing over*—to lead me away from this scene of despair, but— whether he was too tired to truly comprehend what it was that was going on, and the need for privacy inherent in it—he simply stood and stared at the two men, like me and Jessica. All of us there, making this private moment a communal one. It seemed like hours passed before the dust settled on the room, the crying came to a halt, and practicalities were raised.

It was decided, without opposition, that we were to stay the night at the Halloughs' house, as honorary guests. Even if Dante had wished to protest this, he didn't seem to have the energy. He looked as knackered as I can remember seeing him, and I reminded myself that he was still recovering from the gunshot wound—maybe he'd been all too blasé about getting back involved with the spirit world so soon, when it clearly took so much out of him. And, now having seen that other world, I could see how it really could take it out of a person—even one as resilient as Dante.

The Halloughs' house wasn't nearly as spacious as the Finelys' had been, and yet I felt quite snug—and a touch nostalgic—at sleeping in the front room, the same room in which we'd witnessed Dante reaching out for Mrs Hallough. I listened to all the groaning of the house sounds and snuggled up in my blankets. Right above me was the guest room, where Jessica and Dante were staying. I could hear their muffled voices—even through the floorboards I could tell that Dante was exhausted, on the point of falling asleep. I hoped that this frailty would pass him by, that he wouldn't find himself back at death's door so soon. It wasn't that I didn't trust the Halloughs, they'd been kind enough, but I couldn't deny that they had their own issues, their own problems. And I felt it in my bones that if we failed to get Dante away soon enough the whole dreariness of the place would drag him down with it.

I was facing into the fire, rubbing my hands together for extra warmth beneath my covers, when I heard the gruff, now-familiar voice in the doorway. I turned over and looked to him.

Oliver stood up there, one hand resting on his belt, the other clasped around a oil lantern. It was so quiet down here that between the *suck* and *crackle* of the flames I could hear his drawing of breath. I waited patiently for what it was that he had to say. "My ma," he said. "I know you were there with her too. In that other place."

My body seized up and I drew the blankets tighter about me.

"Yes," Oliver said, taking a step into the room. "I *know* you saw here there too—I saw you with your eyes closed, clasped all tight. You were there with him, weren't you?"

I wanted to come up with some excuse, give him some explanation that would make him go away, off to his bed, where I wouldn't have to speak with him till morning, but nothing came to me, and before I knew it I was flapping my gums, saying, "Yes, I was there. With Dante."

He nodded in the half-light, confirming what he had already suspected. He stole a step closer still, and my uneasiness ratcheted up a notch. My heart stopped for several beats then leapt forward, as if catching up with itself. When he spoke again, his voice was quieter, obviously not wanting to be heard by anyone else in the house. "And did you *hear* what it was she said?"

He was close enough now that I smelled his breath, the halitosis revealing that he perhaps didn't always have the energy for a full dental routine in the evenings. Onion, from the stew, lingered there, and that dry, stale milky smell of an empty tea cup hung on his clothes. He inched closer still.

All at once I'm sure that I saw that blinding white light again, flashing before me, I thought that unbeknownst to me, I was going to slip back into the spirit world, be sucked in—and this time without Dante's guiding rope. But I summoned up the strength, deep inside me, and shoved it away, just like I'd push down the urge to vomit. I told myself, again and again, that I could hold it back. That these spirits *wouldn't* control me.

"Yes, yes!" Oliver said, stalking close to me, now an arm's length away. "You are speaking with them, aren't you?"

I hardly had energy to respond, to tell him that I was doing just the opposite—stopping them from speaking with me, ushering them away. But all I could get out was an indistinct *groan*.

He stooped low over me, his eyes wild with interest now, his cheeks stirred back into his face as he smiled broadly. "Please, let me speak to her. There are so many things that I left unsaid." And then his tone hardened. "I have a right—it's *my* right. She was my mother."

With a final effort, I felt the spirit world leave me alone, those endless blank, shadowy faces slip away from me, down into a hole in the pit of my mind. And I was glad. I sensed the tight-ness in my chest and exhaled, feeling the pressure leave me—my muscles unknot themselves, my mind find rest. And then I felt his grasp, strong, pinching my skin against the blanket. He brought his face right up close to mine so that I saw the designs of his irises, all those black lines, and the stubble growing about his chin, sprouting down toward his chest. "Let me!" he said, through gritted teeth, seizing me about the throat, tightening my shirt up to my neck.

I struggled to breathe. Even if I had been free to speak I wonder if I'd even have had the strength to get out comprehen-sible words.

"Oliver," came a voice from the door.

Oliver's grip on me strengthened, got impossibly tight, so tight that I really couldn't breathe any longer. And then, like a receding wave, his grip left me, and he rose.

I gulped down air, lying on my side, staring into the roaringly bright fire. I felt steadier hands on my back, someone rubbing my back. When I got the strength to look back I saw that it was Mr Hallough. He gave me a kindly smile and helped me into a sitting position. "There," he said, "there, there. It's all over now." His smile faded a touch. "I'm sorry about my boy, I think he just got himself carried away—I'm sure you understand. It's not every day that you get spirits and the like about the house, the chance to speak to"—and then out of nowhere he sobbed, long and hard, before getting a hold of himself once again—". . . a chance to speak to your deceased wife."

And then Mr Hallough, too, let me free, took his hands off me. He sauntered out to the door, took up his place beside Oliver. The two of them watched over me and for the most horrible moment I was sure that they would return—the both of them, that they would bear down on me and demand that I indulge them with my gift, that I bring back their wife and mother 'just for a minute or two.' And I knew, even then, that such an act would have killed me in a single, efficient stroke. So I was glad when, after another moment's lingering, father draped his arm around son's shoulder and led him out.

I only allowed myself to stop squeezing my bladder, knuckles long past white from the fists I'd made of them, after I heard that final footstep arrive upstairs on the landing, when the final *click* of the bedroom door drifted into silence.

I bolted up from my place, ran over to the sitting room door, pushed it shut and then drew up the armchair—the same one which Mr Hallough had sat in to receive his wife—up against the doorknob. I stood back to examine my work. I knew that it wouldn't hold a firm shove from the other side, but at least the cacophony of the armchair toppling over would give me some warning.

With this on my mind I returned to my place at the fireside and draped the blankets back over me, feeling the heat of the fire pass over me like a shroud. And despite all that heat, all that physical comfort, I shuddered.

Long and hard.

CHAPTER TWENTY-TWO

THE MORNING WAS SURREAL. I recall coming round to the sound of the *clinking* and *tinkling* of porcelain. My first thought was that they were coming back in—that they'd violated my defences, and then, seeing the armchair was still there blocking the door, another thought dawned on me, that I had to yank it out the way. Because if father and son saw that they might take it for some impertinent gesture.

And so, shivering in the cold draughts floating about that sitting room, I rushed over and moved the armchair out of the way of the door with a woody *scrape* of the chair's feet against the floorboards. I only just managed to return to my place at the fire before I heard the *creak* of the door hinges and felt a gaze rest upon me—where I lay. I squeezed my eyes shut and waited, not daring to breathe.

"Sara?"

It was Mr Hallough.

"Sara? Are you awake yet?"

Not sensing any malice in his tone, but still feeling infinitely wary following the episode from the night before, I slowly stirred—simulating a recently awoken young girl.

This morning Mr Hallough looked plumper, healthier, his eyes—gleaming blue ones which reminded me of Farol—shone. He reminded me of a stuffed animal, a child's toy, that had been taken back to the maker's for its marble eyes to be shined, and to be restuffed.

"You like eggs and bacon?" he said.

I managed to find my voice—no small feat considering the fractured thoughts darting about my brain at a million miles per hour. "Yeah, I do."

"All right," he said, nodding his head and then making to leave the doorway. He faltered, however, and for one horrible second I was sure he would stomp right over to me, grab me and —before Dante could arrive to save me—shake me like a ragdoll until I died. But instead he stayed where he was and said, "I must apologise once again for last night. I—we're feeling much better this morning. In fact, Oliver went off to the workshop early this morning to go get something that might make it up for you."

What could he possibly do to make this up for me? I just wanted to get out of the house, and fast. I listened for any sound above my head—any sign that Dante and Jessica might be rising, but there was nothing. I cursed them in my mind.

Mr Hallough turned in the doorway, headed back for the kitchen. "Whenever you're ready you're breakfast is on the table. I should suppose Oliver'll be back soon after. I'm sure you'll like what he's got for you."

Glad that he'd left me alone, I shrugged out from beneath the blanket, discarding it in a heap, and then pulled back on my trousers and boots, feeling better to be fully dressed—ready to leave at a moment's notice. Dante had only to give the order and I was gone.

I suffered through the breakfast, constantly worried that I might have to face down the two of them—father and son—have them come at me again, wanting me to bring back their dead wife and mother. But there was no further mention of it, and for that I was glad.

I finished off a cup of steaming coffee and crunched through the bacon. Mr Hallough served me rich bread encrusted with oats and nuts. I had never tasted bread so delicious. When I finished I breathed in deep, just trying to savour that smell, to preserve it in my mind forever. And then, breaking through all that sensory delight I heard the *crunch* of boots heading toward the house—Oliver returning.

I thought of places to run, somewhere to hide. I recall very clearly eyeing the large, shining knife which lay on the counter—knowing that in an instant, if I kept my wits about me, I could dash over and snatch it up, run through whoever needed running through, because I was determined to survive. Maybe I was an orphan, and perhaps it was true that no one *really* cared about me, but no way in hell was I going to let death take me without a damn good fight.

I listened to those bootfalls growing louder and louder each time, and then the front door open. I closed my eyes and pressed my knuckles into my eyelids so that I saw stars—almost wishing now that the spirit world would drag me away, keep me safe somehow. I was drawn out of my defensive shell by the tone of Oliver's voice—tentative, a little hurt even. A light jangle of metal on metal sounded, punctuating his words.

"Sara?" he said.

Reluctantly, I opened my eyes, peering out at him.

There, in his hands, he held a saddle. It was made out of sleek black leather, a pair of stirrups hanging down at either side, along with some other straps that I couldn't name. I looked to him, a question in my eyes, and then summoned the courage to vocalise, "That . . . this is for me?"

He answered me with a smile, not a broad one showing off those weather-beaten teeth, but one just far enough to serve a double purpose as an apology.

I found myself up on my feet, moving toward him, eyes locked on the leather, trying to stitch the meaning of the gesture together—what this saddle represented. In the end, I sucked up the courage to look him straight in the eye and say, "What's it for?"

He sniffed a laugh then said, "Why, so you can ride that horse I gifted you—I saw the way you were looking at her."

"But," I said, feeling my throat go numb, "I . . . I don't know how."

Oliver laughed again, throatier this time, more of a bellow really. "Well, I'm sure you'll find the time, during your travels, to learn." He dialled his smile down a notch. "So, what do you say? Am I forgiven?"

I almost asked, 'Forgiven for what?' then stopped myself short, reminding myself how threatened I'd felt the night before. This, though, seemed like recompense enough. I was content that he had managed to empathise with me, to see past his own desires, enough so to realise that he *had* to make an apology.

I reached out and stroked the leather. It was almost impossibly smooth, like my skin felt after I'd taken a bath. "It's beautiful," I said. "Thank you."

He gave me a flash of a grin and then headed back out the way he'd come in. "In that case I'll go load it up, shall I? The carriage is all set to go, horses all bridled up. They're waiting, just at the end of the lane, tied them up to the post." He hesitated a moment and then said, "There was something else."

"What?" I said, still staring at the bridle.

"Look, I know you're on the run, and everything, so I thought it might be advisable to disguise things a little better, you know? What with that carriage, that design, it stands out—lingers in people's memories."

"What did you do?"

"I whitewashed it," he said, his cheeks now colouring. "I *was* going to ask Dante, but the thought just struck me this morning and I had a big pot of white paint . . . so I just did it."

I was lost for words. My mind traced back to that day with Farol, when we'd touched up the carriage. Would those designs be lost forever? I guessed that, really, there was no way of knowing, we could think about that later. Because despite everything, despite the gift of the saddle, I still felt uneasy in Oliver's company. What's that saying about a dog that bites once will bite again?

Oliver headed out to go pack the saddle and, minutes later, to my infinite gratitude, I heard the footsteps on the stairs, Dante and Jessica coming down together. It was all I could do to stop myself from running right up to Dante, throwing my arms around his neck out of happiness. However, when I laid eyes on him, I took stock of his gaunt cheeks, his heavy eyes, and I wondered whether he'd slept at all the night before. Still, though, he raised a smile, and his appetite seemed just as healthy as ever at breakfast. Gently and unknowingly, I cast off my anxieties, again allowing myself to slip into some kind of a relaxed state.

Breakfast was, thankfully, rapid. It seemed that Dante was just as anxious to get back on the road as I was. When I looked to Jessica there didn't seem to be the same opposition to our destination, our determination to help free Farol.

Once we'd finished, all of us, with Mr Hallough walking along beside us, handing over various produce he'd plucked that morning from his garden: peas, carrots, apples, a wicker basket full of blackberries, headed up the road from the house to where the carriage waited—Oliver already leaning up against it, arms crossed.

We got all loaded up and, despite his apparently frail state, Dante demanded that he be allowed to dress in his peasant's garb, and do the driving himself. With everything ready, we bobbed about the carriage ready to say our goodbyes. I received a pair of scratchy kisses—courtesy of his unruly beard—on either cheek from Mr Hallough. When I turned to Oliver, though, he was locked in conversation with Dante. They were apparently speaking about something that carried great gravity, seeing as Oliver's forehead was knitted into a sea of wrinkles. Oliver glanced over at me and I tried my best to give him an innocent smile. But he either ignored me or simply didn't see me, so wrapped up was he in talking to Dante.

Dante seemed to be outlining some proposal or other, perhaps some sort of an arrangement for him to supply us on our return journey—if we ever did get back—when we headed back down toward the south coast and to France. Whatever it was, Oliver was deeply concerned. In the end, after much head-shaking on Oliver's part, Dante shrugged, smiled and then gave him a firm handshake. As Dante passed by me, I looked to him and asked, "What did you want from him?"

"Oh," Dante said, with a light tone of a man shrugging off not receiving something he would've quite liked, "I asked whether he'd be interested in driving the carriage."

My blood froze and my brain felt like a helium balloon, inflating inside my skull, getting too big for me to handle.

"You know," Dante continued. "Just till we get old Farol back."

"And what did he say?"

Dante shrugged. "No."

I resisted the temptation to blow out a sigh of relief. But only just.

"Ah well, guess we'll have to manage for ourselves." He looked over the carriage. "At least he saw the sense of white-washing the carriage, can't believe that I didn't think of doing that myself—an extremely sensible move."

"Yes," I said, only then feeling the numbness lessen its hold on me.

"*Well*," he said, with enthusiasm that belied his obviously fraught condition. "We'd better get a move on, then, Farol's not going to save himself." He gave a light, hollow chuckle. "At least, it would help if he did, but I don't think it's all that likely."

I watched him hoist himself up onto the driver's seat, snub-bing help from Oliver. I noticed the wrinkles around Dante's eyes, the strain showing there, as he plonked himself up on the seat and out of sight. Next thing I knew I found myself staring Oliver right in the eyes and, before I could take evasive action, he had me in a great, big hug, holding me to his chest as tight as he could. Just as he backed off, leaving me with *several* crushed bones, he said, right in my ear so that no one else could hear, "I'm so sorry," and then backed off.

I stood there in a daze for a moment, thinking about why Oliver had said no—was it because he was afraid that he wouldn't be able to control himself, that he wouldn't be able to stop himself from demanding that I share my power with him— bring back his mother? I liked to think so. At least that way, being out of control, he realised it himself and took himself away from the situation. I told myself that he did it for my own bene- fit, although I never had the gall to ask.

I launched myself up into the carriage and listened to the door *whisper* shut behind me, as Oliver treated it with great deli- cacy. Then, I forced myself to face forward, in the direction we were travelling—onward to the Forsneers' estate.

The pace of the carriage was relentless. If I hadn't seen Dante that morning, how he had looked absolutely shattered, I never would've imagined that he wasn't anything but in excellent shape. Me and Jessica found ourselves gripping tight to the cush- ions of our seats as we bounced our way along the road, smashing into and out of potholes, screaming around corners with the carriage along dangling over on its side, two wheels in the air. It appeared that we wouldn't be stopping en route to our destination.

I thought of the new horse, who I'd yet to name. I rolled Susan over in my mind, in honour of the Halloughs, but, to be honest, that was more something that I was looking forward to forgetting. In the end I settled on Honey—like her colour. I liked it, it was feminine, yet sturdy somehow. And I thought it suited a hardened pony like herself fine. I thought that Silver would have his work cut out trying to keep up with her.

Night was falling before I started to make sense of the scenery, to have odd reminiscences that I'd thought to be long-forgotten return to me. And I knew, without asking Jessica, that we were now on the Forsneers' estate. I sank my teeth into my tongue, afraid that from any direction a group of men on horses might emerge—and I worried that I wouldn't be able to summon my power again, that this time they would fire on us, killing everyone in a messy bloodbath.

Dante slowed the pace of the carriage, no doubt hoping not to attract attention from anyone watching on. There would be questions of a carriage going that speed around here—questions as to where exactly it was headed to in such a hurry. I wondered what the plan was, but looking over at Jessica, who stared blankly out the window, I got the feeling that I just didn't want to know. Dante had already worked out just what we had to do to get Farol back, and that's the way it was.

There was a light in the road ahead, off to the side. I heard Dante grunt at the horses and them, in response, slow their gait. It looked like this was where we were going to make our first stop. The carriage wheels tickered along the roadside, getting their first real break since we'd left the Halloughs behind. The light grew stronger and I could make out the sign up ahead jutting out of the building. It was a pub called *The Ditcher's Arms*. Some merrymakers stood spread out at the front door, light spilling out onto the road. Each of them had pints of ale in their hands and, inevitably, great raging beer bellies spilling out over their waistlines. As the sounds of the carriage got quieter I could make out the bellowing laughter. It set the hair all over my body on edge—I thought of myself as a frightened cat.

Dante brought the carriage to a complete stop and set about roping up the horses to a nearby post. I watched on out of the window as a pair of drunks exchanged glances, their smiles slipping off their lips, and approached him. They spoke so loudly, in such thunderous drunken tones, that I could easily make out their words.

One of them had a bowl cut, his hair flapping all about in his eyes and at his neck, while the other was totally bald. Although both were clearly inebriated, they looked pretty heavy, at least fifteen or sixteen stone each, which would be far too much for Dante . . . unless he called upon his undead friends.

"Whatcha doin' here, eh?" the man with bowl cut said to Dante.

The bald one sneered along. "Yeah, ain't a bloody place for beggars this, pal."

Dante eyed the two men, gave them each a bow, and spoke with that guttural voice he had used—dressed as the beggar—on the night we'd met. "I have a proposal."

"Whatcha say?" Bowl Cut said, screwing up his eyes in bewilderment.

"A proposal. A deal, I have something which you might be interested in . . . or which your employer might be interested in."

The bald one gargled laughter. "And what employer's that then, numb nuts?"

However, Bowl Cut failed to see the funny side. "He's talking about the Forsneers, you twat." Still addressing his companion, he added, "Aintcha heard that they've got ears all over the place? I'd be a bit more cautious if I were you, or next time you insult them you might find it's my hands that find their way to wringing your neck."

The bald one's expression darkened and he sipped at his pint, like a wild animal, injured but biding its time, awaiting the opportunity to catch its opponent with a counter attack.

Bowl Cut turned his attention back to Dante, staring down his—not unsubstantial—chin at him. "All right, beggar, you best start making some sense or I'll cripple them both of your legs."

Dante seemed unfazed by this threat, although his tone did quicken, as he became aware that time was a limited resource here. "Right, here's the thing, that little one—what's that little Forsneer called?"

"Adrian?" the bald one said, in a bright tone that suggested he'd already forgotten his companions recent threat on his life.

"Nah," Dante said, closing one eye in thought—or mock thought, "the other one, what's his name . . . Gareth, Grenald? Something like that?"

Once more, Bowl Cut remained focussed on Dante, clearly wanting to cut to the quick as soon as possible. "Gerald Forsneer. What about him?"

"I've got, uh, something that he wants."

"That so?" Bowl Cut said, raising his tone. "And what'd that be exactly?"

Dante knew to bide his time here, and he rubbed one hand against the other, stared off along the road, as if he had somewhere more important to go.

"Out with it, then," Bowl Cut said, pulling the flap of his shirt up to reveal a knife nestled there. Seeing that Dante had noticed the knife, he broke into a grin—bereft of several teeth. "You're in the Forsneers neck of the woods now, beggar. You'd best be careful about how you act or someone's wont to teach you some manners."

"It's a girl."

"A girl?"

"That's right."

My mind spun. I looked over to Jessica. She clutched her arms into her chest, trying to make herself as small as possible. There was no other girl he could be talking about, was there? From the way Jessica was acting I could only infer that Dante wanted to hand her over to Gerald. But why?

Bowl Cut sneered, his fingers now clasping the hilt of his knife—in a single movement he could easily draw it out and run Dante through. I didn't doubt the Forsneers' powers out here, they were the law, if some beggar showed up dead in a ditch in the morning I was sure that it would just as quickly be buried by an obliging, passing serf.

"Look here," Dante said, for the first time a touch of stress entering his voice. "If Gerald Forsneer finds out about you passing up this offer, why I'm sure you'll find yourself at the bottom of"—he turned to the bald companion—"what's the deepest lake on the estate?"

The bald companion shrugged then said, "Fryer's Mile."

Dante turned back to Bowl Cut. "You'll find yourself at the bottom of Fryer's Mile if Gerald finds out that you had the opportunity to give him *this* girl."

Bowl Cut slipped the knife from its sheaf and held it up to Dante's eye. I could make out the shimmer of candlelight, the light spilling out from the pub, wobbling along its blade. "In that case I'd better make sure he never *does* find out, eh?" Bowl Cut said, with a sly tone.

Dante remained measured, even with that blade an inch

from his eyeball. "Wouldn't you like to be the one to give Gerald Forsneer *exactly* what he wanted?"

Bowl Cut kept his same posture. In the gloom I was sure that he moved closer, but it was impossible to know for certain.

"He'd reward you," Dante said.

Bowl Cut remained in his stance and then, very gradually, brought the knife down, replaced it in his hilt. He nodded in our direction and, in a moment of terror, I ducked back inside, afraid that he might see me. "Girl in there?" he said.

"That depends."

"Depends on what?" Bowl Cut said, hand still hovering uncomfortably close to the hilt of the knife.

"It depends whether or not I can strike a deal with Gerald."

Bowl Cut's eyes moved shiftily now, from Dante to the carriage, and back. I could see that he was eyeing up the angles, seeing things from Dante's point of view—wanting to get himself into Gerald's good books. "And what deal would that be?"

"He has someone kept prisoner, a simple man, elderly. He would be quite willing to part with him in exchange for the girl."

"That so?" Bowl Cut said, wetting his lower lip with his bulging tongue. Then he snapped back onto Dante. "And, tell me, *beggar*, what's stopping me commandeering your carriage here, and riding it right up to Gerald—handing the girl over myself." He shrugged. "Might just say that you were trespassing, how about that?"

"Because," Dante said, his tone growing a little sharper, "there are other things which Gerald should fear about me, about who my friends are and what they can do."

Once again, Bowl Cut squeezed the hilt of the knife.

"Do you remember the fire, at the mansion? Those horses

who pursued the vandals, only to end up on their backsides, in blazes of flames themselves?"

I could see this had got Bowl Cut a little uneasy. He blinked a few times, quite rapidly, and then glanced at his companion.

The bald companion broke into a chuckle. "What's he blabbering about, eh? Just rubbish, all of it. I say that you gut him like a fish and be—"

Bowl Cut lashed out at his companion, his fist a flurry of flesh. He knocked the man down to the ground with a single blow, and he lay there, eyes lolling back in their sockets, mouth open, knocked clean out.

Dante continued to stare at the downed man, a reminder of the razor-thin line he was treading himself here. He tore himself away from the spectacle and back to Bowl Cut's piggy eyes, those calculating eyes trying to eke out whatever profit he could for himself.

"I was on that ride," Bowl Cut said, then snorted back some phlegm. "Damndest thing I ever saw, and I seen some damn things on *this* estate." He looked down into his pint of ale and then, with a sure flick of the wrist, poured the contents out at his feet. "Where're your friends, then? Where're they hiding?" He glanced about the road as if they might be ready to pop out of a ditch. "Not got guts or what?"

Dante allowed himself the sliver of a grin. "I think they prefer to say that they pick their battles."

"That's what cowards say, is all that is." He sucked a long breath, his shoulders rising as he went. "Right," he said, puffed up as a bellows. "If the girl's in there, I'll escort you to go see Gerald, see if he's interested in what you, and your *friends*, have to offer. Although you'd best be warned that we're prepared now. Last time maybe your friends caught us off guard, this time, though, you won't be so lucky. Whatever . . . whatever it was you did, we'll be ready, you mark my words." And with a final glance at the trees, and a furtive one at the ditches, he rounded the pub to go and fetch his horse.

I settled into my seat feeling my stomach sink at the prospect of whatever it was that Dante was doing. This seemed nothing less than suicide—pure and simple. I was sure that all of us would be in prison before the night was out.

CHAPTER TWENTY-THREE

B OWL CUT, who it turned out was named Richard—a
fairly noble name for someone who was obviously a
common thug—led us along the main road for a long time before
taking us along a narrow track which bordered a field ripe with
corn. I watched the corn swaying lightly in the breeze, the
moonlight somehow making it seem like an underwater world—
and the corn was seaweed, waving in the current.

Soon after we headed through a forest road which led
upward sharply. I thought that Richard might have been leading
us into this place so that he could quickly kill us when all of a
sudden, up ahead, the trees opened into a clearing to reveal a
structure made up of sturdy blocks—turrets running across the
top. It made me think of a mini castle, out here in the middle of
nowhere. Looking out, over the treetops, I could see that it had
a good view of—what must've been—most of the Forsneers'
estate.

I overheard Richard as he swung his leg around and leapt

from his horse. "Your *friends* have got Master Forsneer all riled up, got him living out here now."

I watched as Richard waved for Dante to stay where he was, on the driver's seat, before slipping off toward the castle, a pair of men—guards—lolling about, each shouldering a rifle. They cast a quick look over the carriage before returning to their conversation.

I counted my heartbeats while Richard was gone inside the castle, anxiety ripped through me. I noticed that Jessica was shuddering beside me, but I was too afraid to reach out and take her hand in mine. It was like she was a bomb, all triggered to go off, and the slightest touch would cause an enormous explosion.

Through the gloom, knocked back only by the pair of lanterns which shone to either side of the entrance to the house, I made out two figures making their way outside. First came Richard, a light smile sketched across his lips, before Gerald Forsneer emerged behind him.

I felt Jessica go all rigid beside me, her eyes skirting about, batting back and forth in their sockets. My own muscles drew taut and I hoped that Gerald wouldn't come any nearer. But, as it turned out, my hopes didn't count for all that much.

After a brief, muttered exchange with Dante—who Gerald failed to recognise in his beggar's garb—Gerald rounded the carriage and rapped his knuckles against the door. My door. I stared out, through the window, into those sly, niggly eyes, which would skitter off to look around him, obviously not quite trusting this encounter—that truly this was happening, that it wasn't some sort of a con.

Before I got the chance to shift away from the door, Gerald was already working the catch loose, opening it up. A cool breeze floated into the carriage, sending my hair sailing about my ears. I looked back to Jessica who simply continued to stare forward, apparently unaware that the carriage had been opened at all.

Gerald sneered at me and looked over me to Jessica. His sneer faltered a little, shifted into a lecherous grin, then he said, "Why, good evening, my dear."

Jessica mumbled something in response, but didn't look around to meet his eye.

"Out you come," he said.

Then I heard the *scuff* of the soles of Dante's boots landing on the earth outside, followed by the sound of his footsteps. He arrived at Gerald's side, still speaking with his rasping, beggar's drawl. "Look, don't touch," he said.

Gerald clicked his fingers.

The guards who had looked so carefree just moments before seized their rifles and rushed over, pointing them at Dante's chest.

"This wasn't the deal," Dante said, through gritted teeth. "This is just so you can see that I have her—you're not to get her till I get the helper, the old man—Farol—yeah? Those were my orders."

Gerald chuckled dryly. "Listen, your *friend* burnt down my home—my family's home, and so I would advise him to not stretch my goodwill." He flapped his hand at me, for me to get out of the way. Not wanting him to touch me, I sidestepped him and stood at the other side of the carriage. He stepped in and reached over to Jessica. "My dear?"

Jessica remained totally still for a few more seconds before seeming to snap out of her daze. When she did look around at Gerald she'd somehow banished that deep, entrenched hatred and forced herself to give him a faint smile—an embarrassed smile, as if she were nothing but a ditsy girl caught up in this filthy transaction.

"Yes," Gerald said, his grin widening, taking hold of her hand in his, "this is much nicer, isn't it? What without that brute storming in with his box of tricks to snatch you away from me."

Jessica left the carriage.

Holding his hands up, obviously afraid that Gerald's guards might shoot at any moment, Dante met my eye briefly, before turning back to Gerald. "Aren't you forgetting something?" he said.

Gerald pouted. "I'll have my men take her possessions down once I have her inside."

"No," Dante said, pursing his lips. "What about her handmaiden?"

My whole body froze up, my breath felt like icicles. How could he? How could Dante sell me down the river like this? And without even *telling* me! I crunched my teeth together and cursed him, turning to Gerald, waiting for his response.

"Don't want her," Gerald said, decisively. "Got plenty of that sort out on our colonies, overseas"—he stared at me and added, pointedly—"where they *belong*."

My body relaxed a touch. That was it. Things would be fine. Gerald hated me just as much as I hated him.

Dante, to my horror, however, shook his head and stamped his feet, flinching a few times—acting out on his beggar's persona. "No, nuh uh, nope, that wasn't what he wanted—he said that the lady simply *must* have her handmaiden. Ask her yourself, see what she says. He'll be angry enough about what you're doing, but if you don't let her have her handmaiden, why he'll be *furious*."

Gerald turned his attention to Jessica, raising his eyebrow.

Jessica nodded dolefully.

Gerald's shoulders rose and fell with a sigh. "Very well," he said. "Far be it from me to inflame the *great* Dante Gobornik."

Even as he said it in that disparaging manner I was sure that I registered a touch of fear enter his eyes.

He beckoned his finger at me. "Come on, then."

I stared at Dante long and hard, waited for him to change his mind, to tell me that I didn't have to go, but, seeing that it wasn't going to happen, I reluctantly skittered out of the carriage and took up my place at Jessica's heels. Where I *belonged*, apparently.

As we headed back inside the castle, I cursed Dante again and again, shaking my head. I don't know what it was that caused me to look up, to catch Dante's eye for one final time before disappearing inside the house, but, when I did, he gave me an assured, ridiculously cocksure wink. Was that his idea of a joke? That he'd been playing me, Jessica, maybe even Farol, all along? I started to doubt my own powers in that moment, to think that—perhaps—he had spun some illusion about me, only made me *think* that there was anything at all special about me. With a heavy heart, I followed Jessica inside the house, the creeping realisation of my future, slowly dawning over me.

I overheard Dante call out to Gerald. "So what am I supposed to tell him?"

Without turning around, Gerald responded, "Tell him that the prisoner shall be at *The Ditcher's Arms* at eight o'clock tomorrow morning—and I would tell him not to be late, that would be most unwise."

"Can't he be brought any earlier?"

Gerald paused midstride and then, rolling his eyes, said, "Fine. Seven. He'll be there at *seven*. Okay?"

And with that, the door swung shut behind us with a woody *thunk*.

I'd hate to say that at that point I gave up hope, but I recall, being led by another of the servants to what would serve as my quarters, thinking that this was the end of my life. What had seen so promising, been such a rush for me, was at an end. Dante Gobornik had studied his options, calculated what he might have to do to get what he wanted, and he had made his choices. I wondered whether he'd had a frank talk with Jessica or if—somehow—he'd caught wind of her intention to run away, and he'd launched a peremptory strike. What had they said to one another back in the Halloughs' house? Had he threatened Jessica, told her that if she didn't bend to his bidding now, so that he might rescue his *one* loyal servant, the one person who—from his perspective—had not betrayed him, plotted against him, he would bring untold miseries from the afterlife down on her. Maybe he told her that she'd regret ever having been born.

I shared my room with five other servants. My bed was to be the one right by the door. I knew that, sleeping there, I wouldn't get so much of a wink of rest. From what I've heard of servants working in these houses for the upper classes, they called them in at all hours. My dreams would be ravaged by the constant coming-and-going of the house staff.

Each of the beds had a chewed-up, stiff turtle-shell green blanket. When I touched the blanket lying draped on my bed—a straw mattress bursting at the seams—it reminded me of a scouring pad.

The servant who had guided me to the bedroom informed

me that I would have ten minutes to get settled before being called to receive my orders from the housekeeper. I don't know exactly what he had in mind for me to do during that time, having nothing on me—not even the hand-me-down clothes Jessica had given me—so I simply sat on that uncomfortable mattress and wept to myself, silently. When the housekeeper came, I turned away from her, wiping away my tears, and ordered myself to grow some steel for a backbone, to face up to what the future held in store for me. At least I wasn't going to starve—going to go begging on the streets of the capital. Relatively speaking, all things considered, I had a better life now than I ever would have had back at home . . . and yet, knowing that I'd been with Dante, been part of his troupe, been that close to something truly great and mysterious, it was as if I tumbled right out of the heavens and landed with a huge *thump*, right down here, back on Earth.

While the housekeeper shepherded me about the house, introducing me to the washroom, the servants kitchens, and various other locations that I added to my mental map of the place as I went along, it only then occurred to me, as she was bringing the tour to an end, escorting me back to my sleeping quarters, to give my powers a try. Surely, if it had all been some ruse of Dante's, that all along it had been him tricking me into believing that I was really special then I wouldn't have any of those abilities now—not with him being far away by now. As she left me back in the servants' quarters, informing me that I would be woken at six o'clock the following morning so that I could be dressed and ready to be of service at my mistress's waking and breakfast, my mind twirled about the opportunities, if I did in fact possess these powers.

I lay on my side, in bed, trying to blank my mind. To block

everything else out and simply concentrate, as I had done before —back at the Halloughs' house, where I'd actually managed to consciously worm my way into the spirit world. I tried and tried for minutes, maybe an hour or more. There was nothing. All that greeted my efforts was a staunch migraine and a collection of scattered thoughts—those stupid thoughts that always come to you whenever you truly attempt to toss everything out of your mind.

My brain felt fuzzy, when I opened my eyes everything was out of focus. And then I realised that I was crying again, weeping at this situation Dante had landed me in. At least, if he'd wanted to throw me away, why didn't he just tell me before-hand, allow me to make my own way? Had he, through some dumb, misplaced fatherly instinct, thought that I wouldn't be able to manage alone, that I needed some sort of *structure* so that I wouldn't starve like a stupid, useless child? The more I thought about it, the angrier I got—I felt a giant ball of hate forming in my chest, nestling down below my ribs, rolling around, spinning, twirling, absorbing everything inside me and making me furious.

There was a *clatter* off somewhere in the house. Instinctively I raised my head to look, even though the door to the servants' dormitory was sealed shut at that moment. As I sank my head back down, brought it back to make something comfortable out of my mattress to lay my head on, I caught sight of her—unmistakable, despite the darkness, *there* in the corner of the dormitory. My mother. Standing, watching over me.

CHAPTER TWENTY-FOUR

I SLEPT ON through the night soundly—despite the fears I'd had before that the servants' comings-and-goings would keep me awake. Perhaps I wouldn't have slept so soundly if it hadn't been for the knowledge that my mother was watching over me. With her there, her gaze resting over me, I felt safe and secure, and I could've slept on forever.

A slither of light burrowed through the tiny, rectangular window in the servants' dormitory, resting across my eyes, making me feel rejuvenated. I knew that I had my power—and that gave me fresh hope. I wasn't like everyone else here. I was something special, although it made me feel a little headstrong to admit it to myself.

Soon after I'd woken, one of the housekeeper's close aides came down to wake me up. When I heard the door creak open I shut my eyes, clasping them shut, not wanting to let her see that I was already awake. Lightly, she rocked my shoulder and whispered in my ear, "It's time to get up and go see your mistress, my dear."

I rubbed the sleep from my eyes, looking about me at the other sleeping bodies, arms sprawling over the edge of their mattresses, faces looking set in stone, the exhaustion long chiselled in around their eyes and mouths. It struck me that the place was like a morgue, and I knew that it would turn me into a corpse before my time if I stayed here. But now I was determined to break out. I knew that I could break out. I had fresh hope now.

The housekeeper's aide led me through infinite winding corridors, past barrels of beer leaking gradually onto the floors, landing in mucky pools. I saw, too, many clothes hanging out to dry—fine-looking shirts, a pair of well-stitched trousers, and I guessed these to belong to Gerald. Now wrapped up in the potential of my power, I felt an almost uncontrollable urge to do something to those clothes, a way of getting to Gerald, having some kind of revenge. But I scolded myself for being rash, reminded myself that I needed to be patient. If I showed my hand too soon it was possible that I might be stopped—Richard, Bowl Cut, had suggested that there were now failsafes in place to prevent against a similar attack, and, to me, knowing the Forsneers, or at least what they represented, that most likely meant bigger and meaner guards with twitchy trigger fingers. And that was one thing that my power didn't provide for me. It didn't make me bulletproof.

As we rose through the house, leaving the basement behind, the light grew brighter, the first morning rays seeping in through the windows. We passed through a drawing room, several sitting rooms, the aide completely focussed on where she was going—

and incredibly not making a sound as she proceeded so rapidly. I felt like a giant in comparison with her, the way that I was clunking my way through the house. A couple of times the aide did swivel around and give me a look of warning, albeit never vocalising a reprimand—although I suppose that would've only made more of a racket.

We padded up yet more spirals of stairs, round and round, till we emerged on a landing carpeted with a beautiful Persian rug—gold and holly coloured designs twirling about. I longed to slip off my shoes, to feel it beneath my bare feet, but now that I was a servant that sort of behaviour would not be acceptable. Perhaps after I had taken this place for my own.

The aide strutted up to a large wooden door, ornate with flowing carvings—although ugly to me, the gargoyle heads, the flickering tongues and the jagged claws, I suppose it appealed to the Forsneers' tastes. She knocked quickly, twice, before turning the handle and heading inside. Not having been given an order to the contrary, I strode in behind her.

The bedchamber took my breath away. The four-poster bed with creamy-white netted curtains flowing down around it. There was an enormous window, currently with the curtain pulled across, which occupied much of one of the walls. Another was replete with a fireplace—only ashes now as the day dawned.

Only when the aide trod over to the four-poster bed, whisked back the curtains and looked over to me, did I realise that Jessica wasn't there at all. The aide, giving me the flicker of a smile, crossed the room and flung open the doors to an enormous red-wine-coloured wardrobe. Inside were nestled countless dresses, blouses and other clothes. I noticed the dozens of pairs of shoes in the bottom, beneath the hanging clothes. The aide began speaking, without meeting my eye. "Now," she said, "when your mistress returns you are to have her clothes all laid out ready for her, is that clear?"

Feeling a little dazed by the whole affair, I found myself saying, "Where is she?"

The aide arched an eyebrow, gave me a narrow smile and then trotted toward the door of the bedroom. "If you find that you need something—anything for your mistress, then you are to ring the bell at the bedside." She pointed out the cable which hung down from the wall, which I supposed jangled a bell somewhere in the depths of the servants' quarters. When she spoke next it was in a more confidential tone, what I thought to be similar to her normal tone of voice. "The housekeeper shall be watching you these first few days, so you'd best do a good job—handmaiden or not, if she's not satisfied that you fit in here she *will* have you thrown out on your backside and another, better candidate brought in. When it comes to Gerald Forsneer's lady companions the housekeeper will not tolerate mediocrity."

And with that, she swished out into the hall, leaving me alone in Jessica's bedroom.

As I stalked back and forth in the bedroom, biding my time, planning what it was that I was going to do, I could feel my mind right on the cusp—I could almost hear those spirits now, all banging on my skull, wanting to get into my mind, to burst through, come back into the real world. I held them back, keeping them squeezed in. There would be a time for them to come out, but not yet.

I busied myself doing as the aide had suggested, organising Jessica's clothes, getting everything ready for when she returned —I guessed—from Gerald's bedchamber. I picked out an emer-

ald-coloured dress and a pair of flat shoes, thinking—mercifully
—of the various stairs throughout the house. It was just when I
was swishing out one of the drawers, pawing through it trying to
locate the make up which Jessica might require that day, when I
had an odd tingling sensation in my hands. The funny feeling
travel up through me, into my chest, down into my legs. My
whole body got caught in a kind of frenzy—my shivering got out
of control and, all at once, I felt those spirits banging on the
door, demanding to come in. And I just didn't have the strength
to stop them. Bright white light flashed through my mind. I saw
the spirit world in snatches, that pale white, the multitudes all
with their heads inclined, tilted up, looking at me. And then,
moving as one, they formed one huge, great black shadowy mass
and rushed me. I covered my eyes with my hands and screamed
long and hard. My defences fell. When I reopened my eyes, I
knew they were there, with me, and I would be nothing more
than a mere puppet for whatever purpose it was they had
in mind.

I wanted to scream but my tongue was reduced to nothing
more substantial than a sodden sock in my mouth. I watched my
arms flailing about as *something* fought to gain control of me. I
knew it was too late, there was no turning back now. Once I'd let
them in I'd lost the battle, and so now I would be reduced to a
mere spectre. My legs moved me over the bedroom floor, toward
the door, I wondered where these spirits intended to carry me—
what destination they had in mind. In that moment I recall
feeling so utterly racked with fear that if someone had asked
whether I would've relinquished my power then and there, to
spend a lifetime in the service of the Forsneers, I think I
might've accepted.

I left the bedroom behind and headed on along the hall. Despite the unwieldy control these spirits exercised over me, they managed to keep my footsteps quiet. And so I paced along that carpet, that deserted landing, swiftly and softly, my heart juddering in my throat, and my whole body sweating, and yet the gestures that these spirits controlled were so gentle—so contrived.

I came upon another door along the landing. There was no polite wait or the steady knock which the aide had made on Jessica's door. This time, I watched my arms simply barge into the door and knock it open, squealing out on its hinges. Another bed, even bigger than the one in Jessica's room, stood up against the opposing wall. Two figures stirred within the netted curtain hanging down there. I felt heat rise through my body. Gerald. Jessica at his side. I fought and fought the spirits, trying to regain control of my body.

"What *is* the meaning of this?" Gerald said, setting one foot out of bed, dressed only in white long underwear.

Jessica remained burrowed in blankets, peering out at me with eyes shining like marbles, fingers clasping the edge of the bed sheet. I saw her lips moving before I realised that she was making a sound, before I managed to make sense of what it was that she was saying. "Too early," she said, and then again, "Too soon."

In that moment my whole mind burnt up. I thought of all the times we'd been through together—me and Jessica—the journeys we'd shared, the frosty silences we'd suffered through together, and then I knew it was all over. That it would be all over right now.

My whole mind flashed white. My eyes felt like burning coals boring their way into my skull, singeing my brain beneath. And then there was a bright white flash. Those shadows scarred the backs of my eyelids. A thousand, a million, crying, mewling mouths. When I opened my eyes again they were dead. Both of them.

Gerald, having stepped out of bed, now lay sprawled on the floor, one arm reaching out across to a bench, on which I saw rested a rifle. I was sure that he'd taken to keeping that thing close ever since the night Dante had burnt down his house. I considered him now, already full of regret for something I hadn't even had any control over, for which there was no murder weapon, no evidence against me—even now I realise that. He looked so meek, so weak. Just a humble mass of blood and bone. Nothing more.

My attention turned to Jessica, still in bed. She lay back, neck bent at an unnatural angle up against the headboard, eyes rolled back in their sockets, looking to the canvas ceiling of the four-poster bed. Her lips were slightly parted. I stood and watched on, sure that I heard words—or perhaps just a gargle—resonate in her throat. Her arms protruded from the blanket, her wrists facing upward, so pale and veiny. So lifelike. And yet . . . so dead.

I had no choice in the matter as I found myself turning on my heel and heading out of the room. It seemed that those two murders—killing those two people—had sated the hunger of the spirits, allowed them to rest a while. But they still had something in mind for me, I knew that, otherwise they would have released me. I was headed back along the landing, going back to Jessica's bedroom. For what reason, I wasn't sure.

I rounded the door and stomped purposefully over to the

balcony where my arms steadied me against the stone wall. Another netted curtain hung there, flapping about in the morning breeze. I recall thinking of how the world just kept on turning, despite that unspeakable thing I'd just witnessed. Those two deaths, murders. Nature was indifferent.

And then, without a moment's hesitation, I jumped.

I landed in a heap in thick bushes. The leaves and branches broke my fall with a cacophony of *rustling* and *crunching*. My heart beat hard in my throat, I could hear the steady *thump-thump*, *thump-thump* resounding in my eardrums. The spirits, I knew, had released me. I could move my arms and legs. Feeling returned to me. I gave a tentative movement of my arm, trying to prop myself up onto my feet, to get some perspective.

Over my shoulder, back within the house, I heard a long, shrill *shriek*. The aide, I imagined, who'd just stumbled into Gerald's bedroom and seen the two of them, lying dead.

Even with my regained capacities, the conscious control of my limbs and thoughts having returned, I found myself frozen there for several moments, paralysed with fear of what I had done . . . or had I simply witnessed? And then, my mind coming back to me, I broke into a run, running into the trees, allowing their branches and leaves to cover my tracks, to hide my escape.

I had only taken a few strides before I heard the *clop* of hooves heading up the drive, going toward the house. I increased my pace, feeling branches scratch my arms, poison ivy brush against my flesh. I would have kept on going—maybe running forever—if only it hadn't been for that all-too-familiar voice. "Sara? Jessica?"

Dante.

Blood flushed through my mind, trying to get a grip on what was happening.

He spoke to me again. "Sara? That's you. Come on, quick!"

I hesitated. I don't know why. Perhaps it was some hangover effect of those spirits' possession of my body or maybe it was something else, something deeper down, buried. I recall how I'd felt when Dante had handed me over to Gerald as if I were nothing more than a mere trinket to bargain away—nothing more than a sweetener of a deal. But, soon, logic found me again, and I rushed in the direction of his voice.

Dante sat astride Honey, using the saddle which Oliver had gifted me. He looked wild-eyed, his hair sticking up all over the place. He wasn't dressed as the Beggar or the Man in Black. He was just Dante. The Dante beneath everything. He wore simply his shirt, trailing out on his trousers, and there was a shade of stubble all around his mouth. He craned his neck back in the direction of the house. "Jessica, where's Jessica?"

My thoughts flurried. The truth was there, on my tongue. If I had wanted I could've told him straight out. But, instead, I found myself simply shaking my head.

"Inside?" Dante said, his tone sharper, raised in a way I'd never heard before—a note of genuine concern and affection for her.

I continued to shake my head and found a sob welling in my throat. Then I managed to say, "She's dead. Gone. Dead."

Dante's eyes bulged from their sockets. His fingers clenched the reins tighter. He glanced back at the house—as if it itself were to blame, as if it hadn't been him at all who had delivered Jessica to her place of death. When he spoke again his tone was cold, harsh, bitter. "Climb on. Quick."

I felt Honey's flank, feeling her stiff hair beneath my finger-tips. I rested my hand there a moment, just enjoying the softness and the warmth. Then I burst back into action, throwing myself onto her, taking up my place behind Dante.

After a final glance off in the direction of the house, Dante swung Honey around and we galloped off down the drive and into the trees.

Our pace was just as relentless as it had been the day before, when we'd headed along the road. I held on tight, bundling myself into the small of Dante's back, pressing myself in there. Only when the smell of smoke wafted up my nostrils did it occur to me to look around, to the hillside where the house sat. I watched those flames licking at the morning clouds. The smoke wafting out over the fields. I turned back to Dante, looking for an explanation, but I could only see his face in profile, his eyes fixed on the path opening up before him, his lips bloodless, and as rigid as his posture.

We bounded along the road and I half-expected to have another group of men careening after us, a similar scene to that which had played out following Lord Forsneer's birthday party. But no one came. We simply galloped on along the road, passing only the odd cart, the few workers in the fields at that time. We passed by *The Ditcher's Arms*, where this had all begun. It was closed, of course. It looked devoid of life in the morning light—all its windows shuttered up, no horses or carriages out back. We kept on going past it, and I didn't notice Dante so much as shift his gaze to take a look.

A bit further on I noticed us passing the fences, leaving the

Forsneers' estate. If only that had meant safety. For this was only the start—we had simply seen off a minor element of the forces hounding Dante, and now me. Gerald Forsneer, and whoever else, was lying dead in that house, but there would be an investigation—police to contend with.

CHAPTER TWENTY-FIVE

W E STOOD on the windswept dock, late in the evening, the freezing mist just appearing on the horizon. Every-thing was grey, dark greys, light greys, metallic greys, brown greys. It was like a smoke in the capital, lingering over every-thing, smothering the life out of all. I would have described it as a deathly grey, but that would have been an incorrect observa-tion—since I knew that the colour of death, the kingdom of the spirit world was white, that all-too bright light blinding every-thing. Grey was just neutral. Nothing at all, really.

Down below a pair of dock hands worked to load the carriage onto the ship, putting it down beneath the ship in the cargo deck. The two horses waited patiently—I read a little anxiety in their eyes—as they watched the men at work. Somehow I'm sure that they knew that they would be next on, sent onto that florid sea, left at the mercy of the waves of the Channel.

I held my copy of *Newbert's* to my chest, as I had done during the whole journey here. It had acted as a kind of stuffed toy, giving me comfort. It's not that *Newbert's* contained the answers I was looking for, or even the questions, but it was just refreshing to know that—other than myself and Dante—there was someone else in the world who *understood*, or who was at least *trying* to understand, what this absurd power we yielded was.

I glanced to my side, to Dante, standing with his hands propped up against the railing before him, staring out to sea—casting his eye over the horizon, who knows, perhaps he could make out the coastline of France there.

The dock hands returned for the horses, one taking a lead rope each. Neither Silver or Honey complained, there were no whinnies, no throwing back of their heads, it was as if they had come to accept their fate, and that there was nothing at all they could do to change it. Then, one by one, they disappeared inside the belly of the boat, neither of them looking back.

Sometimes I wished that I could take it upon myself to act more like them, find it easier to move forward with my life, head on to the next thing. But, standing there, on that dock, waiting to board the vessel after the horses, I found my eyes constantly tracking back to those cliffs—those chalk-white cliffs—looming over us, as if intimidating the breaking white waves rushing about in the harbour. I imagined them saying, 'Sea? What use do we have for sea? You'll never be as sturdy as land. All you reveal to us are mere tricks of the eye, why tomorrow you might be gone, in a fit of rain, a burst storm cloud. And we know your secrets—can imitate them. *We* are more powerful by far. Fixed here, forever. Never changing. Permanent. Authentic.'

I caught myself before I could become to transfixed with interpretation, because this was a day, just like any other, and the reality of it was that the sea didn't care—neither did the cliffs. They were inanimate, had been around for millions of years and would probably be around for millions of years more. As for me, I would only live for a fraction of that time. If I was lucky I might live for another fifty, sixty years—providing nothing saw to cutting away the slender thread which bound me to life . . . or what remained of it.

Dante's gaze was still burnished with shadows, with almost visible mental reflections, moving in and out of his eyes—those jet-black, bottomless pits.

I toyed with telling him, telling him what had really happened back at the house, but I knew that I never could. We hadn't so much as spoken two words to one another on the journey here—so much meaning and misunderstanding must have cropped up in both our thoughts, becoming so thick and unyielding as to almost strangle the both of us. What would happen to us now?

Farol, apparently sensing the funereal tone drifting between myself and Dante, approached with twitching eyes, fumbling his hands together. I felt for him, too, because surely he felt responsible for Jessica's death—the whole reason we'd returned to the Forsneers' estate. But was there really anything I, or anyone, could say to change his mind?

"Sir?" Farol said, risking a glance at Dante.

Dante continued to look out to sea, appearing as if he hadn't heard, or made sense of, Farol just addressing him.

"The captain's ready to sail," he said, then half-turning away, beginning back down the dock, "in your own time, sir, that's what he says."

Dante still remained unmoved, his gaze fixed.

I watched Farol, shoulders hunched, waddle his way back

down to the dock, exchange a word or two with a dock hand, who glanced back in our direction—most likely wondering what the hold up was, wanting to know why we didn't wish to sail right away, for goodness' sake we'd been waiting long enough for the ship to be loaded.

When Dante spoke, he caught me in a daze, as I was looking out to sea, trying to observe what it was he was looking at myself. As he did speak, he continued to look towards that same point. "I'm sorry for what I did," he said.

The first question that sprang to my mind was 'Why?' But before I got the chance to vocalise it, he was already explaining.

"I had to keep you in the dark about what we were doing—there was no other way."

"I . . . I don't under—"

He held up his hand. "I needed someone in the house, well, I needed *myself* in that house, it was the only way I could ensure I'd be able to save Farol, then get you and"—his voice wavered—"Jessica out again."

I had the urge to feed him some sarcastic line, to tell him what a roaring success that plan had been.

"Your power," he continued, "it's unrefined, you struggle to control it. If I'd told you what I required of you—to help get Jessica out—that would only have burdened your mind. You would have been unable to act when the time came."

"But . . . I had no control. It was the spirits."

He tilted his head, about to nod, and then at the last moment gave a very definite shake of the head. "I'm sorry, Sara. It was the only way."

For a long few seconds I pondered this, unable to fathom what it was that he was getting at. And then, up out of nowhere, it struck me. My cheeks burnt and I found myself scowling uncontrollably. "*You*," I said, "it was you, wasn't it? You were controlling me, through those spirits. *You* made me kill them both. It's all your fault."

He slipped into silence, making no comment on my accusations and then, at the end of his pensive pause, he said, "I'd understand if you wanted to stay behind—here. What I did, it will live with me for always. If—"

"But *I* killed them. You weren't even there. It's *me* who has to live with the guilt."

He shook his head. "No." He paused another beat. "No, you don't."

I stewed away, smouldering with rage, angry with myself for having allowed Dante to manipulate me so horribly—unforgivably—not even to extend me the courtesy of telling me what it was he was going to do, not giving me a chance to back out from it. And then another question floated up in my mind. In a funny way, it calmed me, and it showed in the tone of my voice—more collected, more inquisitive than accusatory. "But why did you kill Jessica?"

He kept staring out to sea and then, slowly, he turned around to face me. His cheekbones looked gaunt, as they always did after he'd performed a show, the marks the dead left on him. "I didn't plan on it," he said. "She wasn't supposed to be there—she was meant to be long gone. That . . . that's just the problem with the technique, the *possession*"—that word stabbed at my brain like a knife, and now it was out there, in the air hanging between us it could never be taken back, but how else could it be described?—"it's unreliable, that's why you couldn't know, don't you see? It's like a simple hypnotism, the possessor's thoughts can interfere with the control of the possessor—"

I was already going miles ahead of him, and I cut in. "You mean that it was me . . . I . . . I mean, I killed Jessica?"

Dante broke off eye contract, returning to that point in the middle distance. He swallowed long and hard. "No . . . she, oh . . . I just don't understand what she was doing there!" He caught control of his rising temper. "There's no way of knowing," he said. "But I only set out to just find a way to incapacitate Gerald —and then to get the both of you free. There was interference, right from the start, really. But I just couldn't—"

All of a sudden his words were cut off by a sob. He bowed his head and tried to get himself under control, forehead tucked into his chest, shoulders shaking. He remained there for a good five minutes, letting the tears flow, before he could summon the strength to finish what he'd started. "That morning, I should have stopped it—I know that. But you were both in there, and using you was the only way, a horrible way, but still." He looked me straight in the eye, his own eyes now wet with tears, his cheeks puffy and sore. "I want you to know that I take full responsibility for both their deaths, they were my fault. But it was an *accident*, I hope you can see that, I didn't mean for it to happen."

My heart jigged up into my throat and I shook my head. "If you were really sorry why not hand yourself into the police?" I said. "Tell them what you've done."

He gave a half-sob, half-chuckle. "Yes, I can see just how that might work—oh yes, officer, that's right, I was just possessing this girl, having spirits control her body, and then I had her kill them." He shook his head. "No," he said, "there's no way that they'd take me—or perhaps they would have me put in a mad house, and I may be a lot of things but I am not a madman."

I wasn't sure how I saw that personally.

"You have to trust me that they will forever be with me—more literally than that's usually meant. Whenever I step into the kingdom of the souls, they shall be waiting for me, the same questions on their lips. And I will never be able to explain, never be able to reason with them. That, you must believe me, shall be my punishment."

Those hundreds of words settled between us, God knows that their burden was a heavy one. And I was getting uneasy, trying to make up my mind whether I should step onto that ship, take off with Dante, or should I go my own way—escape his overbearing influence, not tempt fate by having him take control of my body and mind so easily a second time. Then the perennial question returned to me, the one that had bothered me throughout our relationship, and which he had always so neatly dodged. For this I leant back against the stone wall, my back to the sea and looked up into his face, not caring whether or not he looked me in the eye—I would have an answer now, I was sure of it. "My parents," I said. "How did they die?"

Like everything else we had talked about up on this windswept harbour wall, Dante took it without emotion, but clearly turned it over in his mind. I knew that I had to give him some time so that he might get his thoughts in order—express it in the right way. Finally, he spoke. "I never told you how I ended up an orphan, did I?"

"No," I said. "You just told me that an English gentleman took you in."

He nodded at this, pouting slightly. "Yes," he said. "I suppose it's time you knew."

"No, Dante," I said, flinching as I said his name, and berating myself mentally for fearing it, "tell me about my parents, how *they* died. You were responsible, weren't you? You killed them—

you saw that you wanted me, needed me, another just like you that you could manipulate into your bidding, that you could use just as you wanted. Admit it!" I said, my voice rising almost to a shriek.

Again, Dante nodded to himself, as if accepting some truth to himself, some unchangeable situation. "What I will admit is that I saw you, Sara, and I knew what you possessed. Yes, it's true that I saw you as one like me, that I thought it might be . . . *handy*, having you around. But, please believe me, that was at the start, later, over these weeks, never had a thought been further from my mind, until . . . until it became unavoidable."

I scoffed. "It wasn't unavoidable, we didn't *have* to go back for Farol—that was your choice, nothing to do with me or Jessica, you just drew us in, took us along for the ride. We were nothing more than stepping stones you used to get across a stream. Farol," I said, looking down on the dock, where he sat up on a bollard, back to us, out of earshot, waiting for us to come down and board the ship, "Farol *killed* that man. He *deserved* to be locked up, he *deserved* to go to prison for it. Why did you free him? Was his life worth Jessica's?"

"Farol didn't kill anyone. That man, the man he struck, he was knocked out for all of five minutes, and he got up fine—I asked last night in *The Ditcher's Arms*. For what I know he's at his guard post right now. No, Farol did what he had to, and his hands are clean, which is much less than can be said for mine."

"Or *mine*," I said, with spite.

He glanced at me, but didn't dare deny it this time. He sighed hard and then turned to head back down the dock.

"Stop!" I said. "You still haven't answered my question."

"Because you have no patience for the answer."

"I've waited what seems like forever."

"Then perhaps you would prefer to wait just a little longer."

I lurked back there, thinking to myself, considering my options. I had to know—there was no doubt in my mind—but why couldn't he just tell me straight, stop all this beating about the bush. I stood there, waiting for him to go on.

A light mist blew over us, and I tasted salt water on my tongue. It was cold enough to sting my cheeks.

Dante pushed back his hair, smoothed it down, pulled at the tips. When he spoke again, it was in a pointed manner, as if he had already gone over this a million times before. "I was at school, just a normal day. I'd had some bad dreams, but nothing more than that, and then . . . and then, on the way back home, I was walking along the cobbled streets, down a back alley, the same route as always. And that was the first time that I saw one of them."

My anger rose higher, but I kept it out of my voice. "A shadow?"

He nodded then continued, "When I got back home I thought I could smell the stench of death, even before I walked in the door. And there they were, my mother, my father, my two brothers. *All* of them dead. I . . . I just ran. I never returned—could never return."

Silence broke out once again, and this time I embraced it, taking Dante's story, blending it into my own—trying to work out how it fit. And then I had the answer. That, my parents, my little brother, that they had been killed by this . . . this power.

It was like a weight lifting off my shoulders, as if the sky simply retreated several thousand miles. I could see more clearly, my hearing was more acute. When I looked at Dante I was no longer marinated in bitter rage.

"Sara," he said, "what you must understand is that this power is bigger than any one practitioner. It does not simply give, it takes away . . . oh, how it takes away. We cannot wish for more except to understand it." He nodded to the copy of *Newbert's* crutched in my arms. "There is no control—control is just an illusion. I hope you can see that. This power is a curse and it shall follow us to our graves, perhaps beyond. Do you see now? Do you understand?"

"But . . . but why me?"

Dante shook his head. "I don't know—no one does, not even Newbert." He gave me a sliver of a smile. "But maybe, one day, we shall be able to answer that question. *That* is my dream."

Farol called up to us and, when I looked down, I saw that the captain was standing on the deck of the ship, looking impatient, head lolled to one side.

Dante looked to me. "It seems that we are ready to sail, Sara." He shoved his hands into his trouser pockets and shuddered. "I have to say I am looking forward to leaving the British summer behind—getting some warmth into my bones." He stopped shuddering and then looked me, for the longest time, in the eye. "So, if you really see the two of us as equally culpable—as equally compliant in murder, in death—wouldn't you also say that we might be better off together? In that way perhaps we can find the answers together, learn to share the burden?"

I turned the idea over in my mind and, before I had truly scanned all the implications, the captain of the boat blew the whistle, long and hard. For a few seconds my ears rang, my mind got cluttered. I thought, with disgust, that Dante might've been getting into my head again—and then the sensation passed. I knew that my body was my own—my thoughts free of *possession*. I exhaled hard and then looked to Dante. "Okay," I said. "I'll go with you."

Dante gave me a hardy grin and then stepped forward, offering his hand. I accepted it, feeling those fingers, which felt worn down before their time, rub against mine like rough wood cuts. As we headed down the dock to where cargo waited to board boats, to head out across the Channel, I looked to the horizon, our destination, and thought—just for a second—I saw a shadow hovering there. And, if I did, I know precisely who it was. There's no doubt in my mind, to this day. My mother—my good omen. Or was that just an omen? I guessed that I would soon find out.

And so, with Dante gripping my hand tight, we stepped over the groaning gangplank and boarded the ship, leaving England—and all that had passed—behind us. Onward, to a new future, a hopeful future, although—I thought with a little tightness in my throat, a little heaviness in my heart—an uncertain and possibly dark one. There would be no way of knowing, and I would guard myself against, remain wary of, any sleights of hand.

AUTHOR'S NOTE

Thank you for taking the time to read one of my books. If you would like to hear about my latest releases you can sign up for my newsletter here: www.raymondsflex.com

Thanks for reading!

Raymond S Flex

A Sleight Of Hand
A Novel